the sunday girl

the sunday girl

pip drysdale

SIMON & SCHUSTER

London · New York · Sydney · Toronto · New Delhi

A CBS COMPANY

First published in Australia by Simon & Schuster (Australia) Pty Limited, 2018
This paperback edition published by Simon & Schuster UK Ltd, 2019
A CBS COMPANY

1 3 5 7 9 10 8 6 4 2

Simon & Schuster UK Ltd
1st Floor
222 Gray's Inn Road
London WC1X 8HB

www.simonandschuster.co.uk

A CIP catalogue record for this book is available from the British Library

Paperback ISBN: 978-1-7608-5144-6
eBook ISBN: 978-1-7608-5145-3

Printed and bound by CPI Group (UK) Ltd, Croydon, CR0 4YY

For the wild ones

War is a grave affair of state; it is a place of life and death,
a road to survival and extinction, a matter to
be pondered carefully.

MASTER SUN TZU, *THE ART OF WAR*

sunday

Master Sun said: *'The Way of War is a Way of Deception.'*

5 FEBRUARY

Some love affairs change you forever. Someone comes into your orbit and swivels you on your axis, like the wind working on a rooftop weather vane. And when they leave, as the wind always does, you are different; you have a new direction. And it's not always north.

But you learn that this was their job, their role in your life. You should let them go; you cannot blame the wind for leaving, for that is what wind does. I know all that in theory. I'm not an idiot. I'm well versed in contemporary wisdom and the inspiring nature of Instagram memes. But here's the thing: in real life, in the sphere of true human existence, theory holds an old quill pen, while a broken heart wields a gun. No competition, really.

So, that covers the *why*: love – broken love – made me do it.

Love. And a sex tape.

The *how*, on the other hand, is a bit more complicated.

And the *when*?

Well, that's the simplest of all: it started four days, eighteen hours and twenty-three minutes after the strongest gust of wind I'd ever known decided to leave me.

And like all snowballs, it started small.

It was February in London, so cold. The rain was tapping lightly on the window, folded newspaper stuffed into the edges to fix the leak, and I was sitting on a beige-and-red hand-me-down rug on the floor in the middle of my apartment. I'd drunk most of a bottle of chardonnay and was conducting what I thought at the time to be a reasonably justified Sunday night Google search: *how to ruin a man*. Or, if I'm being truly faithful to history: *gow yo ruin a nan*. Luckily Google can quickly decode drunk-girl speak.

Type that in and the following two main sets of results appear.

One: pages full of concise, step-by-step instructions in tepid psychological warfare against your ex (most of which involve posting provocative photographs of yourself with other men all over social media; except for one page, which, if you find it, provides detailed instructions on how to acquire an undeserved restraining order).

Two: pages full of concise, step-by-step instructions on how to win said ex back (mostly suggesting the 'no-contact rule' in conjunction with intermittent and low levels of those tactics outlined in option one).

Both of these were useless to me. I refused to believe I wanted him back, and I needed something a bit stronger than the no-contact rule to inflict the kind of damage I was yearning for; I wanted ashes. Flaming ashes. The kind that only a woman truly betrayed by the man she loves can crave. I was done with making excuses for him, done with being a casualty, done with playing nice.

The question I keep asking myself is: would I have stopped right then and there if I'd known how things would turn out? But I don't suppose it matters – I didn't know. Besides, I wasn't really open to rational argument: I was fuelled by the white-hot fury known only to the young, the oppressed and the broken-hearted. And so all Fate had to do was set up her cosmic dominos around me and then wait until I let the first piece fall. Which I did, right on cue: the moment I pressed 'enter' and let my will to destroy him escape into the ether, that first domino toppled irrevocably and one thing led to another.

Because that's the thing with dominos: easy to start, hard to stop. And impossible to know where they'll lead.

Of course, the easy answer to 'Would I have stopped?' is: *Yes. Damned straight I would have stopped*. If face-to-face with a jury I would surely say just that. But if I am truthful, really truthful, the hand-on-my heart answer is: no, probably not.

It was too late for that.

Because I'd always been the good girl. The amicable, pliable, understanding girl. The kind of girl you could take home to meet your parents, introduce to all your friends and keep around long after the love faded to beige, simply because she was (I was) so very amenable. And that's precisely why Angus loved me, needed me, why we were 'meant to be together': I was the 'perfect yin' to his yang, he was 'a better version' of himself when I was in the room. Kinder. Or at least, that's what he'd always said.

But everybody has their limit, a boundary you just can't cross, and Angus eventually found mine.

And so, two days before the above-mentioned Google search, that amicable, pliable, understanding girl finally snapped. A rubber band, stretched a millimetre too far. And in that moment, Life lifted the veil of saccharine I'd been hiding beneath and forced me to come face-to-face with the other parts of my psyche. The darker parts. The ugly parts. The fragile, petty, venomous parts.

The parts I may never have found if it wasn't for him.

And those parts didn't cower. They fought back.

It's not that I wanted to be a bad person – nobody wants to do bad things. And if it had just been our dark and distorted history, the secrets that bound us and a shitty break-up, I may have held it together. I like to think I would have just moved on. But it wasn't. There was something else. Something more.

And I learned about it via a Facebook message.

At first I presumed it was spam – the title was *XXX* – so I deleted it. Adjusted my privacy settings accordingly, and went about my workday. But then came the email to my work address. From a different man. It read: *Hi Taylor, I loved your tape*. And this time, it came with a link.

I sent it to my phone, clicked on it and a video filled the screen.

A video of me.

A video of me that nobody else was ever meant to see: my ruffled dark blonde hair falling over one eye as I smiled coyly at the camera. My co-star's name was Holly. We'd met her in a club at

3am. It was Angus's idea. I'd never even kissed a woman before her, but it was nice. Soft. She tasted of berries and salt. And the footage, dimly lit and shaky, was never supposed to leave Angus's possession.

He'd promised.

Yet there it was, staring back at me, my full name included in the video's description – this must have been how the two men found me. Google is good like that.

My cheeks turned hot. My heart thrashed against my chest walls. And as my mind registered the horror of what I was seeing and I pressed the cross in the corner of the screen, removing it from my phone before any incriminating sound played, something broke inside me. Something vital. It was almost audible: *snap*.

Maybe it was trust. Perhaps it was virtue. Or maybe it was my sanity.

But after twenty-nine years of embracing the virtues of kindness, tolerance and forgiveness – of living by *two wrongs don't make a right* – I'd finally had enough. All yin has a little dot of yang in it, after all. And so, as my boss tapped away on her keyboard just a metre away from me and I stared blankly at my computer screen, pretending everything was fine, Life whispered a new mantra in my ear: *survival of the fucking fittest*.

Hence, the Google search. And everything that followed.

monday

Master Sun said: *'Victory belongs to the side that scores most in the temple calculations before battle.'*

6 FEBRUARY

It was the Monday after the break-up when I called in sick to work. Google had kept me up till 2am and I woke feeling raw and reckless, craving anaesthesia. Anything to help me forget. And so I lay in bed till 11am, staring at a crack in the ceiling and downing the bottle of champagne I'd been keeping in the fridge for a special occasion.

Then, at 11.03am, I texted Jamie. I thought I'd deleted his number when I first met Angus, but apparently not. Because there it was, cleverly disguised under the pseudonym 'Never-call-he-just-wants-sex Anderson'.

I'd met him two years before at a street-art exhibition in Brick Lane and we'd gone on two dates. The first was magical, the second was tense. Our brief affair had ended in an overly dramatic row in a backstreet of Soho – I didn't want to have sex just yet and, well, he did. But maybe I'd had it wrong all along: maybe romance really *was* dead and a casual hook-up was just what I needed. So when Jamie texted back with his address I went straight over.

'How was therapy?' he asked, eyes to the ceiling, menthol cigarette between his lips and a sheet barely covering him. I watched his right hand toy with his cigarette, guiding it theatrically from his mouth and letting it dangle over the side of the bed. By 'therapy' he meant him. Sex. I wanted to tell him that his mouth tasted of oranges and that Life reminded me of a Rubik's cube, not because of its complexity, but because of its complete pointlessness. And that no amount of therapy, or sex, could ever cure that.

Instead I said: 'It was good.' Lie number one.

I reached for my phone: nothing.

Silence put its pretty hands around my throat, its thumbs into my windpipe and my chest grew tight: it was Angus's forty-third birthday that Friday, 10 February. My gift for him, a carefully selected cashmere jumper in heritage green, was already wrapped and scorching a painful hole in the top of my wardrobe. He'd never wear it now.

I lay back down and Jamie slung his free arm around me in a half-hearted embrace, the charade of intimacy making me feel more alone than any amount of isolation ever could. I reached across, took his cigarette and inhaled. Angus hated me smoking – cigarettes, weed, whatever – said it made me taste trashy, and so I'd stopped doing it for the most part while we were together. Anything to fit into his shimmery world of high-grade cocaine and Chivas Regal.

But I'd missed it. And I liked watching the cloud of smoke dissolve above me as I exhaled. It felt like a symbol of my flickering spirit, the one part of me I'd never let even Angus touch.

'Are you going to tell me what happened?' Jamie asked, reaching for his cigarette, taking one last drag then stubbing it out on a CD cover beside the bed. Coltrane, *Blue Train.*

'Nope,' I replied.

He looked at me with clever eyes, and I couldn't help but laugh.

'What do you think happened?' I said, sitting up and looking at him over one shoulder. 'We broke up.' I glanced around the room, searching for my underwear. The air was like ice and giving me goose bumps, so I wrapped my arms around my breasts and stood up. 'Aren't you supposed to be a barrister? How the fuck do you piece together a defence with a brain like that?'

'Idiot,' he replied, burying his face in the pillow. It was lemon-yellow. I remember that. It seemed an oddly feminine touch for the bed of a self-proclaimed confirmed bachelor.

'Oh, don't be so hard on yourself,' I said.

'I meant him,' he mumbled, turning his head to the side so he could see me.

I wanted to crouch down and look under the bed but I couldn't; I was naked. Instead, I walked through to the living room – I could feel his eyes on me as I moved.

'Where are you going?' came the muffled voice.

'I'm looking for my shoes,' I replied, locating my underwear on the edge of his caramel leather sofa. My handbag lay on the floor beside it. I put on my pants, threaded my arms through the loops of my bra and reached back to fasten the clasp.

Our two empty glasses sat on the coffee table in front of me: vodka and orange. Basically brunch. And beside them lay a half-eaten block of dark chocolate and two copies of a book.

I picked up one of them.

'What's this?' I called through to the bedroom as I read the cover: *The Art of War*.

'What's what?' he replied, appearing naked at the door.

'This,' I repeated, holding up the book.

'I have a student shadowing me this week – it's supposed to help him with strategy.' He walked over to me and wrapped his arms around my waist. I could feel his breath on the top of my head. 'Why don't you take one? It'll give you a head start.' I could hear amusement in his voice.

'Oh, ha ha,' I said. 'Maybe I will.' I put it into my handbag.

And that's how it happens, how the dominos fall. Within the five days since the break-up, a sex tape had led to a drunken Google search, a drunken Google search had led to a sick day, a sick day had turned into a drunken romp with a scoundrel, a drunken romp had turned into a free book and that free book would soon turn my life upside down. Forever.

My dress was draped across a dining-room chair. I moved away from his embrace, slipped it on and then returned to him.

'Do me up?' I asked, presenting him with my open back. And he complied.

'Can you get me a car?' I asked sweetly as I put on my shoes.

'Of course,' he said, dialling already. 'Do you think the patient will need repeat therapy sessions?' he asked, holding the phone to his ear.

'Maybe.' Lie number two. It had left me feeling worse, not better. Every moan reminded me of Angus and every time I closed my eyes I could see Holly's body pushing up against mine, the warmth in my hair turned red by the low light as her fingers ran through it. I wouldn't be doing it again. I chewed slowly on a piece of dark chocolate and listened as he ordered the car.

—

By the time I got home my eyes were as heavy as suburban windows tired of holding up their blinds all day, my tongue was dry and my nose was running from the cold. The three flights of stairs to my apartment felt like six, I kept trying to put the wrong key in the lock, and the booze had worn off. But my mind was awash with inspiration.

I moved over to the heavy blue curtains and pulled them shut: the sky outside was glowing blue-grey as it moved from dusk to night-time, and it was just starting to rain. Then I stripped off my clothes and put on one of Angus's old work shirts – a relic from happier days that had taken on a second life as my pyjamas. It smelled like soap. It used to smell like him. I made a cup of Earl Grey tea, climbed into my unmade bed and pulled the covers up to my chest. My toes had gone numb from the cold and I could hear the upstairs neighbour getting home from work, her high-heeled shoes tapping on my ceiling.

That was the first time I opened *The Art of War*.

Chapter one: Laying plans.

Master Sun said: *'The Way of War is a Way of Deception. When able, feign inability, when deploying troops, appear not to be. When near, appear far, when far, appear near, lure with bait.'*

That sounded sensible enough. But far more complicated than it needed to be: I really only had one objective, and that was to destroy him in the way he'd destroyed me. Insidiously. Irreparably. Like a puzzle he slowly disassembled over the course of our eighteen-month relationship, stole a vital piece from, and then discarded, knowing that nobody would ever be able to put it back together again. But I needed a plan. A strategy. Something solid. And so, I did what I always do when I need a solution: I made a list.

Reputation.

Work.

Money.

Family.

Health.

Home.

Sanity.

Sex.

Other.

This, I scrawled in my journal. Actually, it wasn't my journal at all, it was an old purple leather notebook I'd bought with the intention of jotting down useful French phrases I wanted to remember. I'd taken it to Paris on our first weekend there. And as I held it in my hands, the memory made me wince. We'd been dating for two months, were lying naked in a hotel room, bathed in a sort of pink light, the lace curtains wide open and the tip of the Eiffel Tower in the distance. He'd just announced that he wanted me to meet his parents, and I was high on hope as I traced the edge of his face with my fingertips. There was a small white scar on his upper lip, as though he'd split it as a child. 'What happened here?' I asked. And there was a flicker behind his eyes. A jolt. 'Cricket,' he said, swallowing hard. But something about that flash in his eyes told me he was lying. That was the first time I glimpsed his vulnerability, and the memory stayed with me: the flicker, the pink light, the lace. It made me want to protect him.

That was the night I jotted down the first entry: *la magie dans la lumiere*. Pages one through three were filled with similar phrases, but I suppose I lost interest by page four, because it was blank from there.

But it would no longer be my French phrase book. From that moment on it would be a written account of my plans and progress. The sort of stupid mistake I'd never make now.

I continued reading: *'Heaven is yin and yang, cold and hot, the cycle of seasons.'* My face flushed hot: that description fit my former relationship perfectly. The words stared at me from the page, little cacti just waiting to make me bleed. I sipped my tea. And my mind struggled to make sense of the decay.

Because it had all been so promising at the beginning: he was a banker and dazzling and passionate and bold. With Angus, life was like a movie: a dozen red roses at work for no reason, phone calls from the restaurant bathroom in the middle of a business lunch just to say that he missed me, long baths together chatting about nonsense. And it was sex: sometimes gentle and tender, sometimes rough. I never knew what was coming next and I'd never been so sure somebody loved me. He used to say we were the last two romantics in a time of swiping right, which suited me just fine.

Because I wanted more than anything to believe that love was real and the words 'I do' meant something; that my parents were the exception not the rule. And Angus did that for me. We were picnics by the Seine on a stolen hotel blanket, sex in public places when we just couldn't wait, late-night conversations about what our children would look like (my eyes, his hair) and inside jokes nobody else could understand. He could make me laugh with a single look across a dinner-party table. At the beginning everything was so simple: I was his, and he was mine. Within a week we were spending almost every night together. And after two I'd met most of his friends and his parrot (Ed). It was magic, like living in perpetual dusk.

But then, after a few months, the night set in.

A tapestry of darkness began to weave itself around us. It started with the prostitutes in his internet search history, the silent treatment and the realisation that his 'occasional line' was actually a daily habit. Then came the slap, the mind games and the affair with Kim. The sex became rougher and I let it happen, so maybe that's why he thought it was okay to grab me by the throat when we fought. Soon it was all just apologies. Excuses. Make-up sex and tears. But every time I went to leave I'd catch a glimpse of the man I'd fallen in love with and be stung by the certainty that it was at least in part my fault; because I knew how wonderful Angus *could* be if he was happy. And so I'd stay.

Until one night everything culminated in a final, irrational argument and the choice was taken out of my hands.

It was the night before our ski trip. And in the beginning it was about stacking the dishwasher: he preferred the handles facing upwards, and the fact that I consistently didn't comply was proof I didn't respect him. But it had escalated quickly and before long he was delivering the news that 'we' as a concept was shot to shit. I didn't argue – he needed time to calm down – I just gathered my things, he picked up my suitcase (already waiting by the door), and we carried them in silence to his car. What followed was a tense drive to my flat, a tearful late-night phone call to my best friend, Charlotte, and an emergency rescue mission.

When morning came, I didn't know what else to do, so I dragged myself to work. Told my boss that the ski trip had been cancelled last minute. Tried to gloss over it – surely we'd make up – and waited for his call. But when I received the sex-tape link, my focus shifted entirely. I no longer wanted him back, I no longer wanted to talk about 'us'.

Because he'd begged me to make that film and I, wanting to be more exciting to him, hoping it would curb his wandering eye at least for a bit, had complied. I'd been frantically emailing the site since I'd received that link. Imploring them to take it down. Calling Angus and pleading with his voicemail. But nobody answered.

By the time Sunday rolled around I must have clicked on that link at least a hundred times, checking to see if it was gone yet. But it wasn't. And then Charlotte pointed out that every time I clicked on it I was probably pushing it up in the rankings. So I stopped.

Chiara, the neighbour's cat, was meowing at the front door. So I put down the book and let her in. She wove a figure eight through my legs and followed me back to my purple notebook and *The Art of War*.

Step 1. Reputation.

This seemed like the best place to start because our lives had been so intertwined – I knew so many of his secrets. Surely there was *something* I could use against him: I knew his work credit card details, his email password, his PayPal password, where he kept his cocaine, who his friends were, where his parents lived and that he'd gone to prostitutes …

Prostitutes.

That had to be it.

We'd been dating for five months when I first found them in his search history. I'd hoped that I was wrong, so I confronted him about it. He got angry, so very angry – a side of him I'd never seen before – and told me I was impinging upon his privacy. That it was just free porn. I accepted that and apologised – maybe I really *was* over-reacting. He was wonderful in so many ways, and nobody is perfect.

He didn't speak to me for ten days after that. When we finally did make up, he told me that was how he coped, that he shut down when he was deeply hurt and waited until the hurricane passed.

I told myself that the anger was probably just embarrassment: he'd been caught looking at porn. That there were always bumps along the road to intimacy, that passion was a double-edged sword, and that if I wanted the intensely loving parts of Angus, then I needed to accept the darker parts too. But that was the first time I experienced as an adult the gnawing pain that only a sudden silence can impart. And all it did was make me more certain of my love for him. My need for him.

But I never really trusted him again after that. Instead, my paranoia grew: I started going through his pockets and glancing over his shoulder under the guise of giving him a neck rub every time he sat down at the computer. Carefully watching which keys he tapped. Piecing it all together, letter-by-letter. Until soon I knew that his email and PayPal passwords were one and the same: Supercock88.

The next time I found prostitutes in his search history, I kept it to myself: it was just porn, after all. Nothing important. Nothing worth causing a fight over. But the third time was soon after I'd found out about his affair with Kim. And so that time I clicked on the pages. All of them. I just couldn't help myself: I needed to know *why* he needed them. Why I wasn't enough. That was when I noticed that they were all from the same service, located just around the corner from his flat. We'd been dating a little under a year by then. And while I still didn't mention it – what was the point, it wouldn't change anything – I took down the details. Phone number. Address. Email. And the names of the three girls whose pages he had visited the most: Christy, Madeleine, Heather.

Just in case.

And now I finally had the chance to use them. But as I sat there listening to the rain dripping down from the upstairs gutters in thick loud streams as Chiara purred beside me, I was filled with a poisonous and bubbling frustration. Because even after everything Angus had done, even with everything I knew about him – even with the girls' names and the agency details – what could I do about it? I couldn't just tell people about them. Firstly, if I did that he could simply deny it. His word against mine: he'd say I was unbalanced, vindictive, making things up. Secondly, who was to say anybody would even care? No, I needed to get a bit more creative. I needed to make them care. To make it something they *couldn't* just ignore.

A bit like I *couldn't* ignore a sex tape uploaded to the internet.

tuesday

Master Sun said: *'I have heard that in war haste can be folly, but have never seen delay that was wise.'*

7 FEBRUARY

I shut the door quietly behind me and slipped off my shoes. It was 7.01pm. I had half an hour until the night-time stairwell CCTV switched on and Jake came on duty.

Jake was the most astute of Angus's doormen and seemed out of place so close to the handbag dogs and navy blazers of Sloane Square. He was an aspiring DJ with tattoos peeking out the end of his shirt sleeve and a first-class degree in Philosophy – he'd mentioned the latter twice. He had the eyes of a dreamer; they had that kind of sparkle. But the mind peering out from behind those eyes – fuelled by a steady diet of conspiracy theories and Red Bull – was razor sharp.

And he watched those security screens like a hawk. So, the moment he clocked on, a portion of the stairwell became officially out of bounds.

And that would factor into my exit strategy.

–

Nine hours earlier I was at my desk recovering. The Tube ride in had been brutal: fluorescent lights, a lack of space, the combined smell of body odour and takeaway curry and newspapers made damp from wet umbrellas – all amplified tenfold by my hangover.

I worked as a research analyst for a property company just off Berkeley Square, and so a vast spreadsheet detailing house-price growth across London over the past five years glared back at me from my brightly lit screen. It was making my head throb: what I needed was coffee, two paracetamol and a time machine – to be able to go back to that night we met Holly and say: 'no'.

I switched to my inbox, my nausea deepening as I scanned the subject titles. Nothing more about the sex tape. Maybe it had dropped in the rankings.

'How's the Turner report coming?' That was Val. Valerie. My boss. Although she sat a mere metre away from me, we were separated by a blessed cubicle partition. And so she couldn't see me staring blankly at my screen, trying not to cry.

'Coming along well,' I lied. It wasn't – I'd barely started. And it was getting urgent. There was a promotion to Senior Analyst I wanted – I needed the money – and Val was immovably in my corner on that front. I didn't want to let her down but I was finding it hard to concentrate on anything other than Angus, the sex tape and the icy loss that pumped through me with every heartbeat.

'Okay, well, I need to send whatever we have across to his office this afternoon,' Val's voice continued, 'for tomorrow.'

The photocopy machine buzzed behind me. 'Sure,' I replied. *Shit. Tomorrow. The meeting.* I needed to focus. To find an idea. But instead I pulled up a browser window and did the one thing I'd promised Charlotte I wouldn't do: I signed into Facebook.

It was the only social media platform Angus used and my last remaining window into his life. I knew it was dangerous, but I couldn't stop myself. After eighteen months of talking to him almost every day, the silence was excruciating.

I wonder if he's changed his relationship status yet.

My jaw clenched at the thought of the steady stream of emails – mostly from people I hadn't seen in the flesh in over ten years – that would follow that click of his mouse: *I'm so sorry … I thought you were so happy … That's too bad, my marriage is going great.*

And to an outsider, Angus appeared too picture-perfect for our demise to be his fault, so everyone would presume it was mine, something I'd done wrong, some fundamental flaw within me. I couldn't even tell them otherwise – I couldn't tell them about the video, or any of our other secrets – without humiliating myself in the process. No, all I could do was stay silent and hope the conclusions they drew were less damning than the truth.

Eyes narrowed and forehead tensed, I typed his name into the search function: A-N-G-U-S H-O-L-L… A moment later there he was.

Angus: my Facebook friend.

I clicked on his little face – I'd taken that profile photograph. We'd just come back from five days in Gran Canaria. Sand beneath our fingernails. Sunburned shoulders. And me, in the orange string bikini he always loved me in, my legs wrapped around his waist as he carried me through the waves. His skin was tanned, his whiskey-coloured eyes bright and his dark hair still smelled of sunscreen when I'd taken that shot – and we were happy.

'Do you want to chat about it, see if I can help?' Val asked. Her head appeared above the partition. I minimised the browser and glanced at the time: It was 9.43am.

'Sure, I can walk you through what I've got at around 2pm?' I suggested, willing her to leave me alone to focus. *Walk you through.* That was an Angus-ism if ever there was one – whenever I did something he didn't like, he'd gently ask me to 'walk him through' what had happened just so he could walk *me* through why I was wrong. It had fast become my least favourite phrase. And yet there I was, using it like I owned it.

Val smiled and her grey head disappeared once more. My eyes, hungry for information, returned to my screen. And as I glanced down past his birthday and place of work, I saw it:

In a relationship with Taylor Bishop.

He hadn't changed a thing.

My forehead softened. My lungs relaxed. And all the thoughts I'd worked so hard to push aside flew back at me with renewed force: *Maybe he still loves me … Maybe this is just a phase … Maybe Charlotte is right and he has that attachment-issue thing – the one that makes you push people away when they get too close … Maybe he uploaded the tape because he was angry and upset when we broke up and he'll take it down.*

Soon. People do all sorts of awful things to those they love. Especially to those they love.

Yes, avoidant attachment style. That was a mainstay of Charlotte's rookie diagnoses of Angus. She'd been psychoanalysing the world since the day we met: first day of First Form at the boarding school her parents could afford and mine couldn't. I was there on an academic scholarship (I was always the girl with potential) and over the past year and a half we'd spent many evenings analysing Angus and his behaviour. Or rather, she had. I'd spent many evenings drinking too much pinot grigio and listening to her with what I liked to think of as a healthy dose of scepticism. Her diagnosis always bounced between three main hypotheses: avoidant attachment style, malignant narcissism and the fact that he was an Aquarius. For some reason the latter held the most weight with her. But then, I hadn't told her everything. I'd skirted around the darker details and only mentioned his garden-variety offences: the affair with Kim, the drugs, the lies, the silent treatment. There are some things that you can't un-tell, and I didn't want her looking at me – at us – that way.

In a relationship with Taylor Bishop.

As I re-read that phrase my resolve softened, my respiration slowed and my desire to destroy him, so overpowering just hours before, began to cower. My feelings for Angus were always like that: tangled and complicated. Love tinged with fear. Rage laced with longing. And the sadness of what we'd become always giving way to the hope that we might somehow find our way back.

Maybe it all just got out of hand. I need to talk to him.

I stared at the screen, trying to make sense of everything. But then something bright blue and sparkling caught my eye. It was right at the bottom of the page. I scrolled down further.

And there it was: a bright blue sky above a sparkling white snowy slope. And there he was, grinning back with those bleached white teeth of his that glowed in the dark like a Halloween costume whenever we went to a nightclub. And there she was. Grinning alongside him.

His ex. The one he 'never spoke to' anymore. Kim.

—

Which is how I ended up breaking into Angus's apartment that evening. Did I know I was doing the wrong thing at the time? Absolutely. Of course I did. I just didn't care anymore.

The first thing I needed: gloves.

I hadn't had a lot of time to prepare (it was Tuesday and he was due back on Thursday), so I'd overlooked the issue of fingerprints. In hindsight, mine were probably still justifiably strewn throughout the apartment – we'd been a couple just a week before – but there are some lessons we learn from TV crime shows that we simply can't unlearn: *fingerprints are bad* is one of them. *Never leave an e-trail* is another.

I left the lights off: I didn't want anything drawing a neighbour's attention to my presence. But I knew that flat well – the creaky spots in the floorboards, the sharp edges to be avoided. And there was just enough artificial light streaming in through the balcony window to allow me to make out shapes in the dark: the coffee table, the cold marble kitchen counter and the black leather sofa we used to binge-watch TV series on. I could still feel his arms wrapped around me, the warmth of his breath in my hair as I leaned back into his chest and told him who I thought the bad guy was. I'd learned a lot from those bad guys. From their mistakes.

I slid towards the kitchen, opened the stainless-steel fridge door for extra light and peered into the cupboard beneath the sink. Kneeling on the cold floor, I found what I was looking for: the box of surgical gloves he kept for dirty jobs. I put a pair on.

A low, dark shuffle. Movement. Behind me, to the left.

I swivelled my head.

My heart ping-ponged in my chest and my eyes searched for a form in the darkness.

The shuffle came again; it was coming from the window.

My breath stopped. I froze. And then he moved through a beam of light.

Ed. Angus's pet parrot.

His large cage was periodically moved around the apartment, and its current position was on the living-room floor by the window. He was standing in a spotlight cast by the globe outside: a rash of green and yellow feathers and two black eyes. And he was staring at me. He knew I wasn't meant to be there.

The beeping of the open fridge drew back my attention, and my eyes scanned the brightly coloured bottles, dirty sponges and scouring pads beneath the sink. A plan was forming in the back of my mind, but I didn't know what it was yet. My eyes landed on the white piping that wove its way down like a fat snake from underneath the sink – it gleamed in the fridge-lit darkness.

There'd been a leak in that piping the previous November. It wasn't a big job – it only took five minutes to fix – but the plumber had charged a £150 call-out fee. And so I'd watched carefully how he'd fixed it. Just in case it ever happened in my flat – I could barely afford toothpaste.

It wasn't complicated and he was a willing tutor: there were three nuts on the pipe, one of them was loose, and it just needed to be tightened a bit. Easy.

So, in theory, in order to create another leak, all I needed to do was loosen it again. I reached towards it, and with the same force and determination required to open a stubborn jar of strawberry jam, I unscrewed it. The middle nut. Not entirely, just enough to let a steady trickle free. Then I nudged the bucket of cleaning products to the left so it wouldn't catch the drip.

I watched a small puddle begin to form at the base of the cupboard. With a little luck that steady stream would find its way through to the apartment below long before Angus got back from skiing, pissing off his already angry downstairs neighbour Mrs Clifton – the vice chairperson of the tenants' board.

That may seem like a petty way of inflicting revenge, and my being there may seem crazy – but I had to do something. I couldn't just let him get away with it all. And I wasn't crazy per se – there's a reason 'crime of passion' is considered a viable defence – I was just pissed. Really pissed. Can't-see-past-the-haze pissed. The photograph I'd seen of Angus and Kim, the realisation that he'd taken *her* away on *our* holiday while leaving me in London alone, heartbroken and bitter and writing streams of emails to RedTube while he ignored me, had left me seething in a way I hadn't known since I witnessed my father betray my mother.

And so my plan (concocted that afternoon while staring at a spreadsheet through a blur of tears) was simple: break into his apartment and get a key to his building while he was away.

That way when they changed the access code to the side entrance of the garage – something that happened every month for security reasons – I'd retain access. Not only would that allow me to use the key I still had to his apartment, should I need it, but it would also grant me access to his post box, located just inside the door that led to the garage. And that would open up all sorts of avenues for mayhem.

I shut the cupboard door quietly, moved towards the beeping fridge, closed it, and reached my hand into the little terracotta bowl above it where he kept the spare keys. My fingers, desensitised by the rubber of the gloves, fumbled around, searching for what I needed. Large. Hard. Metal. And lying loose. There, among the rogue elastic bands, a set of three smaller keys on a metal loop, a promotional bottle opener and a couple of broken pens: the key.

I slipped it into the front pocket of my handbag and looked around the room.

Socks.

His lucky socks.

I could get inside his head.

His bedroom was dark, aside from the orange digits that flashed back at me from the alarm clock beside the bed: 7.13. My clothes were no longer hanging in his closet, but nothing else had shifted. It still smelled like him – the spice of his cologne, fabric softener on the towels – and the bed still wore the same gown-like grey metallic bedspread it had the first night we 'made love'. His words, not mine. He'd turned to me afterwards, wrapped his arms around me and whispered: 'Where do I sign?'

I'd never felt so safe.

But then behind it hung the ugly painting – all dirty-greens and greys – that he loved and I hated. He said it was Rothko-esque. Whatever. That was the same wall he'd held me against the first time he grabbed me by the throat.

And there, facing the bed, stood a big chest of drawers. Mahogany. Brass handles. We'd picked it out together – our first piece of furniture purchased as a couple. I opened the top left drawer and reached inside.

For, while I've learned that there are many things that can be hidden in a relationship, there are others that simply cannot. Things like: Does he snore? How does he take his coffee? And which are his lucky socks? The socks he pulls out only for important meetings or golf with his father. The socks, which if they were not clean when he needed them, would elicit a slap across the face.

They were nothing special to the untrained eye – just a brown-and-black pinstripe – and I could barely identify them in the low light. But I didn't need to. They lived in a very specific place: on the left side of his sock drawer, always rolled into a pair, right at the back and separated from the rest by a small silver cigarette tin.

I took the socks out, used the light on my phone to double check it was the right pair, and placed them in my bag. Even then, without him in the room, I was careful with them.

I reached my hand back into his open drawer and felt for that hard, silver cigarette tin. Because that tin was not just a marker for his lucky socks: it was also where he kept his emergency cocaine – his main supply being duct-taped to the underside of the sofa. I opened it, picked up that little white bag and wandered through to the living room.

Turning the rusty key that lived in the lock to the balcony door, I moved outside towards the railing. And as I stood there looking out over London's jagged horizon, I thought of all the evenings I'd spent out on that balcony with Angus as he sipped his post-work Scotch. 8pm. Every night. All those wasted hours. All that wasted love. And so I took that little bag of white powder and dropped it over the edge.

I meant to simply waste it, for it to fall to the pavement below, but my aim was unintentionally impeccable. Olympics-worthy even.

It landed on the balcony of the flat downstairs. Mrs Clifton's balcony.

And I think that was when the plan formed. The leak. The bag of coke that she'd find waiting for her on her balcony floor.

I'd get him into trouble with the tenants' board.

Still small. Still petty. But those dominos were falling with gathering speed.

I checked my phone: 7.17pm. I had thirteen minutes left and I could see his study door ajar so I quickly moved towards it.

His aged leather chair stared back at me with accusation as I entered. We'd made love in that chair. I looked around me: the chair, the bookcase, the desk, a pad of post-it notes and a small ceramic coffee mug containing two highlighters – pink and yellow. Beside the mug lay a small pile of papers.

And on his desk, emitting what appeared within that darkened room to be a religious glow, sat his computer. I went straight to his search history out of habit: Agent Provocateur, Ocado, Hotmail, Amazon. And then it occurred to me: maybe he was still logged into RedTube. Maybe his password was saved in the keychain. Maybe I could delete the tape for myself. I typed RedTube into the address bar. Went to the log-in screen. Entered his email address. Then slowly, taking care not to hit the wrong key, I typed in the one password I knew of his: S-u-p-e-r-c-o-c-k-8-8.

My pulse sped up.

The screen went white.

I held my breath.

But no.

Invalid username/password!

My face grew hot, my stomach twisted and I wanted to cry. All I could think of was my naked body – all pale skin and shy smile – and Holly with her sticky lip gloss and long dark hair that hung to the middle of her back. The awkward movements. The knocking of teeth. The noises. That video. And Angus holding the camera.

Fuck him.

I went back to his browser history and clicked on Agent Provocateur.

What I needed was something expensive, something that showed thoughtful consideration, something that showed intent – something like the outfits worn by the models on the welcome page. Red, lacy and destined for Felicia, the beautiful – but engaged – woman who lived next door to Angus in Flat 81. I chose the 34C bra, small panties and a garter belt, and moved swiftly to the checkout stage. I ticked the box for gift-wrapping and added a personalised note: 'I hope to see you in these soon. Love, A xx'

Then I entered his PayPal information. And just like that it was done.

Downstairs neighbour: tick. Next-door neighbour: tick.

Adrenaline sparkled in my veins as I sat alone in the silence, staring at the semi-clad women smiling back at me from the screen. I thought of Felicia receiving her gift, then of of Angus's birthday in just three days' time – the one he'd spend with Kim instead of me – and his birthday jumper sitting wrapped in my closet. Then I thought of the slap, the drugs, the apologies, the promises that he loved me and how easily he'd forgotten me. A heat pulsed through me: I wanted to hurt him. I wanted everyone else to see who he really was. And that's when it happened.

That's when I had the idea that would change the course of my life forever.

I pulled up a private browser. Went to Hotmail. And slowly entered: S-u-p-e-r-c-o-c-k-8-8.

This time it worked: I was in.

My pulse beat hard against my inner wrists as I opened a new message and began to type. I kept it short. Specific. A booking. This Friday coming. 8pm sharp. *Please send Christy and Madeleine. Or Heather if need be. It's my birthday*, I typed, pausing for a moment to think, *so please have them come dressed in just boots, a coat and a yellow silk bow wrapped around their waists. Have them only say three words to me all night no matter what I ask for: 'Happy Birthday, sir'. Feel free to charge the all-night rate.*

Send.

I included his work credit card details: he'd given me that card to use months before – for a flight booking when Candice, his team secretary, was taking too long. And there was no way I could have remembered the details after all these months if I hadn't stored them in my phone. So he'd never suspect it was me.

And then I sat there, staring at the screen, a little stunned by what I had done. Waiting for the obligatory reply to arrive, confirming his card had gone through and giving me the total. Imagining the scene when they arrived in their yellow bows. Would Kim be there to meet them?

Four minutes passed, then five, and the email still hadn't come in. I caught sight of the time in the upper right corner of the screen. *Six minutes left.* I would struggle to get out in time. I almost lost my nerve. Almost wrote back to them to say it was a mistake, to cancel. But then at minute eight, there it was: the confirmation email.

It was organised. It was paid for. And the total would definitely be flagged for investigation – anything above £1000 always was and the all-night rate was quoted as £3580. I added the escort service's email address to his black list, ensuring nothing further would find its way to his inbox. Deleted the confirmation email. Deleted it again out of the deleted folder. And followed the same process with the original email I'd sent. Then I cleared the browser history, stood up and headed for the door.

Slipping on my shoes, I opened the front door and shut it gently behind me. Then I walked calmly to the stairwell and, as I moved inside, checked the time on my phone. It was 7.39pm. I was nine minutes late. I couldn't risk the CCTV that operated on the stair-well between the ground and second floors after 7.30pm. I'd have to go to Plan B. I walked quickly down the three flights of concrete stairs to level two, took the lift to the basement, moved past the post boxes – his was empty – skirted the camera, and let myself out the way I'd come in.

As I closed the heavy garage door behind me and moved onto the dark street, I heard the sound of traffic in the distance, buzzing from King's Road, and I moved quickly in that direction. The night air was cold against my cheeks and it was drizzling. I pulled a small black umbrella from my handbag, opened it and used it to obscure my face. And as I got to the corner of the road, I saw the empty bus stop ahead and walked towards it.

It was Angus who'd taught me about the placement of the two CCTV cameras. Most of the residents didn't want CCTV throughout the entire building; they liked their privacy. And so in order to keep surveillance to a minimum and security to a maximum, the camera locations had been decided like this: robbers don't take the lift. In order for them to get higher than the ground floor they'd need to take the stairs between ground and second. Clearly, therefore, that was the only place that required a camera. This logic was reasonably sound, provided the perpetrator didn't know about it. And so camera one had been strategically placed in the corner of the first-floor stairwell platform and took in most of both staircases – ground to first and first to second, give or take a step. That one operated after 7.30pm every evening. Camera two had been placed in the basement facing the cars – the most likely object of theft – and was on permanently. I'd avoided the camera on the stairs simply by taking the lift two floors, and the one in the basement by using the coded side exit – the one I now had a key to – that was in the camera's blind spot.

This in-depth understanding of the building's CCTV had been imparted to me quite early on in our relationship. We'd just got home from his parents' fortieth wedding anniversary dinner – he wanted to have sex in the stairwell but I didn't want to end up on YouTube. Irony at its most acidic. Eventually, after much discussion about security-camera placement, I had complied around floor seven.

I remember hearing the sound of wedding bells chiming in my naïve imagination as he thrust himself into me that night. But as my knees knocked against those concrete stairs, not once did it occur to me how important that knowledge would prove to be.

And I can only presume that not once did it occur to him either.

wednesday

Master Sun said: *'Know the enemy, know yourself, and victory is never in doubt.'*

8 FEBRUARY

'Where the hell is he?' whispered one solemn girl to another. 'I have a ten o'clock.' They were sitting on the other side of the table. Serious types: born in corporate attire and could never be coaxed into a threesome. The type I wished I was right then. But instead, I was the break-and-enter-ordcr-prostitutes type.

And they were my direct competition.

We'd piled into the boardroom, all seven of us: the two solemn ones, Val, me, Nigel – the head of research – and two people I couldn't account for. But the reason we were sitting there, under bad corporate lighting amid flaky, day-old pastries, hadn't arrived yet.

He was late. Twenty-eight minutes late. We had nothing to do but wait, chat and consider whether the indoor plants that sat by the window were real or plastic.

Not that it bothered me: I was too tired to care, and I had Felicia from Flat 81 to occupy what was left of my lucid mind. The lingerie was a good first step, but I needed to up the ante, let her know that it was not just a one-off event. Get her fiancé properly cross. Show them that there was ample reason to be concerned.

I was staring at my phone, scrolling through my junk emails in the hope that I'd missed one from RedTube, when the door opened and he walked into the room.

So, this is David Turner?

He wasn't anything like I'd expected. There were no glasses, no beard, no £400 ripped jeans – no awkward attempt at cool. Instead, he wore a suit. And a big silver diving watch on a strong, solid wrist. He was a bit too pretty for my taste – thick brown hair that struck gold in the light, strong jaw, straight teeth, wide shoulders and blue–green eyes – but he walked with the self-assurance of a man who would turn up on your front lawn with a boom box if you'd had a fight.

And that made me like him immediately. Until he spoke.

'Let me be frank,' he began, before sitting on the edge of the table, 'I expected more.'

There were three spare chairs at that table.

Cock.

There we sat, in the sort of anxious silence usually reserved for the morning after a one-night stand; a silence so potent you can hear your neighbour swallow. We were part of a relatively new division of the company, set up to research and isolate untapped property investment opportunities. David Turner was the biggest client we'd ever had the chance to work with. None of us wanted to lose him, but he clearly wasn't happy.

My mind raced.

Val had briefed me a week before, handing me a business card that read: *David Turner, The Turner Group, Property Investment and Development*. 'He's looking for new projects, something unexpected, something *fresh* that will take his business to the next level,' she'd said. 'He thinks we might find something nobody else has. But we don't know who else he's gone to with this, so it's important that we impress him.' Then, lowering her voice slightly, she'd continued: 'You know, he grew up with seven brothers and sisters.' She'd said this as though multiple siblings posed a serious threat to success in life. 'And *now* look at him. Such a good man, too – always contributing to charity.'

So, three of us (me and the two solemn ones) had the same assignment: find him something nobody else had.

Essentially what I'd interpreted that to mean was that I had to go through London with a fine-toothed comb and find the un-findable. It was an impossible job at the best of times and we'd been given it just as the Angus-shit-storm hit me. So when this man said he'd expected more, from my corner it wasn't entirely unfounded. I *should* have done more by then, and under normal circumstances I would have. Professional inertia was completely out of character for me: I'd always been the conscientious and committed one. But I was off my game. And it stung to have that acknowledged out loud.

'Mr Turner, this is just the preliminary stage of our research.' That was Val, ever the diplomat. 'We're sure to uncover more soon.' She shot me a look that said: *say something*.

'Yes, you asked to see where we were with it,' I said. 'This is in no way a reflection of what we expect the final findings to entail. It's only been a bit over a week.' My voice was steady. I sounded sure. But my pulse was fast. *Just focus on your breath, darling.* It was Angus who taught me to hide my nerves.

'It was quite disappointing,' David said, rephrasing his earlier sentiment.

And then his eyes, navy with green in the middle, made their way to mine.

Bang.

Fuck. Don't you dare blush.

The silence was thick as I swallowed and waited for somebody else to step in and say something. But they didn't. And he didn't. He just sat there, watching as my pale skin turned pink. I had no choice but to continue.

'As I'm sure you can appreciate,' I said, holding eye contact, 'if the opportunities we are looking for were immediately apparent and could be isolated within a week, then everyone would be capitalising on them. By their very nature they're difficult to find. But we *are* making progress. It just takes time.' I waited for him to look away but his eyes didn't waver.

'Let's just try to be a bit more … innovative, shall we?' he said. Then he smiled. *That* smile.

'Of course,' I replied, breaking our gaze. I hated the word innovative – it reminded me of team-building days where everyone has to wear a name badge and share a secret with the group.

'Great, glad we're on the same page,' he said, still smiling.

'Great.' I shot back a polite smile of my own.

Val had clearly decided the meeting wasn't going at all to plan, so it was she who led the evacuation.

But as I walked past David Turner, who was now talking to one of the solemn girls by the door, I will never forget the look he gave me. In a Teflon world, it stuck.

A minute later we were back at our desks – aside from Val; she was at mine, wringing her hands like Lady Macbeth.

'We're going to need to do something,' she said, looking at me. 'This is important.'

'I know,' I replied.

Then she went to her side of the carpeted partition and I sat down heavily in my seat.

I set my browser to private, and then with clumsy fingers I opened 192.com, typed *Felicia* into the 'name' field and *SW3* – Angus's postcode – next to 'location'. Then I clicked 'search'.

Up came a screen asking me to log in.

Shit.

I wanted as light an e-trail as possible. Below the log-in screen was an offer to 'register for free'. My mouse hovered over it. I hesitated.

Fuck it.

I filled in the fields:

Name: Angus

Surname: Hollingsworth

Email: MrHollingsworthtoYou@hotmail.com

Password: Supercock88

Submit.

Up came another screen, prompting me to log into my email to finalise the registration.

Shit. Shit. Shit.

My stomach flipped: I was walking deeper and deeper into quicksand and I wanted to stop. But I couldn't. I knew logging into his email account from work was a bad idea, it was too traceable, but the confirmation email was already sitting there in his inbox, just waiting to be discovered as Angus scrolled through his messages in his white robe and slippers from the hotel room – I had to follow through.

And so, watching my screen for any reflection behind me, anything that spoke of prying eyes, I opened another tab. I navigated to hotmail.com. And logged into his account.

There it was, right at the top, the 'Please confirm your 192.com registration' email. I clicked the 'Confirm registration' button and was taken back to their site.

I took a deep breath, turned back to my screen, blocked any future emails 192.com might send, deleted the confirmation message from his inbox and trash, and logged out of his Hotmail account.

My hands were trembling and my jaw was tight, but as a newly registered user I was free to search 192.com for Felicia at my will. And so I did.

There were two Felicias in that postcode district, but only one who lived in Angus's building. Her full name was Felicia Bronwyn Jones. She was registered to vote. She owned her home – joint ownership, presumably with her fiancé – and her landline was: 0207 946 0139.

I'd just scribbled that down on a pad beside my desk when a small notification popped up in the lower right-hand corner of the screen – an email had come in from Charlotte.

You okay? FH is going to have the worst karma. xx

FH was an abbreviation for Fuckhead – the nickname she'd given Angus immediately following the break-up. I'd learned the awkward way that my work email had a swear-filter.

I typed back: *Hey honey, thanks, am okay. Am sure karma's got it covered ;)*

'Karma' being me and Master Sun Tzu.

It was dark outside and I was lying in bed, the whir from an electric heater coming from the floor beside me as I scrolled through old photos of Angus and me on my computer. My phone buzzed from the bedside table: a text message from my mother.

Please just let me know you're all right, sweetheart.

I typed back: *I'm fine, love you. xx*

But she'd know the truth.

She'd warned me of the danger Angus posed long before I'd experienced it. 'He worries me,' she'd said. 'Why?' I'd asked. And she'd replied, 'He injects you with sunshine, and that can never end well.'

At the time I'd thought she was projecting, presuming all relationships would end up the way hers had with my father. How could sunshine possibly be bad? And when she'd said it I was still high on the warmth of his gaze, the honey in his voice, my laughter as he tickled me and the smell of his hair on the pillowcase. There was nothing like it on earth.

But she wasn't projecting: my mother just knew the agony of a cold world when the sun went down and the wind and rain set in.

And soon enough, I did too.

Because the more powder that went up his nose the worse he became.

I cast my mind back to the last time I'd looked into his eyes – they were the colour of whiskey when held up to the light. It was just before I got out of the car, grabbed my suitcase from the back seat, rolled it inside and he drove away …

I stared back at my computer screen: selfies we'd taken in bed. Always smiling. Me: kissing his cheek. Him: winking at the lens. Screen shots of things I'd considered for his birthday present: a wine aerator, a flying lesson, a money clip. A couple of dick pics. Another screen shot, this time of a loving message I'd forwarded to Charlotte to prove that he wasn't all bad. He'd sent it to me a few months before, when he'd been away on business in

Hong Kong: *If I had one wish right now it would be that you were next to me. A xx*

I closed my eyes and clenched my jaw: I was softening.

I could feel it.

My resolve was slipping away. I could feel nostalgia's riptide tugging at my ankles, trying to pull me under – I couldn't let that happen. And so I did the one thing that I knew would fix it: I clicked on the link to my sex tape. It stalled for a moment – my wifi connection was slow – then loaded and started to play. The red hue of the footage, Holly's hair, my coy smile. I closed the window quickly and went back to my photos.

Then, selecting every photograph in the album entitled 'Angus and Me', I pressed 'delete', plugged my phone into the computer and let them sync. Now there was nothing left to taunt me. No happy memories to pull me under.

My purple notebook was lying beside the bed on top of a pile of books: *The Unbearable Lightness of Being*, a book about fashion written by a TV costume designer, an unread copy of *The New Yorker* and *The Art of War*. I reached for it, picked up the pen that lay beside it and began to write.

I could hear the bubble and hiss of the boiler spilling through from my little kitchen and see a mounting pile of dirty laundry in the corner of the room.

Angus would still be living his life of dry-cleaning – the only thing that had changed was the woman collecting it – while after eighteen months of service I was back to watching my clothes spin round and round in the big steel machines in the laundromat on the corner.

I pressed hard into the paper as I crossed things off my list that night, making notes in the margin. And I can only presume that if Fate was looking on, she must have been clapping her hands with glee as the ink flowed: her dominos would continue to fall unhindered. But as I read back from it I couldn't help but wonder: what had I actually accomplished? The prostitutes. The leak beneath the sink. The coke on Mrs Clifton's balcony. Felicia. And his lucky socks.

It was all so petty, so silly – and I wanted to do something that truly made a dent.

But what?

thursday

Master Sun said: *'The art of war is governed by five constant factors: 1) Moral Law, 2) Heaven, 3) Earth, 4) The Commander, 5) Method and discipline.'*

9 FEBRUARY

'Right. Lay it on me,' Val said, arms crossed. 'How bad is it?'

I hadn't slept properly and was staring out the window at the building across the road trying to focus my eyes.

'Taylor?'

'Sorry. Not great,' I said, looking at her. 'I really have no idea where to start.' The tan leather skirt I was wearing had mistakenly found its way into one of the industrial-grade washing machines at the laundromat a few days before. It was now too short and too tight, and made me shuffle as I laid my research out on the table. I shouldn't have worn it.

We were in a meeting room on the client level: three glass walls separated us from a steady stream of grey suits, ornate stitching and shiny shoes. And Val was circling the table in silence, nervously double-clicking a pen with her thumb as she took in everything I'd found. A nod here. A small grunt there. The brightly coloured charts; the bullet points; the maps; the countless red stars intended to mark something important. To the untrained eye it looked like a jumbled mess. It *was* a jumbled mess – but not to Val.

'Hmm, this one is interesting.' She picked up a page showing two line charts. I'd scribbled a couple of notes underneath it. 'What's going on here?' she asked.

'Value growth,' I said. 'The blue line shows properties with some kind of green space, and the red shows those close to schools. The top chart is West London and the bottom one is East. But there's nothing new there, Val. Nothing we don't already know.'

'We could try combining them,' she said, 'create some sort of index. Maybe include proximity to grocery stores?'

I felt my pocket vibrate.

'Oh, look who it is,' Val said through a clenched smile, her eyes following what I presumed to be a figure walking past the glass behind me, her thumb giving another double-click of her pen. 'What's he doing here again so soon?'

'What? Who?' I asked, turning around before she could answer.

David Turner was walking past slowly, watching us, one of the solemn girls by his side. He was waving, smiling, and it made my pulse jump, so I looked away and pulled my phone from my pocket as a distraction.

'I wonder what she's been suggesting,' Val said, eyeing the solemn girl. 'Can I keep these?' she added, nodding towards the papers.

'Sure,' I said as I stared at the screen. It was Charlotte, checking we were still on for yoga that night. It was Thursday. We always did yoga on Thursdays.

~

'They haven't written back yet?' Charlotte asked. 'That's ridiculous.' She was wearing a charcoal woollen dress and thick black tights, her beige coat hanging on the back of her chair. She chewed on the lemon from her gin and tonic, swirled the ice in her glass, and her small engagement ring gleamed from her finger as she moved.

Charlotte: the girl who introduced me to boys, booze and the joys of downing half a bottle of cough syrup while lying in the sun.

Charlotte: with painfully rich parents and a soft spot for the esoteric.

Charlotte: my best friend.

Arguably, my *only* friend following the break-up. The few acquaintances I'd had in London before Angus and I got together had fallen away through lack of care – at the beginning he was all I needed, and by the end I didn't have the energy for small talk and pleasantries – and his friends were just that: his friends. But Charlotte was Charlotte and didn't give up.

She was tall and ethereal, her light brown hair cut into an angled bob that highlighted her eyes: hazel, round and glittery. She was one of those people whose life never seemed to fall apart and yet she never judged me when mine did. So when Angus pulled the plug the week before, the first thing I did after he dropped me home and I shut the door behind me was dial her number.

It was 10.30 on a Tuesday night, she was a high-school teacher so had to be at her desk by 7.30 the next morning and was leaving a fiancé at home, but forty minutes later she was on my doorstep with a bottle of gin, a packet of weed and a sleeping bag I hadn't seen since our Eighth Form ski trip. And she didn't leave my side until the Sunday afternoon.

Which is how Monday, Jamie and *The Art of War* happened.

'No, not yet,' I replied. Charlotte had helped pen my series of incensed letters to RedTube, peppering them with phrases such as 'blatant disregard', 'unconscionable conduct' and 'culpability'. She watched a lot of law TV and was a connoisseur of alibis, missed clues, foiled plots and legal jargon, so by virtue of conversation, so was I.

'It's not legal. They *have* to take it down. You could probably sue Angus,' she said, looking around for the waitress.

We were huddled in a dark corner of Nam Long. This was 'yoga'. We used to actually get dressed in stretchy pants and turn up at the yoga studio with our mats and the best of intentions – but it always ended the same way: with us escaping through the emergency exit that led from the women's change room into an alleyway and onto the street. Eventually we just cut out the middleman and met at Nam Long instead. 'Seriously, we need to find you some kind of legal advice. I'll ask Ben if he knows anyone. Angus truly did outdo himself this time.' Ben was her fiancé. Beautiful. Kind. The sort of bone structure and skin colour only mixed-heritage can give you. Actor by trade, corporate health-and-safety filmmaker by economic necessity. And a member of Shoreditch House.

'Do you really think I need a lawyer?' I asked. The thought of having to show that video to yet another set of eyes left me feeling defeated. Ashamed. How had I agreed to that threesome in the first place? Why had I let him tape it? And how had that mistake ended up in the public domain?

'Well, if they won't reply and Angus won't talk to you, I don't see that you have any other choice,' she said, taking the last sip of her drink then sucking on an ice cube.

'I just wish I could get back at him,' I said. Then I waited for her response. Maybe she'd agree, help me plot.

'No, don't do that,' she said, biting down on the ice and shaking her head. 'He'll twist the whole thing to make it your fault. Best thing you can do is walk away and let a lawyer deal with it.'

And for someone like Charlotte, that would be true: she had the money and the clout behind her to hire the kind of lawyer that would turn a sex tape into a profitable lawsuit. I didn't. But what I *did* have was Felicia of Flat 81's phone number. And on the way to meet Charlotte, I'd used it.

Having booked Angus's return ticket for our romantic ski trip, along with my own, I knew what time he was due into Victoria Station from Gatwick: 5.30pm. I probably wouldn't have remembered that time so clearly if he hadn't made such a fuss about having to be at the station at rush hour. But that was the train that worked with the flight. And so it stayed.

There were two phone boxes on Buckingham Palace Road just outside Victoria Station, both of them fully functioning. I knew that because I'd seen people in them, people I'd always regarded with a certain level of suspicion, talking on the phone. *Who uses a phone box unless they are up to no good?* But a public phone box is a wonderful tool for a stalker: it could be anybody calling. And so there I was at 5.45pm, surrounded by the business cards of sex workers and strip joints, dropping three 20p coins into the slot and pressing the grimy keys.

All around me, tourists hurried along the grey street wheeling suitcases, balancing take-away coffee cups or examining maps on phones. I was wearing a black baseball cap and kept my face angled away from the pavement, towards the road and the line of parked tour buses on the other side. Angus would need to wheel his suitcase down that pavement to get a cab home from the station. Hell, that was the precise reason I'd chosen *that* phone box at *that* time: it gave total plausibility to Angus having placed the call when Felicia finally put two and two together. I wasn't sure how to help that penny drop yet – how I'd link the lingerie and the call to Angus – but I knew the answer was out there somewhere. Waiting.

I dialled slowly: 0207 946 0139. Felicia Bronwyn Jones.

The line rang twice and then it went to voicemail: 'Hi, you've called Felicia and Joe, we're unable to get to the phone right now, please leave your name and number after the beep. If it's urgent please call Fee on: 0770 090 0007.'

Beep.

Deep breath in. Deep breath out. Deep breath in. Deep breath out. Deep breath in. Deep breath out.

Then I hung up. Felicia officially had a stalker and I officially had her mobile number: *zero-double-seven-zero-zero-nine-zero-zero-zero-zero-seven.*

It was as memorable as a pizza-house jingle.

Twenty seconds later I was exiting that phone booth, closing its dirty red door and crossing the busy road away from Angus's path home. The air was thick with exhaust fumes, and the sky dark and starless. I kept my head down and made my way to meet Charlotte at Nam Long at 6.30pm.

'Babe, it *will* be okay,' she said, reaching across the wooden table and squeezing my hand. And I wanted her to be right. But Life had taught me that the converse was more often true: it was always the exact moment I began to believe the carpet was real that it was yanked from beneath my feet.

She turned her head to face the bar and waved to get the waitress's attention: dyed black hair and a silver nose ring that caught the light. 'She'll have another pina colada and I'll have another gin and tonic,' she called to her with a smile.

'No, I'm okay, thanks,' I said to the waitress. Then I turned back to Charlotte: 'I can't have any more.'

She looked at me with concern.

'I haven't eaten all day and it's burning my stomach,' I said. But it was nice to have a fuzzy head, the details of my life scrambled for a short while.

'Okay,' she said. 'Burger?'

'Burger,' I agreed, sipping the dregs from my glass. Then we both moved to the bar, my ears latching on to the song that was playing – 'Satisfaction', The Stones – as the waitress moved to the till.

'Well, I hope he has a horrible holiday,' Charlotte said, pulling her money from her purse as the waitress passed our bill across the scratched wooden bar.

'Me too,' I said, pulling a twenty-pound note from my purse to pay my share. I looked down into my handbag, carefully choosing my words. 'But I doubt he will.' I paused for a moment. 'He took Kim.'

She stared at me, eyes flaming: 'What?'

I hadn't wanted to tell her that. Because then she'd ask how I knew and I'd have to admit to looking at his Facebook page, something we'd agreed I wouldn't do.

'I looked at his Facebook page,' I admitted, crinkling my nose.

'Babe, I'm so sorry,' she said, exhaling loudly and putting her hand on my arm. Then we turned and headed for the door.

Old Brompton Road was alive with the red flare of tail-lights. As we turned left and headed past the dry-cleaner, the international-newspaper vendor and a dimly lit pub with noisy people spilling out onto the street, I buried my cold hands deep in my pockets.

We walked in silence for a little while, past the naked winter trees, across a road, over puddles turned amber by the streetlights above us, and eventually Charlotte spoke. 'I can't believe he took her. I mean, what the fuck?'

'I know,' I said.

I couldn't figure out what Kim had that I didn't – why he'd chosen her over me. All I could presume was there was something calming about her that didn't translate to the photographs I'd seen of her; something that made him treat her better than he treated me. That was the only thing that made sense. Because she was so processed: all bleached hair, fake smiles and shiny dresses that barely covered her boobs. She didn't seem like Angus's type at all. *I* was his type: naturally dark blonde hair that brushed my collarbones, medium height and slender, well read, high cheekbones and grey–blue eyes he'd once said were the colour of the ocean in a winter storm.

He'd *told* me I was his type. Many times.

I couldn't see him taking her to a business dinner; I couldn't see his demure mother or elitist father warming to her the way they had to me – discussing the meaning of Turner's early artwork over dinner and beaming at the fact that I, a property researcher, knew who that was. But then, he'd dated her for the two years before we'd met – and for a brief spell after that – so, clearly I was wrong. I'd found the photographs I was basing those assumptions on in a shoebox at the bottom of his cupboard. Her name was written on the back – *Kimmy*. I'd never mentioned that box to him. Instead I'd just hoped she'd fade from both our memories in time.

'That's precisely why you can't look at his page,' Charlotte said, breaking my train of thought. 'It'll just torture you.'

My skirt was creeping up as we walked, so I adjusted it and pulled it flat. 'You're totally right,' I said, 'but it's like I can't stop myself.'

The pina coladas were wearing off, and the sadness I'd become accustomed to wearing was returning. The yellow-and-red lit-up signage of our burger place glowed from the street corner ahead and we walked quickly towards it, pushed through the wooden doors and sat at a table by the window. It had fogged up at the edges, but I could see a couple outside, kissing by the traffic lights. Her hands were in his back jean pockets, and they missed the green man. But they didn't care.

'What you need is a distraction,' she said. 'What about that guy from last week – the lawyer one?'

'Jamie?' I asked. 'No, he just wants to hook up. I need for them to at least pretend to want to date me.'

'Okay, give me your phone.' Her hand was out in front of her.

'What for?' I asked, pulling it from my bag.

'Just trust me,' she said as she took it.

I watched her busy thumbs with suspicion. I could smell French fries and was hungry. 'What are you doing?' I asked. 'It's almost out of charge.'

'Just wait,' she said.

My eyes moved back to the couple outside. They were crossing the street. Then they were gone.

'Two seconds. Seriously.' She was concentrating, her fingers moving quickly.

'You're not texting anyone, are you?' I asked. The last thing I needed was her sending a piece of her mind to Angus from my phone.

'No,' she replied, 'calm down. Okay, I need you to enter your Facebook info.' She lifted her eyes and handed me my phone.

'What?' I asked.

'Just sign into Facebook.'

'What for?' I asked.

'Taylor,' she said firmly.

'Fine.' I signed in and handed it back to her.

'Okay, all done,' she said as she leaned across to me so we could both see the screen. A picture of my face stared back at me, my name underneath it.

'I don't want to be on a dating app,' I said, looking up at her.

'I know,' she replied. 'But you don't want to be pining after an arsehole, either.' She swiped across, and a man's face – mid-thirties, good hair, the sort of self-conscious smile that said he didn't enjoy having his picture taken – filled the screen. 'You know how this works, right?'

'Sort of,' I said.

'It's easy: press the heart if you like them and the cross if you don't. We like him because he's hot.' Her finger loitered over the heart and it turned red. Another picture appeared.

'Yuck,' we said in unison and she pressed the cross.

'See? Easy. Then when they like you too you get a match. And then they can message you. It's like dating for dummies,' she said, handing me my phone.

'How do you even know about this stuff?' I asked, eyes narrowed. 'You're about to get married.'

'Yes, but I *am* a high-school teacher. I know everything.'

That was true. She knew about things I'd never even thought about: the newest apps, slang, and a series of sex tips she'd acquired via eavesdropping in the girls' bathroom. Those, I'd tried to forget.

'So, here's what's going to happen,' she said. 'We're going to eat our burgers, when they finally take our bloody orders,' she looked around for a waitress, 'then you're going to at least try using that app before you go to bed tonight, and then try again in the morning. And when you match with someone cool you're going to go and meet them. You won't want to, but just go. Maybe you'll get a date for Valentine's Day. And maybe you'll surprise yourself.'

So, that's what we did. We ate our burgers. She ate my fries. And then we both went home: her to the lovely Ben, and me to an empty bed and my purple notebook. And in it, I scribbled an account of that evening. Not because it was a diary, but because I needed to tell someone, and there was nobody there to tell.

Saw Charlotte tonight. It was fun but I'm still so sad. It's like a rainstorm is following me around and I keep ignoring it, waiting for it to pass, but it doesn't. It just grows darker and heavier. I just can't believe he'd do this to me. Any of it. Tomorrow is Friday, his birthday. And I keep thinking about last year, wondering where we went so wrong, and about the prostitutes turning up, wondering if I did the right thing. I want him to pay for what he's done but I hate the thought of him with someone else almost as much as I hate him. Anyway, bed now.

Raindrops beat against the window as I squeezed my eyes shut and tried to fall asleep. I was wearing a pair of tartan pyjama bottoms and an old T-shirt – his shirt had been relinquished – and I was cold. I pulled the duvet up towards my chin and waited for the thoughts to stop. But they didn't. They just kept swirling. I could feel him there beside me, his warmth, his weight. I could hear him breathing. His voice. All early-morning gravel: *'Sunday Girl'*. He used to call me his Sunday Girl. *'You always know where your heart belongs when it gets to Sunday and there's only one person in the whole world you want to curl up with on the sofa.'* And that was a crown I wanted. I tried to block it out and rolled over. But I couldn't, it kept drawing me back, startling me like a motorbike backfiring. My eyes flicked open: there was light streaming in through the crack in the curtains and landing on my phone by the bed. So I reached for it and opened the app. What could it hurt to follow Charlotte's instructions?

A parade of faces appeared on the screen. And names. James. Peter. Walter. Dave. Lars. Cedric. Funny blurbs. Souls for sale. Some were handsome. Some were not. But nobody was him, and I ached.

Still, I forced myself to press the heart a few times. And the cross a few more than that. And eventually biology won over and a deep sleep found me. And when I awoke the next morning … I had a match.

Actually, I had six.

friday

Master Sun said: *'The skilful warrior stirs, and is not stirred.'*

10 FEBRUARY

Perhaps if I'd seen David when I first walked in, I wouldn't have got so drunk.

But I hadn't. So I was.

It was 8pm, I'd been there since 6.30pm and Walter, my shitty entrée back into the dating world, was mumbling something inane through his teeth. We were surrounded by low lights, silver ice buckets and a sea of yellow napkins – all folded into origami witches' hats – but he had one of those monotone voices that even atmosphere and wine can't fix.

And I'd know, I was on my fourth glass.

At 8am, when he'd suggested dinner, it had seemed charming. At the very least, his photos had looked promising. But by 8pm, the un-retouched, un-filtered version was watching me from across the table and it felt creepy. Still, there we were: two ill-matched strangers at Signor Sassi. It was well reviewed and in Knightsbridge – just one Tube stop from work – which all sounded good in theory, but the longer I sat there the more I flinched every time that wooden door opened. I didn't want anybody to see me there. Not with Walter.

'Really, how very interesting,' I said. He was in the middle of explaining what he did for a living – something about derivatives – and I was on my third bread roll, thinking instead about the fact that it was Angus's birthday – Christy, Madeleine and their yellow silk ribbons would be turning up soon and I still wasn't sure how to feel about it.

Walter had a mole to the left of his lips and it jiggled when he spoke. I kept watching it and was worried he'd think I was looking at his mouth. Small. Dry. So I averted my eyes and let them scan the room.

And that's when I saw him. The other him. Four tables away. His face was slightly obscured by the back of a blond head but it was definitely him.

David Turner.

My eyes met his before I fully registered who he was. *Fuck.* I looked away and tried to focus on Walter. On his mole. But David had clocked me and I could feel him watching me. I willed my face to relax, my heart to calm down, but it wouldn't.

Walter continued his monologue and I smiled. Nodded.

What's David Turner doing here?

I watched him from the corner of my eye: talking, smiling, shuffling in his seat. Then I focused on the blond head sitting across from him: it appeared to belong to a man, not a woman.

Interesting.

'How was your ravioli?' Walter asked.

'Great,' I said, and took another sip of wine.

How was your ravioli. That was as interesting as Walter was going to get. Not like Angus. Fifteen minutes into our first proper date, he'd leaned in towards me, looked me in the eye with that whiskey stare of his and said, 'You're dangerous.' Then he'd smiled and added, 'But that's okay, so am I.' I guess I knew it was a line, but I didn't care. It was electric.

There was nothing dangerous about Walter.

My eyes were drawn back to David. He was dressed for a business meeting – all pink shirt, tie and tailored stitching – and was pouring wine for the table. Red. The muscle in the left side of his jaw was twitching beneath the stubble. And he was sipping from his big glass, focusing intently on what the man in front of him was saying. Then he was squinting. Feigning interest. And as I watched, his demeanour changed in the subtlest of ways, a minute shift in the way he was sitting – taller – his forehead furrowing, his laugh masculine, and I knew: he knew I was watching him.

'Mine was great too,' said Walter.

'Great.' I smiled, rearranging my cutlery.

'Anyway, I feel like I've done all the talking,' he said. 'Tell me all about you.'

'What would you like to know?' I asked.

'Everything,' he said with a smile. 'Why don't you start at the beginning?'

Shit, he thinks this is going well.

I laughed nervously. 'Okay … Well, you think of a question, I'm just going to pop to the ladies' room for a moment,' I said, standing up and laying my yellow napkin down on the table – I needed to escape, even if just for a moment.

'Okay,' he said.

Then I headed towards the staircase: it was steep and spiralled and lined with mirrors, and I could see the restaurant reflected in it. I led myself upwards, took a deep breath and let my fake smile relax.

And as I pushed through the heavy doors that led to the ladies' room with one arm, I used the other to retrieve my phone from my handbag.

You bitch! I typed with clumsy, drunken fingers. *He's so awful! xx* I managed to type enough of Charlotte's name for the software to do the rest, and then I pressed send, but it didn't go. No reception.

'Perfect,' I said out loud. A girl in silver shoes exited the cubicle behind me, and moved towards the basin. 'No reception,' I offered as she turned on the tap. She gave a half-smile, dried her hands and left.

Putting the phone back into my handbag I moved my face close to the mirror: I looked haggard. The red wine had left my teeth a funny colour, my face looked pale against the black dress I was wearing and the unforgiving lights made the skin under my eyes look crepey. *How the hell did I get here?*

Two minutes later I exited, my drunken eyes guiding me towards the spiral staircase that would deliver me back to dear Walter.

Now, you wouldn't think destiny intervening would have a sound, but it does: a high-pitched clang. Like one of Fate's dominoes had fallen over a teaspoon, or banged into an empty ceramic cup. And if you close your eyes you can feel it on a cellular level.

'Taylor Bishop,' he said.

Clang.

Of course, maybe it wasn't destiny at all. Maybe he'd just followed me. But it sure as hell *felt* like destiny. I looked up, my hand grasping tighter to the flimsy banister for stability. And there he was, passing me on that narrow spiral staircase.

David Turner.

I'd never had a thing for the Pierce Brosnans of the world; I was wary of their smoothness, their lacquered veneer and the wholeness that I sensed lay inside them. Wholeness meant they didn't need me. It was always the inwardly broken and unpredictable ones who won my heart, the poetry of their jagged edges catching on my imagination as I tried to walk on by. And there was nothing broken about David Turner, so he wasn't my type. Not at all. And yet there I was, trying to remember to breathe.

'Hi,' I said. Surprised. His reflection was splintered in the shards of mirror that lined the staircase.

'What are you doing here?' he asked.

'Eating,' I replied. 'I'm with, ah,' I didn't know what to call Walter, 'a friend.'

'Right. Going well, then?' he joked. And a new smile, a less rehearsed smile, flashed across his face.

I laughed. 'No. Terrible. What about you?' My voice was low. Almost a whisper. And my pulse was fast – I could smell the alcohol.

'Same,' he said, 'but mine actually *is* a friend. Recently separated.' His head motioned down the stairs. 'I'm trying to cheer him up so he doesn't top himself on Valentine's Day.'

'Oh, I'm sorry,' I said.

'I know, it's all so shit,' he said with a smile, his eyes holding my gaze. 'Shall we stage an escape?'

And I couldn't help myself. 'Definitely,' I laughed.

And then we stood there, silent. I could feel his body heat, smell his shampoo – spiced limes – and all I wanted was to reach out and touch him. But I couldn't: he was a client, and Walter was waiting for me downstairs. I started to walk away.

'Well, have a nice evening, David,' I said. 'It was nice to see you.'

Good save. Professional.

'Nice to see you too,' he said.

I could feel him watching me as I moved down the stairs back to Walter. And I liked it.

'The pudding menus came while you were gone,' Walter said as I sat down.

I smiled in reply.

'I'm thinking cheesecake,' he continued.

I pretended to study the menu, my heart beating hard against the soft spot in the middle of my throat.

'What are you going to have?' he asked.

'Same,' I replied, placing the menu back on the table and crossing one hand over the other in front of me.

'So, tell me about your job,' he said. Then one of his hands – soft and flat – reached on top of mine. My jaw clenched and my skin recoiled. All I wanted was to pull my hand away, but I didn't want to be rude. I'd forgotten how awful first dates could be.

'I work in property.' I forced a smile.

'Really?' he replied.

'Yes,' I said. 'I mainly do research.'

My eyes scanned the room. I was searching for David's face among the remaining diners. They landed on his seat. It was empty. He was gone. And so was the man he'd been dining with …

Fuck.

'Oh, right.' Walter took a sip of wine, let go of my hand, narrowed his eyes and smiled. He was trying to flirt.

Shit.

'So, markets. Property markets,' I said, keeping it deliberately vague.

Then I saw it: a flicker of movement in the corner of the room. And I allowed my eyes to follow it.

Just for a moment.

One. Single. Moment. A solitary marker amid the white noise.

Because that flicker of movement could have been anything: a waiter returning from a smoke break, a diner who'd taken the wrong route to the bathroom, anything. But it wasn't. It was David Turner, eyes smiling, hand beckoning.

To me.

And I knew that I shouldn't go. That it wasn't sensible. That he was a client. But I was drunk. And he was an unexpected shard of light, piercing through the darkness Angus had cast. And everybody needs the light sometimes.

'Sorry, I need to go back to the loo quickly,' I said. 'I feel like I have something stuck in my teeth.' I pulled my hands back and covered my mouth with one of them. 'Need to floss,' I said. Then I grabbed my handbag and got up.

'Let me see?' Walter offered but I shook my head and made my way across the room, tugged by an invisible wire lodged deep within my chest. Past the staircase. Past the mirrors. And into the narrow, darkened hallway where he stood. David grabbed my wrist and pulled me out of sight. We were standing side by side, hiding in the darkness. He already had his coat on – black – and a light grey scarf hanging from his neck.

'What are you doing?' I asked with a laugh, dizzy from the wine.

'Staging our escape,' he said as he peeked his head around the corner, back towards the tables.

'This is nuts,' I said. But it was also fun.

'Shh,' he hissed, forefinger to mouth.

'Where are we going to escape to?' I whispered.

'Anywhere,' he said.

'What happened to your friend?' I asked.

'He's in on the plan. Fully endorsed it. He happily went home to drown his sorrows and drunk dial his soon-to-be ex-wife. Poor fuck.' Wink.

'Are you drunk?' I asked. He seemed so different from the man I'd met just days before.

'Very. Are you?' he asked with a smile.

'Yes,' I said, 'quite.'

'Good,' he replied. 'Okay, this way,' he said, leading me away from the tables and towards what sounded like the kitchen. 'I know a secret exit.'

'Oh really?' I said. 'Done this before, have you?'

'I am deeply wounded by your insinuation,' he said. Then the corner of his mouth turned upwards.

'But my coat …' I said.

'Oh fuck, where is it?' he asked.

'The hostess took it.' We were standing outside the kitchen and I could smell garlic and hear sizzling.

A young, timid-looking waiter walked past us and David touched his arm: 'Please would you get the lady's coat and meet us out the back with it?' he asked, his tone polite and kind.

'Which one is it?' the waiter asked.

'Darling, what does your coat look like?' David asked me. All conspiracy and secrets.

Darling.

'Navy. Size 8. Big gold buttons,' I replied, tracing the pattern of the buttons with my hand.

The waiter nodded and we parted ways: him to the coat rack, us to the emergency exit marked by the dark green sign that hung from the ceiling, suspended by a rusty chain. David was leading me by the hand.

We got to the end of the hallway, pushed through the heavy metal door, and out into an alley lined with rubbish. The air was cold and clung to my skin, and it had been raining.

To our right lay a smelly darkness just beyond a noisy pub. In front of us lay a red and yellow intermingling of lights, and the tyres and horns that spoke of a main road. The waiter emerged from the back door behind us, my coat held out nervously in front of him.

'Is this it?' asked the waiter.

I nodded. And as David handed the waiter £10, took the coat and opened it for me to put on, I saw Walter through the window, sitting under dimmed lights, waiting for my return. *I should have said goodbye*. But then David took me by the hand again, and led me to Brompton Road.

'Where do you want to go?' he asked me. He was hailing a cab. The streets were full and a car alarm sounded in the distance.

'Anywhere,' I replied. 'Anywhere else.' I was breathing fog and doing up the buttons on my coat.

'Good answer,' he said, pulling out his phone.

'Why?' I laughed suspiciously.

'You'll see,' he said, dialling a number on his phone: 'Hello, I need a room.'

My ears pricked up. *A room?*

'What?' I asked and he shushed me. Forefinger to lips again.

'Turner. Thank you, see you in five minutes,' he said.

'David, I'm not going to a hotel with you,' I said, warning bells ringing loudly in my ears.

'Relax, I just need a shower,' he said. 'I've been on the go since 5am. Then we'll go to a bar or something.'

A cab approached and pulled up beside us on the kerb. And the driver, about sixty with a tight mesh of pink veins glowing from his cheeks, rolled down the window. 'Where you going?' he asked.

'South Kensington,' David said, leaning forward to speak through the open window. 'The Ampersand.' The driver nodded, rolled the window up again, and David opened the door for me.

I stood there on the curb, my blood pumping fast. *Am I about to make another bad decision?*

'Are you always this difficult?' he laughed, threading his arm around my waist and scooping me into movement. 'Really, I just need a shower. That's all.'

So I got inside, then he climbed in after me and slammed the door shut. The car pulled away from the kerb and I could feel him beside me, the warmth of his hand on my knee. Raindrops clung to the window, gathering in streams, and I looked through them at pedestrians running across the street, holding hands and hopping over puddles. It was four days from Valentine's Day, so most of the shop windows boasted some sort of red-love-hearts-and-roses display, matched perfectly by the glistening wet tar of the road: red tail-lights reflecting off it in long and jagged lines. As we approached

Harrods, all grandeur and white globes marking its structure in the dark, we pulled to a stop at the traffic lights. I could make out a homeless man asleep in a doorway, lying beneath a cardboard box and a pile of clothes. Then the lights turned green. I lay my head back and squinted slightly so the images and lights all blurred together. It was prettiest that way. Like a photograph taken with the shutter speed low.

Before long I could see the National History Museum up in the distance but we turned left before we got there, heading down a small street lined with thick white pillars and Victorian houses.

'It's just up ahead,' David said to the driver, 'on the right.' My heart sped up as we pulled up. 'Great, thanks,' David said as he passed him a £20 note through the small opening in the glass.

It was a grand, white building with a black number ten on the pillars either side of the entrance. There were manicured garden boxes, all white and green, sitting outside the ground-floor windows, a lit-up British flag above the entrance, and the type of ornate black railing one usually associates with Paris running along the edge of each balcony. I looked inside: small yellow lights glowed back at me and it looked warm.

David put his hand on my lower back and we moved inside.

The lady behind the small front desk eyed me from beneath bronzed lids, judgement in her eyes. It made me uncomfortable.

'Hi, I just called for a room? The name is Turner,' he said.

She tapped away on the keyboard and handed him a keycard. 'Room 303,' she said.

'Could I get a toothbrush?' he asked, and she handed him two.

'Oh, I don't need one,' I said to her.

'Don't be so selfish,' David said, turning his head to grin at me. 'Maybe I want to give the other one to my mother for Christmas.'

'Third floor,' said the woman behind the desk. But he was already guiding me towards the elevator, the warmth of his hand on my lower back.

'Where are your things?' I asked, as the elevator pinged open and we stepped inside.

'I don't have any. I was planning on heading home to the country tonight,' he said.

I watched the lights flicker as we ascended in silence. Second floor. Third floor. The doors opened: burgundy carpet with an ornate gold-and-black pattern running through it. Paintings on the walls: landscapes, horses. And series of doors on either side of that hallway. All containing people with secrets I would never know.

He led me to the room: 303.

As he pushed open the door, the lights – warm and low – switched on and he moved to the side so I could enter. There were two big windows behind heavy navy curtains, drawn to the side with ornate gold ropes. To the right lay a huge dark-wood four-poster bed covered in crisp white linen and a single mustard throw pillow. In the middle of the room sat a neutral leather sofa with a coffee table in front of it and a small chandelier overhead. And to the left was a mustard-and-gold King Henry style chair.

'Welcome, madam,' he said, following me inside and closing the door behind him. 'Make yourself comfortable.' He took off his coat and threw it onto the bed. 'I'll be five minutes.' He walked towards the bathroom. 'But there's the phone next to the bed, order some champagne or something,' he said with a smile. And then he closed the bathroom door and I was left alone.

Picking up the receiver, I pressed 0 and a woman's voice, presumably belonging to the one who checked us in, answered.

'Hello?' I said.

'Hello, this is reception,' said the bronzed lids and judgemental stare.

'Hi,' I said. 'I'm in room 303. Could I get a bottle of champagne, please.'

'Certainly,' she said, her tone clipped. 'Which one?'

'Veuve?' I suggested.

'Of course. Anything else?'

'Do you have some sort of chocolate cake?' I asked. I could hear her tapping on that keyboard.

'Certainly,' she said.

'Thanks.' And then I hung the heavy receiver back on its cradle and looked around.

It was beautiful. Magazine worthy. But the more I drank it in with my eyes, the faster my thoughts became. What was I doing? A low hum of panic started to rise from my belly. *I shouldn't be here. What if it goes badly? I could lose my job. And if it goes well, it will look like*

I was trying to sleep my way to success … Val's face flashed before me, her grey head shaking, her lips pursed.

But my head was fuzzy and my brain too soft to make a decision. I needed water. So I moved towards the minibar, opened it, and grabbed a bottle of Evian from the top shelf.

I could hear David in the shower. Water hitting tiles. *He'll be out soon.* I sat on the sofa with my water, one of my legs folded demurely beneath me – I didn't want him to think going to a hotel with a client was business-as-usual for me – and reached into my handbag for my phone.

It was 9pm.

The prostitutes would have arrived.

Electricity stormed through my stomach, my lungs clenched and my hands ached.

There's no going back now.

I took a sip of water – it was wonderfully cold – and imagined the scene. The girls, the ribbons, Angus's face. What would he do? What would Candice do when she saw the bill? Would she tell his boss, Henry, immediately?

Then the shower faucet turned off. I heard David moving out of the shower and onto the tiled floor, so I dropped my phone back into my handbag, covered my knees with my dress, and waited for him to emerge.

His hair was wet and stuck to his head and he was wearing a hotel robe. Thick and white. Steam trailed out from behind him as he stood in the bathroom doorway, his feet bare and his legs hairy.

I looked up at him and smiled as he moved towards me, his arms to the side in a 'ta-da' gesture.

'Seduced yet?' he asked. He was using a second towel to dry his hair, and as he sat down next to me, the sofa moved with his weight.

'So, Taylor Bishop,' he said with a grin.

'So, David Turner,' I replied. I was trying to act cool but the air between us was thick.

'Truth or dare?' he asked.

'Truth,' I said with a laugh.

'Perfect,' he laughed. 'How the fuck are you still single?'

I've always hated that question. It sounds like a compliment but it feels like an accusation of either psychological imbalance or bad fellatio technique. For all its faults, my relationship with Angus had shielded me from those sorts of questions for the past eighteen months, and in that moment I missed the protection he'd offered.

So I answered a question with a question: 'Why are *you*?' Then I took another sip of my water.

His eyes shifted, his forehead creased and he said: 'How old are you, anyway? Twenty-six?'

'Jesus,' I laughed, 'that's more than one shitty question. But I'll be thirty in June, if you must know.'

'Bullshit,' he replied. 'You look much younger than that.'

'What about you? How old are you?' I asked. His dressing gown had fallen open and I could see his chest hair peeking through.

'Why don't you guess?' He was still drying his hair with the towel.

'I don't know.' I cocked my head to the side and took a sip of my water. 'Forty-six?'

He stopped dead. 'Are you fucking serious?'

'Why?' I laughed.

'I'm fucking thirty-eight,' he said.

'No way,' I said, grinning. 'I don't believe you.'

He walked over to the bed, reached into his coat pocket and pulled out his wallet: old black leather. Creases from overuse. Then he handed me a small plastic card with an expressionless photo and proof of his ability to operate a motor vehicle.

I looked at the birth date. He was telling the truth.

'Right, your turn,' he said, hand outstretched. 'I want to see yours.'

I reached into my bag, looked down and searched for my wallet in the darkness. I could see my phone. The screen was lit up. And there was one missed call: Angus.

The blood drained from my heart.

'Oh, just show me,' David said, his hand reaching out for my licence. 'It can't be that bad.'

I handed it to him and tried to breathe. It was impossible.

Why is he calling?

'Shit,' he said, looking at it, 'this photo does not do you justice at all.'

I didn't reply. I couldn't. I just sat there smiling, watching as David scanned my licence for details. 'Bolton Gardens? How the hell can you afford to live in SW5?' he asked.

'Give it back,' I said, reaching for my licence, but he pulled it away like it was a game.

'I live in a shoebox that's falling apart, that's how,' I said. The truth was I'd moved there for Angus. It was closer to him and more in line with the version of me he wanted me to be than my previous flat allowed. And all I ever wanted was to be the version of me he needed. The well-heeled version. The one that slotted easily into his picture-perfect life. And so I maxed out my credit card to cover the deposit and moved from my affordable, sensible, spacious flat in Greenwich – just 30 metres from the Welcome to Lewisham sign, with a cutlery drawer that didn't fall apart if I tugged too hard – to my studio flat in Bolton Gardens that cost me 65 per cent of my salary and required me to dislocate my shoulder just to fit into the 'bathroom'.

I reached for my licence again. David went to move it but I caught it this time and yanked it from his fingers with a laugh. We were close and he was looking at me. I could smell his hair, feel his heat, and I was smiling. But it was dangerous to be there with him, so I pulled back and sat deeper into the seat.

I slid my licence back into my wallet and then looked up at him. He was holding his phone. 'What are you doing?' I asked.

'Just a second,' he replied, eyes down and smiling, 'I'm looking for something.'

'Are you texting?' I asked.

'Of course not,' he said with a grin. And then a Latin version of 'Sexual Healing' started to play, all rhythm and cymbals and brass. It sounded like summer on an island. I started to laugh and he reached out his hand. He was looking at me with happy eyes and laughing one of those wide-mouthed, can-see-your-bottom-teeth kind of laughs.

He reached for my hand.

'I can't dance, I'm drunk, David. I'll fall over,' I said.

'Rubbish,' he said, his fingers grabbing hold of mine and helping me up. He twirled me once, twice and then again. And a beautiful dizziness fell over me, blurring all the lines and taking away all the pain. He pulled me to him and we swayed, I could smell his cologne on his neck, his body warm and pressed against mine. Then he flicked me away, I laughed, turned, and he drew me back towards him. Our faces were close, his hands on my waist and his breath smelled of metal, wine and man. And I was laughing.

'Room service,' came a voice from the door. It was loud, as though they were already inside.

I fell back onto the sofa as I watched him move towards the door. All business. All grown up. Everything he wasn't.

A small man with a big tray walked into the room. He placed the champagne in a bucket on the table along with two glasses and the cake. He opened the champagne with a loud pop and poured two glasses.

'Chocolate cake?' David asked as soon as the door closed behind the waiter.

'One always needs chocolate cake, David,' I replied.

'Very true,' he said as he handed me a glass of champagne, sat next to me and raised his glass to mine. 'To one of those rare fun nights you don't see coming.'

'Cheers,' I said, then we clinked our glasses and sipped.

I could feel his heat beside me – he was sitting so close, naked beneath his bathrobe – and the music was still playing in the background. And I thought: *He's right, it* is *one of those nights.*

'So,' he said, his voice low and rough, 'truth or dare?'

'Truth.' I smiled back at him.

His eyes had gone pink around the edges from the booze. 'Now, you can't lie …' he said, leaning in. 'Did you plan on using that cake for something specific later?'

I started to laugh. 'Oh shut up, David, we're going to a bar, remember. Get dressed.' But that was the last thing I wanted him to do. I just didn't want to make it too easy. Then he wouldn't take me seriously.

'Well, that's disappointing,' he said, wandering over to the window. I watched him open it. Imagined his arms straining under that dressing gown.

'Do you smoke?' he asked over his shoulder as the window released and a gush of cool air flew in.

'Sometimes,' I said, as I walked towards him.

He moved over to his coat, still lying on the bed, and pulled out a small packet of cigarettes – Camels – and one of those cheap transparent lighters you can buy at any corner store. It was a dark red. Then he leaned out the window, lit a cigarette, took a drag and then handed it to me. I leaned out with him and there we were: both leaning on the rough windowsill, smoking one cigarette between us, and in that moment there was nowhere else I wanted to be. I looked down onto the street. Rubbish bins. Couples stumbling home hand in hand from the noisy pub down the street. And everything bathed in silver light.

'Okay, one more,' he said.

'One more then it's my turn.' I smiled.

'Fine,' he said. 'Truth or dare?'

'Well, as I'm hanging out a window I'm going to go for truth again,' I laughed. My hands were resting on the rough stone of the windowsill. It was cold.

'Did you know you fancied me the very moment you met me?' He exhaled and handed me the cigarette, all the while watching me. 'You have to answer truthfully, remember.'

'Who says I fancy you?' I asked, inhaling and looking away from him towards the road below.

'I knew I fancied you,' he said, reaching for the cigarette. 'But that's how it is with love, I guess: it's either there, or it's not.'

I felt my mouth turn up at the edges as the smoke escaped.

'So, you love me?' I teased. 'Wow, that was fast.' I grinned at the road.

'You know what I mean,' he said and he looked down at the road too.

And I did know what he meant. It was there with Angus from the first time I heard his voice.

It was getting cold, so I pulled my head back in through the window and David stubbed out the cigarette on the windowsill and followed me. I was facing inside, looking around, but I heard the window slide down, felt the breeze cut off, and then his hand was on my lower back, the heat from his fingertips. Then I was turning to look at him. Feeling his chest as it moved towards me, then his breath was on my neck, on my chin, beside my mouth.

And then he kissed me. Soft tongue. Rough cheek.

He tasted like cigarettes and smelled like spiced limes. And everything else melted away.

'Do you really have seven siblings?' I asked softly, pulling away, trying to puncture the intensity of the moment. Our lips were still touching. I could feel his breath.

'Have you been stalking me?' he laughed gently, his hands on my waist.

I smiled. 'No, I wouldn't have bothered, I thought you were a bit of an arse actually. My boss has.'

'An arse?' he asked, his lips touching mine.

'Yep,' I said. 'So, do you?'

'Sort of,' he said. 'I have one full sister and six half-siblings from my father's first two marriages … but you shouldn't believe everything you read, you know.'

'I know,' I said.

He kissed me again. The tip of his tongue was touching mine. His hands were around my ribcage. I pulled away from him. Just an inch.

'Truth or dare?' I asked.

He took a deep breath. 'Truth.'

'What's your favourite …' I let the question linger. 'Colour.'

He started to laugh and I could see his teeth flash in the low golden light. 'Would you please shut up?' He grinned and then his lips were back on mine. Stubble on my cheek.

He walked me slowly backwards, one hand on my back and the other in my hair, until he pushed me down onto the bed and then lay on top of me. I was lying half on his coat, so he grabbed it from beneath me and threw it aside. His chest was heavy and warm; I could feel it through my dress and our mouths were almost touching. Then he smiled and I smiled, and he kissed me again. His hands moved beneath my dress, tugging at the waistband of my pantyhose. He knelt by my side and peeled them slowly from my calves, my ankles, my feet.

'Hey,' he said and smiled down at me as he kissed my foot and threw my pantyhose to the floor. His voice was croaky and his eyes kind. Then he lay back down beside me, his hand stroking my face.

'Hey,' I said, my voice small and my lips parted. I was still lying on my back and my hand reached up and stroked his cheek. Rough stubble on soft skin. And I remembered the way it glinted when I first saw him in the restaurant, his jaw clenching as he tried to pretend he hadn't noticed me, so I laughed.

'What are you laughing at?' he asked as he turned his face and kissed the palm of my hand, his eyes still on me.

'Nothing,' I said.

'I'm funny, am I?' he asked as he moved on top of me, now propped up on one arm.

'A bit,' I said. My hands were in his hair – it was soft – and then his mouth was pressing against mine as his hand reached down and undid the tie around his waist and the bathrobe fell from his shoulders. His hands were on my hipbones, peeling off my underwear. He moved my legs apart with his knee and his eyes looked into mine.

And then he was inside me.

My breath was fast and my heart beat hard. I put my arms above my head out of habit and he grabbed my wrists, and for a moment I thought of Angus, but then I could smell David's hair – spiced limes – and our hipbones melted into each other and his breath was loud and hot in my ear. And for just a little while, I forgot.

I slept soundly beside David that night. Completely unaware of what the following week would hold; but then, there was nothing to warn me. Except, perhaps, the imaginary voice that tore me from my contented state at around 6am whispering: *Happy birthday, sir …*

And then I remembered.

saturday

Master Sun said: *'Rashly underestimate your enemy and you will surely be taken captive.'*

11 FEBRUARY

I awoke to a mouthful of pillow and hair. A faint smell of cigarettes filled the room, the curtains were half-open, and the grey morning light streamed through them, gently drumming on my eyelids. I felt the warmth of his body behind me, his arm around my waist, its soft hair beneath my fingertips.

'Good morning,' he whispered into my ear.

'Good morning,' I croaked back. The untouched cake and empty champagne bottle sat on the coffee table in my eye line. And the chandelier that hung above it caught the light in its crystals, reflecting it onto the wall.

His breath was on the back of my neck, his lips barely touching my skin, and it gave me goose bumps.

I rolled around to face him and he reached up to remove the hair from my mouth and tuck it behind my ear.

'How's the head?' he asked, his eyes inches from mine.

'Okay,' I whispered. His arms were around me. His body was encasing mine. It was one of those hugs that tells you almost everything you need to know about another person in a fragment of a second.

'God,' he said, rolling onto his back, 'last night was amazing.' He was grinning at the ceiling.

'Mmm,' I replied and rolled over so my back was facing him. I was looking at the window, at the light bouncing off the edges of the champagne bottle and at my black dress hanging over the side of the chair in the corner of the room. It was one of those moments I would remember forever. Even lying there, I knew that. A mental Polaroid to be added to the deck I carried with me everywhere. Because it was one of those rare moments in life when everything was fine.

'I haven't had that much fun in ages,' he said with a heavy sigh. 'I just want to stay in bed with you forever.'

I turned to look at him – his free hand was running through his hair. It was that colour that straddled dark blond and brown. What do you even call that?

'So, let's do that,' I replied, then I looked back out the window.

'Deal,' he said. His lips started to kiss the back of my neck again. His breath was warm and his stubble prickly. And I could hear the faint hum of traffic coming from a cold road somewhere outside.

'So, tell me something I don't already know, David Turner,' I said.

He laughed and I could feel his breath on my ear. Then his teeth. Gently.

'Well, you appear to already know almost everything,' he laughed, 'but what do you want to know?'

'Anything,' I said. He was so warm on that cold February morning.

'Anything?' he replied.

'Yes,' I said, 'anything.'

'Okay,' he said, taking a deep breath. 'I have syphilis.'

'Oh shut up,' I laughed. 'No seriously, tell me something. I want to know you.'

'Like what?' His voice sounded hesitant here. That should have warned me.

'Like the thing you least want to tell me,' I said, turning my head to face him.

And he was silent – not the thinking kind, the loud kind of silent that is always painfully pierced.

'Seriously, tell me anything,' I continued.

His lips were slightly parted. 'Actually there *is* something I should tell you,' he said.

'Good,' I said. 'What is it?'

His Adam's apple bobbed and he cleared his throat.

'Oh hurry up,' I said, panic moving through my veins. 'Too much suspense.'

'It's not as bad as it sounds, so please let me explain.'

There was something cautious in his eyes and he'd moved a little further away from me so he could properly focus on my face.

'Fine, but what is it?' My smile was now turning to a frown.

'Don't scowl,' he said, his thumb massaging the lines out of my forehead.

'What is it?' I asked again. My tone was getting darker.

'I'm …'

'You're what?' I said. 'David?'

'I'm married.'

'You're *what*?' The blood drained to my feet. 'What is fucking *wrong with you*?' I hissed, pushing his chest away from me and wrapping myself in the tangled sheet. I stumbled out of bed, leaving him naked, exposed and watching me move across the room.

'You said you'd let me explain,' he said calmly.

'That was when I thought it was something fixable,' I said. My heart was racing but my voice was low and steady. A veil of ice had fallen over me – I was tired, so tired, of men deceiving me – and I just wanted to go home.

I walked quickly to the bathroom, grabbing my dress from the chair, my pantyhose from the floor and my knickers from the edge of the sofa. Then I closed the door heavily and slipped them on.

My mascara had smudged around my eyes during the night, so I wet a tissue from a box below the mirror and tried to dab my face clean. The bathroom was vast and white, with a big clean mirror, thin white curtains covering a small window that looked out onto a backstreet and a huge old free-standing bath with clawed feet. It was the kind of room good memories should be woven in. The kind I had shared with Angus many times.

David was knocking gently on the door. 'Taylor, it isn't how it looks,' he said.

'No?' I retorted, giving up on the tissue and splashing my face with water. I grabbed for a towel to dry it and stared at my reflection in the mirror. Pale. Sad.

'We have an understanding.'

'Oh my God,' I said loudly through the door. 'Seriously?' Kim's face appeared in the mirror before me. Then Angus's. Then my father's. And then my mother's, cracked with her tears. 'Why didn't you say anything, David? You didn't think that our little why-are-you-still-single chat last night might have been the ideal opening to mention it?'

'I didn't want to ruin things,' he said through the door.

'Ruin what?' I replied as I roughly rubbed my face. 'Your affair?'

'No,' he said as I unlocked the door and pushed past him, avoiding his gaze.

'Well, there's nothing to ruin,' I replied, putting on my coat. I grabbed my handbag, opened the hotel-room door, slammed it behind me and moved quickly down that gold and black patterned hallway towards the elevator. My shoes were dangling from my hand and I felt stupid. Really stupid.

And David? Well, he let me leave.

—

The tears waited politely until I was inside my flat before they decided to fall. But fall they did: me crumpled on the floor like a discarded poem that never quite made it to the wastepaper bin. It seemed that no matter where I turned, no matter whom I trusted, men lied to me. And it had always been that way. Starting with my father.

The first seven years of my childhood were idyllic, at least in my memory: beachside holidays, laughter, blown-out birthday candles, Christmas trees decorated with garish tinsel, even if Christmas Day itself was just me and Mum. But around the same time that I learned that Santa Claus was definitely not real – a fact I discovered via a girl called Emily at school, not a realisation I came to on my own – I discovered something else was not real: the other magical man in my life. My father.

Or rather, my mother discovered it. And then through her tears, the sound of his footsteps leaving, and the fact that his newspapers lay piling up near the front door until a kindly neighbour brought them in, I discovered it. Because we were not his only family. She was not his only wife. The only thing common to both his lives was his name – and that's the thing that eventually got him caught. A credit card sent to the wrong address. I guess he must have filled in the form too quickly. Forgotten what was what. Or maybe in some way he wanted to get caught. But it was one of those situations you see on daytime TV talk shows and presume the people presented are all out-of-work actors: because nobody could be *that* stupid, could they? You would *know*. Of course you would know. But between travelling a lot for his work and the fights he would instigate with my mother in order to have a reason to be absent for a few weeks – or vital holidays such as Christmas – we didn't know.

My mother never recovered from the shock, and when I went off to boarding school I started telling people my father had died when I was seven. Even Angus thought that. Because he did, in a sense. I never saw him again. But brief as his cameo spot in my life was, Charlotte's poignant diagnosis was: he'd shaped me. Because of him, my life was an endless quest in search of a happy ending for which I would endure anything. Just to prove to myself that it existed after all. And so marriage, weddings, rings, flowers and dresses always mattered more to me than most. As though somebody promising to be with me forever and meaning it was the only thing that could adequately fill the void my father gouged when he left.

A void that remained long after my memories of him faded. But there is one image of him, one memory, I have never been able to shake: he's wearing a red-and-green checked shirt, a cigarette hanging from his lips, his eyes a sparkling green. About ten vinyl records are lying scattered on the muted brown carpet in front of him and he's making me a mix tape: The Stones, Coltrane, Leonard Cohen, The Doors, Bob Dylan, James Taylor – my namesake – and some of the Beatles' later work. He's singing along and I'm trying to sing too, but I don't know the words. The tune. And it's just me and him and the carpet and that mix tape. That was the last time we were alone together.

My mother threw that tape away, along with boxes and boxes of anything else he'd ever touched, soon after he left. But there are some photographs we snap with our mental camera that are branded onto our minds for life. And that image of my father remains the uncontested king in the pack I always refer to in my darkest hours, either for confirmation or solace. At that moment, my father's polaroid was held beside that of David, in bed, just before he told me he was married.

I stayed there, in that pitiful crumpled position, for about ninety minutes. That's how long the tears lasted. But eventually they dried up and I made my way over to the kettle. Made a cup of tea. And opened up my computer: I needed to focus on work. It had been slipping and I needed that promotion – it would mean paying off my credit card, no more living hand-to-mouth and maybe, with that on my resume, even being able to move to another industry in time. And work was something constructive I could focus on. Something unrelated to men.

Because ever since the break-up I had been consumed with either hating Angus or sedating myself, yet none of it had worked. Booze was just a Band-Aid, and my attempts at revenge hadn't proven to be the salve I'd thought they would. Instead, an image of Angus in bed with two prostitutes and yellow bows haunted me whenever I let my guard down. My daylight romp with Jamie had simply confused me further, and my night with David had torn the wounds open wider than they were to begin with. I was better off just leaving it all behind me. Drawing a line in the sand. Stepping over it. Nothing before that line had ever happened.

Yes, work was the only thing I could count on. That one thing I could control. And the sole part of my life that Angus couldn't touch. I would focus, get back on track and get my damned promotion.

It was around 4.30pm. After five hours of intense concentration I was taking a break, staring into the open fridge, its chill on my face. My hair still smelled of cigarettes and I was wondering if I should wash it. That was when I heard a faint noise. A gentle tapping: knuckle on wood. I ignored it at first, but it grew louder. More urgent. It was my door.

Someone was at my door.

I closed the fridge and walked towards the sound.

'Who is it?' I said through the wood.

'Me,' came a voice.

I looked through the peephole, and there he stood.

Angus.

My ears buzzed. My vision swirled.

Shit.

Why is he here? Is it about the prostitutes?

Does he know it was me?

'Hi,' I said through the door.

Fuck.

'Are you going to open the door?' he asked.

My teeth were chewing my inner cheek and my ribcage pounded.

I looked through the peephole again. And his hands, formerly behind his back, were in front of him now: he was carrying roses.

Fuck.

I read once that a spider's silk is stronger than steel. My love for Angus was always like that: barely visible to the eye but unbreakable. And the more I struggled, the more stuck I became. But I really thought he'd snapped that thread, finally gone too far. It was only when he was standing there on the other side of the door, his presence palpable, that I realised some threads fray but never break. And the longer he stood there, the tighter that thread wrapped around my heart.

'What do you want, Angus?' I asked sharply. But I sounded stronger than I felt.

'Darling, please just open the door?' he said. He didn't *sound* angry.

'I'm busy,' I said. Then I stood there watching him, waiting for him to leave.

'Taylor, please,' he said. His voice cracked and his eyes implored me through the peephole. But then an image filled my mind: Holly's nipples pushing against mine, the smell of her musky perfume and the way her dark hair felt as it brushed against my face. My cheeks grew hot.

'There's nothing to talk about, Angus,' I said, my voice calm and low.

'Can I just give you these?' he asked, holding the flowers up in front of him.

Fire swelled inside me. 'Well, unless they're magic flowers that can take sex tapes off the internet, I don't want them,' I said, my voice less calm.

'Darling, I know you're angry,' he said, 'but we really need to talk. Please.' There was kindness in his eyes, vulnerability, and it reminded me of the man he was when we met – the one who organised spontaneous picnics by the Seine.

But I hesitated.

'Baby, it's *me*, you need to at least talk to me,' he said. 'This is silly.'

I let out a sigh and opened the door just a crack. He smelled the way his pink work shirt used to smell before the laundry detergent robbed me of that, and it hit me. Hard.

'Hi,' he said. He was pushing the flowers towards me. He looked tired, like he'd been up most of the night. My mind moved to the prostitutes and the yellow ribbons and my throat grew tight.

'So?' I asked, my voice rough. 'What do you want?'

'Darling, I'm trying to make things right,' he said, nodding at the flowers.

'How will *they* make things right?' I was attempting to speak softly – the neighbour's bay window was wide open – but it came out as a hiss. 'If you want to make it right, take the tape down and never speak to me again.'

There was a dusty breeze blowing in towards me and the light was low and grey. He wore blue jeans, a cream pullover and a navy scarf. His skin was tanned and his head was hanging, eyes on his feet.

'I have,' he said. 'Of course I've taken it down.'

That caught me off guard and my head grew light.

'When?' I asked. *It was still up on Wednesday when I checked.*

'Yesterday,' he said. 'I wanted to do it sooner. But I was away in the mountains and the connection was non-existent. I tried to call you last night,' he continued. Small. 'It was my birthday and it felt so wrong without you there …'

I opened my mouth to speak but didn't know what to say. David's eyes flashed before me, and then two yellow bows. I tried to control my expression: I couldn't let him know I knew about the prostitutes. That I knew how he'd spent his night.

'Please,' he said. His lip was quivering and he couldn't hold my glance: 'You don't have to take me back but please let me try to make you understand why I did what I did.' He looked up and there were tears in his eyes.

There had been many apologies, but in eighteen months together I'd never seen him cry. It threw me off balance.

But then Holly's naked shoulders and the sound of her laugh filled my head. 'Angus, you know I didn't want to have a threesome. I did it for you.' My voice was so low it was almost inaudible. 'And then you uploaded it onto the internet.'

'Baby, I was high when I uploaded it.' The tears had started to fall and he was trying to stabilise his voice.

'You were high?' I said. '*That's* your excuse?'

'I don't expect you to forgive me.' His voice was a whisper. 'But I need you to understand *how* it happened. I was coked out of my head after we broke up. I'd just dropped you home and didn't know what the fuck I'd done. How I'd ruined everything. So I was watching it because I missed you so much, and I fucking uploaded it. I have no idea what I was thinking,' he said, sobbing, his head shaking. 'I was just so fucking angry about it all. Angry at myself.

'I was hoping you'd never know. And then you *did* know and you were calling me about it but I just couldn't face you. I was so ashamed.' He paused and clenched his jaw. 'So I just did what I do and blocked it all out. Pretended it hadn't happened. I knew you'd never forgive me – how could you?' He looked up at me, and the pleading in his voice seeped like molasses through the cracks in my armour. Then his eyes dropped once again to his shoes.

'Angus, it's not just about the tape,' I said. 'It's about everything.'

'I know it's all my fault.' He stood there, shaking his head. 'You deserve better. But that's why I'm in NA, Taylor.' His voice was so small. 'Narcotics Anonymous. Going to meetings, got a sponsor and everything.' His shoulders were slumped. His dark hair greasy. 'I know things have been bad and really hard for you. But I want to be the man you deserve. Darling, think about it, things are only ever bad between us when I'm on it.'

He was right: the drugs made everything worse. And as I stood there watching him, I ached for the way things might have been.

The way they were supposed to be. But that was dangerous. I was weakening. I needed him to leave.

'That's great, Angus,' I said softly. 'I really hope the meetings help, but I really have to go.' Then I went to shut the door.

'Darling,' he said, his hand reaching out to stop the door closing, 'you know me. You know how hard this is for me – to reach out, to show weakness. I'm not in NA for the tea and biscuits. I'm doing it because I can't lose you. I just can't. You mean too much to me. But I don't think I have the strength to do this without you. God, I don't think I can …' His gaze landed back on the floor between his feet. 'I don't think I can live without you. I mean, look at me: I can't even sleep without you in the bed. These last ten days have been hell.' He looked up at me and his eyes cut straight through to my core. 'You're my Sunday Girl, darling. You always will be.'

I took a deep breath and steadied my thoughts. Ten days? It had felt like ten weeks. And I'd never wanted anything the way I wanted Angus. He was my happy ending. But then a hot gust of anger blew over me: him, Kim, a sparkling white ski slope …

'And what about Kim, Angus?' I asked, acid in my voice. 'I know you took her skiing; I saw the photos. What day is she? Monday?'

He looked like he'd been punched.

'That was a mistake,' he said, eyes to mine.

'Yes. Well, you've been making a lot of mistakes lately, Angus.'

'She means nothing,' he said. Slowly. Like he needed me to understand.

'Well, it's nice to know that you sacrificed me for something that meant nothing,' I said, dropping the roses at his feet.

'Jesus, how can you be so cold?' he asked, moving towards me and cupping my face in his hands. 'I just lost my way, darling.' I made a half-hearted attempt to pull away but my heart was beating fast and hard as he guided my gaze to his. 'But I need you to understand this. Because you're right, I've made too many mistakes. Big ones. Frankly, my whole life feels like a fucking mistake sometimes. Everything except *you*. I love you.'

His breath smelled of peppermint. And he was so warm.

'But Kim is not you. Nobody is you. You are my fucking home, like it or not.' He was shaking as he kissed me. A gentle kiss. It was so tender, he tasted so familiar, and the strength I still possessed began to dissolve like rice paper on my tongue.

I pulled back and looked up at his face – the little scar on his upper lip – and my heart panged. That was the thing about Angus: there was always this emptiness, a brokenness, a vulnerability about him that I just wanted to heal. And so it was impossible *not* to forgive him. Even when my head begged me not to.

'Can I come inside?' he asked, his voice a deep whisper.

And I could feel the pull of the sofa behind me, the one we would surely make love on if I let him in. The same sofa he'd whispered 'I love you' on for the first time. There was a deep sharp pain in my chest. I almost let him in. But I could hear my mother's voice in my ear. See the cracked salt from tears on her face. I had to be strong.

'No,' I whispered back. His body was straddling the doorway, so I pushed him aside and shut the door.

'Darling, this doesn't change anything,' he said from outside, his voice breaking. 'I'll just come back tomorrow. I can't help it. I still love you.'

I stared at the door, my hands pressed against it, and I listened for his retreating footsteps.

'I love you,' he repeated, louder this time.

'Go home, Angus,' I said. I knew if he didn't leave soon I'd give in.

And for a moment he was quiet. I could hear him shuffling on the other side of the door. 'All I want is to start afresh with you, darling,' he said. 'A blank canvas. Pretend none of the bullshit ever happened and do it right this time. I feel like we deserve that.'

I waited for him to grow tired and go home.

'Fine,' he said, and then there was silence. My heart shook inside me as I waited again to hear the sound of him giving up, his footsteps leaving. But that sound didn't come. So I was the one to walk away from the door. I was looking for my phone – I wanted to check the link, to make sure he'd really taken the tape down.

I found it charging by the bed, went to the email with the link, clicked on it, and nothing came up. The link was broken.

It was gone.

My forehead relaxed and I took a deep breath as the weight lifted.

'Darling,' Angus was banging on the door, 'it's fucking cold out here. Please let me in.'

I moved over to it.

'Seriously, can I at least have a blanket or something?' His voice was coming from lower down, so I imagined him sitting on my doorstep. 'I don't think you understand, darling, I don't give a shit if I just live here forever.' And he must have heard my footsteps moving up to the door because his voice got softer, he was no longer yelling. 'Fine, leave me out here to freeze to death,' he said. 'But could I make one last request?'

'What's that?' I said through the door.

'I want the orange string bikini,' he said. 'To keep me company.'

And that was all he needed to say.

Because David had provided me with a dangerous comparison: he was a married man with an 'understanding' with his wife about dating other women, a man who'd just let me walk away that morning without so much as following me into the hallway. While Angus, despite all our problems and all his failings, *needed* me. More than that, he'd proven he was willing to fight for me.

And so, I reached for the cold metal deadbolt. Turned it. And let him in.

sunday

Master Sun said: *'Take a roundabout route, and lure the enemy with some gain.'*

12 FEBRUARY

I was wearing his green birthday jumper and nothing else, my naked legs wrapped around the twisted sheets. The tinkering sounds of coffee being made floated through from my sliver of a kitchen, drawing me from sleep. I glanced around the room: a small pile of ripped-up blue-and-silver wrapping paper lay in the middle of the coffee table, a block of hardening brie and some crumbs on a breadboard to one side, the roses in a water jug to the other. And a moment later there he was, walking naked towards the bed, two cups in his hands. And I remembered: I'd let him in. He put them down on the (still unread) copy of *The New Yorker* beside me, then jumped on the bed, making it creak.

Then he lay down next to me and nuzzled his nose into my hair.

'God, I've missed the way you smell,' he said. My eyes drew shut.

I'd missed him too. His gaze was so warm and the past ten days so turbulent; I felt like a flower that had only just survived a winter storm.

'It's so early,' I replied, my voice as creaky as the bed. He hugged me tight over the covers, his leg slung heavily over mine. I gazed towards the window: a slice of bright white sky was visible through the curtains. And, in front of it, flashing and buzzing from the bedside table, lay my phone. I reached for it: Charlotte.

'Hey,' I said, clearing my throat.

'Shit,' she said, 'you sound like you just woke up.' I looked at the time: 10.07am.

'I did,' I said, propping myself up on my side and reaching for my coffee. 'How are you?' I took a sip – strong, hot – then put it back down.

'I'm fine, but how was Friday? You were supposed to text me and let me know what he was like, remember?'

'Oh,' I said. Angus's hand was now beneath the covers, warm on my hip, rubbing my thigh. 'I tried to but they had bad reception,' I said. 'He was awful.'

'Who was awful?' Angus asked and I gave him a wide-eyed *shush* look and held the phone away.

'Is someone there?' Charlotte asked, amusement in her voice. 'Well, now I know why you didn't call me yesterday.' She laughed.

I took a deep breath. 'Yeah,' I said.

'Is that Charlotte?' Angus asked loudly. 'Hi Charlotte,' he said into the phone.

She was dead quiet. I could almost hear her mind clicking into gear. 'Is that Angus?' she asked.

'Yes,' I said, my voice small.

'What the fuck?' she said.

'I know,' I said, 'but there's more to it than we knew.'

I could hear her swallow. She was choosing her words.

'I'm sorry, but I'm gobsmacked. Have you told your mum?' she asked, her tone controlled.

'No,' I said. 'It only happened last night. And she won't understand.'

'Damned straight she won't. Honey –' Her voice was high-pitched and she took a moment to calm herself. 'Aside from the fact that he took some other girl skiing just after you broke up, he uploaded a sex tape of you to the internet. Have you forgotten?'

Angus was kissing my neck from behind, his head close to the phone and I didn't want him to hear what she was saying, so I pulled away and leaned further towards my side of the bed.

'I know, but it's really complicated, and he took it down.' Even as I said it I sensed that she was right.

'Oh, he took it down? What a gallant gesture,' she said.

Then we sat in silence, just her breath then mine, hers then mine, until she finally spoke. 'He's a dick, babe. I'm sorry, but you need to get away from him. Now.'

I took a deep breath. 'Can I talk to you about it some other time? I really think you'll understand when you hear the reasons for it all.' I looked back at Angus, now lying on his back, arms crossed.

'I fucking *won't* understand,' Charlotte said. 'But, sure. What about tomorrow night? It's half-term this week, so I leave for Scotland on Thursday for four days. So, no yoga this week.'

'Sure, tomorrow sounds great,' I said.

'Fuck, babe,' she said, exhaling loudly, 'you worry me sometimes. But love you and chat tomorrow.'

'Love you too,' I said. And then we hung up.

I rolled over to face Angus and he reached his hands beneath his jumper, tickling my ribs as he pulled me to him.

'No,' I laughed as he hugged me.

'Yes.' He laughed back. Then the tickling stopped and we lay there for a few moments while Charlotte's words echoed in my head. Was she right?

'It'll be fine,' he said into my hair, as though reading my mind. 'She just needs to get used to the idea.'

I pulled away and looked at him: tanned skin, thick lashes, strong jaw, dark hair now greying at the temples and a little flat bit at the end of his long and refined nose.

'Maybe,' I said. Then I let out a sigh and nestled my head back into the warm space between his chest and his chin.

'What do you want to do today?' he asked, his hand stroking my hair.

'I have to do some work,' I said. 'It's important and I'm really behind.'

'Big project?' he asked.

'Really big,' I said. 'Promotion big.' My mind moved to David. I'd slept with our biggest client and we hadn't even swapped numbers. *How?*

'That's great, darling,' he said. 'What is it?' he asked, sitting up.

'Long story,' I said, 'and it's supposed to be a secret. But … we've got this new client. I'm supposed to find him something to invest in – a load of us have the same project.'

'Oh, sounds exciting. I'll bring you your laptop,' he said. Angus had never shown any real interest in my work before. It felt like he was really trying, like things really *would* be different.

'It can wait till later,' I said, touching his arm.

'No, do it now, I'll make brunch,' he said, walking over to the bookcase to pick up my computer. When he leaned down and placed it on the bed beside me, I could smell him: sweat, musk and coffee.

'Who's the client?' he asked, walking through to the bathroom. He left the door ajar and I could see his reflection in the shower door as I pressed the power-on button.

'A guy called David Turner,' I replied. It was jarring to hear myself say his name in full and out loud, as though he were just another client.

I could hear Angus pee – water on water – and he felt so close. 'David Turner …' he repeated. 'Never heard of him.' He flushed, washed his hands, wet his hair, and came back to stand next to the bed. He picked up his phone and started typing.

'The Turner Group,' I said, relieved that they hadn't met at a business dinner by some shitty trick of serendipity.

'Oh my God, what a bore,' Angus said, squinting down at his phone screen. 'Nobody should be a philanthropist until they have grey hair. It just seems wrong. I mean, what is this guy? Forty?'

Thirty-eight.

'So, what have you got so far?' he asked, looking up at me.

'Fuck all,' I said with a smile.

'Hmm, so, just any investment? Provided it's in property?' he asked, frowning.

'Yes. But it also has to be clever, something nobody else has thought of.'

'Okay,' he said, sitting down beside me. 'Well, I might actually have an idea for you … It might work – what about Eastbourne?'

'What, the town on the coast?' I asked, sceptical.

'Yes. There's a big development in the works down there,' he said slowly. 'Nicolai Stepanovich has already bought up most of the land. It's part of another place-making scheme. This one's aimed at the over sixty-fives: built-to-rent apartment blocks, a hospital, that kind of thing. He had all the investors already lined up but one of them pulled out unexpectedly.'

I was listening, nodding, taking it all in. I knew of Stepanovich: his last development had entirely transformed an outer part of Oxford, tripling house prices in the area within five years and turning a dilapidated red-brick shopping area into a large-scale mall. The ripple effect was huge. But that scheme had been funded by a very select circle of high-end investors; it was never even taken to market. To get David involved in this one would be a huge win. It would be exactly what he was looking for.

'Construction is scheduled to start in May, so they'll already be looking for new investment. And it was a large sum they lost, so they'll need a few investors to make up the deficit: if your David Turner wants to take things up a notch, this is his chance.'

'How do you know about it all?' I asked.

'We vied for the mandate. It was worth a mint but the idiots went with someone else. An old school chum told me about the investor falling through; it's properly confidential but he knew how pissed I was when Stepanovich passed on us, and he thought it might cheer me up. Which, to be fair, it did. Now,' he said, all seriousness, 'there is something much more important we need to discuss before you even think about doing anything else.'

'What's that?' I asked.

'I want you to really think about this before you answer,' he said. 'No reflex answers.'

I knew what was coming and laughed. 'Scrambled.'

'Very good.' He grinned as he turned and walked back through to the kitchen.

'Thank you,' I yelled after him as I went to my emails, opened up a new message, typed in Val's email address and told her about the Eastbourne scheme. I suggested it might be the perfect opportunity for David. And as I typed his name an image of his eyes – navy and at close range – flashed before me. I pushed it aside, mentioned that we'd need to act fast. And then I pressed: send.

Angus flicked on the light as we walked into his apartment. Its familiar smell filled my nostrils and my shoulders tensed. I felt wrong being there. Angus closed the door behind us, rolled my suitcase full of toiletries and the excess clothes I'd always kept at his place through to the bedroom, and then moved over to Ed. His cage was still sitting by the window. I glanced to my left at the kitchen, the site of the leak I'd created – there wasn't any evidence of it now.

Angus walked over to me, wove his arm around my shoulders and led me through to the bedroom.

'Welcome home,' he said, smiling.

I smiled back and my eyes darted to the mahogany chest of drawers – his lucky socks were still in my flat. And Mrs Clifton would have found the cocaine I threw onto her balcony by now. I looked at the bed and flinched: had he slept with the prostitutes on it? A hot wave of anger washed over me at the thought. But then, who was I to judge? I was the one who'd ordered them. And I'd hardly been the poster girl for chastity in the time we were apart.

He leaned down and cupped my face with his hands. Then he kissed me. And it occurred to me that he tasted of peppermint chewing gum instead of his habitual Scotch – he really *was* trying.

'Get undressed, darling,' he said as he moved to the wardrobe. 'I have a surprise.' My pulse sped up as I unzipped my dress and it fell to my feet.

He looked back and smiled at me. 'Underwear too.'

'What are you doing?' I asked as I took off my bra and knickers.

'Looking for something …' he said. 'Here we go.' He walked over to me and I looked down at his hands: a big yellow ribbon was lying across his palms, its ends dangling down on either side.

I looked at him with confusion, my breath catching.

'Oh don't worry, it's just a game,' he said as he reached down and tied it around my waist.

My mind raced.

Does he know?

'Now, I'm going to lie in bed and I want you to walk through the bedroom door just like that,' he said.

I heard myself swallow. I was blinking fast. 'I feel silly,' I said, my throat tight.

'You'll be fine,' he said. 'It'll be fun. Trust me.'

He went and lay down on the bed, reorganising the pillows behind his head, and I walked out of the room. I was shaking as I turned the corner and crossed the threshold. But he was lying there waiting for me like nothing was wrong. *Why is he getting me to do this? Is it a test?*

'Come here,' he said, patting the side of the bed. I walked around and stood beside him. The bedside light, a green metal lampshade over an amber globe, cast a strange shadow across the side of his face. And my pulse beat fast in my mouth.

He reached up and gently tugged at the bow, and just like a Christmas present I unravelled. He took my hand and drew me to him, then down onto the bed. And then he was on top of me, his hands between my legs.

—

Lying in bed afterwards, his arm around me, my head on his chest and his fingers stroking my shoulder, all suspicion had evaporated. *He doesn't know. I would have felt it.*

'Angus?' I asked.

'Hmm?' he replied. His eyes were half-closed and he was breathing heavily, drifting in and out of sleep.

'Can I ask you something?'

'Of course,' he said. 'That's the great thing about bust-ups: they make a relationship stronger if they don't destroy it. I want you to tell me and ask me absolutely anything and everything.' His eyes had opened. They were focused on the ceiling. And he said it in such a way that made me think he wanted to ask me something too.

Swallow.

'What happened with Kim?'

His breath got deeper and his chest raised high as he inhaled.

'It was a mistake. A reflex. It was stupid,' he said. Then he breathed out.

'Was she why we broke up?' I was looking at him, watching for a flicker of truth.

'No,' he said, rolling on top of me and looking into my eyes. 'Of course not. I am just an idiot. I was terrified. You know me, I'm forty-two years old and –'

'Forty-three,' I reminded him.

'Forty-*three* then, smarty pants, and I have never been in anything as serious as us. I know it sounds clichéd but I really was scared.'

'Of what?' I asked. I could smell his skin, the spice of his cologne.

'That I would disappoint you,' he said and his voice cracked.

'How would you disappoint me?' I asked.

'Well, look at some of the things I've done, they were terrible. I know that. I didn't trust myself. So it seemed easier to just end it.'

'And Kim?' I didn't want to labour the point, but I needed to know for sure.

'Kim was just there. But I love *you*,' he said, 'and I'm not going anywhere ever again.'

And I believed him.

And then his lips – dry but soft – found mine, our fingers intertwined, and all the questions were gone.

—

'Now it's my turn,' he said. He was lying on his back, my head on his shoulder. 'Can I tell you something?' It was around midnight and my eyes were almost closed. We'd made love again and the apartment was silent. All the neighbours were either out of town or had gone to bed. And it felt as though the light beside the bed was the only light still on in the entire hemisphere.

'Of course,' I said, my fingers stroking his chest.

'Would you want me to tell you if something happened that would really upset you, or would you want me to keep it a secret?'

'What?' Suddenly I was thinking of David and Jamie and how Angus would feel if I told him about them. I could feel my heart-beat waking up. 'Like what? What do you mean?' I asked, severing our embrace so I could look at him.

'Nothing that bad, really,' he started and then trailed off.

'No, Angus, I would want you to tell me,' I said. *Hypocrite.*

He looked at me, unsure. 'Really?'

'Really.'

He swallowed loudly and the open bedroom window rattled in the wind.

'You know the thing we did earlier? The ribbon?' he asked.

'Yes,' I replied in a small voice.

'Well, I didn't make that up.'

'Huh?' I said. *Shit. Shit. Shit.*

'I didn't think of that, someone else did,' he said, looking away from me. 'Please promise me you won't get angry.'

'I promise,' I said. *Fuck.* 'I want you to tell me everything.'

He looked back at me cautiously. 'Okay, well something happened on Friday.' He shot me a pained look. 'It was on my birthday.' He took my hand. 'These two women turned up to the flat dressed in overcoats and wearing just yellow bows around their waists.'

As I stared at him, my mouth started to feel weird and paralysed, the way it always does when I lie. I willed it to relax.

'I don't know how to say this nicely, darling: they were hookers. Someone had sent me hookers for my birthday.' He was looking me dead in the eye.

'What? Who?' I asked. Indignant. *Liar*.

'I honestly don't know, that's a whole other story, but let me finish this part.'

'Okay,' I said. I was watching him, trying to figure out whether he'd slept with them.

'I just want you to know, I didn't let them stay, I didn't have sex with them, I just sent them on their way. They were in here for about three minutes max. I thought they were lost or something at the beginning.'

'What's that got to do with the ribbon?' I asked.

'Well, they left. They were annoyed, but they left. Except one of them threw her ribbon at me in a strop.'

'The yellow ribbon? *This* yellow ribbon?' I said, reaching down to grab it where it had been discarded on the floor.

'Yes, that yellow ribbon.' He said, looking away.

'Yuck, Angus, how could you have asked me to wear it?'

'Because it was – God this sounds so bad, but it was a turn on. I couldn't go through with it because I kept thinking of you. I knew that would be the end for good if I did that. But I wanted to.'

'Oh,' I said.

'I still don't know who sent them. At first I thought it was Harry,' he said. Harry was his closest friend, but I'd never warmed to him. Mainly because sending prostitutes as a birthday present was precisely the kind of stunt he'd pull. 'But then I got a call yesterday morning from Candice, who said the charge had come through on my work credit card. Must have been one of the jealous fucktards at work, right?' he asked, glancing across at me. 'It's the only thing that makes sense. Or maybe Candice. Let's face it, she'd love to catch me out. I told her it wasn't me, but she said she'd already called the agency and they insisted I'd ordered them. That if I didn't pay they'd press charges.' He swallowed. 'I mean, what the fuck is the world coming to? They won't even take our calls now.' Deep breath. 'I should report them for running a brothel,' he finished.

'God,' I said, guilt gnawing at me from inside, 'what a nightmare. Can you just stop payment anyway? Then if they try to press charges just say you sent them away?'

'We've already done that. But that's not the point. Ordering hookers on a company card looks pretty bad – they'll make an example of me if I can't find a good excuse. I mean, it was *my* card.' He let out a deep breath. 'God, I'm dreading work tomorrow. It's going to be so fucking tense. You know what Candice is like.'

'Yep,' I said.

And I did. That was why I'd ordered them in the first place. I knew that she would flag them. She was far more officious and conscientious than her name sounded.

'She's such a bitch. Already emailed Henry about it and cc'ed me into the email!' Henry was his boss.

'How much was it for?' I asked.

'Over three-and-a-half grand.'

'Hang on, so they were here for three minutes … that's over a thousand pounds a minute …' I improvised. 'I'm in the wrong job.' Smile.

'You are,' he said, rolling over to face me with a smile. He watched me, and his eyes flickered. 'What would your prostitute name be?' he asked. It seemed like a strange question but I was keen to get a break from the lies.

'God, I don't know, Candy Cane?' I laughed.

'No, you have to take your favourite pet as the first name and then the street you grew up on as your last name – you must have done this?'

'Oh right,' I said. 'Fluffy Kramer.'

'Hot,' he said.

'Thanks, Jenkins Leigh,' I teased.

'How do you remember absolutely everything about me?' he asked, leaning forward to kiss me.

'It's easy,' I said. 'I love you. But what are you going to do?' I asked. 'About the credit-card charge?'

'Baby, I actually have no idea. But I have to do something. I can't afford to lose my job.'

And in that moment it felt like we were as bad as each other: he'd uploaded a sex tape of me to the internet and I'd ordered two prostitutes on his work credit card.

'Yes, I can see that,' I said, eyes down. 'Are you sure you didn't order them, Angus? Maybe when you were high, before you gave up?' *Lies, lies, lies.*

'No, I've never paid for sex,' he said. 'I mean, I've looked at the websites, you know that, but I've never actually pulled the trigger.'

And I thought back to the tone of that confirmation email: polite, yet familiar. It was equally fitting for both a returning client and a new big spender. What if Angus was telling the truth?

Shit.

'So, no, I promise I didn't order them, darling,' he said, his hand ceremoniously drawing a cross upon his heart, 'but I need to find out who did.'

monday

Master Sun said: *'Words of peace, but no treaty, are a sign of a plot.'*

13 FEBRUARY

'Are you ready?' Val asked and I swivelled my chair around to look at her. She was standing behind me holding a Starbucks cup on which was scrawled a smiley face and the word 'Val' in thick black magic marker. Under her arm was a grey plastic folder full of papers and she was wearing her jacket. That was a problem: a jacket meant a meeting.

I looked at her blankly.

It was Monday morning. A lot had happened since Friday afternoon. And my mind was too busy focusing on yellow ribbons and the idea of Felicia pulling red lace from a pink box to have even checked my diary yet.

I hope to see you in these soon. Love, A xx

Fuck.

'The meeting with David,' she said. 'It's in your diary … but we have to hurry, he's only got fifteen minutes free, we're lucky he could fit us in so quickly.'

'Oh,' I said, eyes wide. Shit. *Shit. Shit. Shit.*

'He doesn't need both of us, why don't you go and I'll keep working on it all,' I offered, turning back to my computer.

'No you don't.' She smiled. 'You found this, you'll be taking the credit, like it or not.'

I clenched my teeth and smiled.

Shit.

As we rode the mirrored elevator downstairs to the meeting rooms I stared at my reflection – burgundy dress, navy cardigan, pink cheeks – and tried to calm my breath. My pulse. But I couldn't.

The elevator doors opened and we walked in silence down that grey hallway towards the door at the end. Val opened it and we walked inside. David was already there, seated at the big table and staring out the window at a sky the colour of steel. Dark grey suit, navy tie and a white shirt. There was a white china coffee cup in front of him. No papers, no pen: the true mark of importance.

'Hello David,' said Val as we walked in.

He turned his head to greet us and I immediately looked down: it was worse than I'd expected. I felt naked.

'Hello,' I said. My eyes refused to meet his.

'Morning,' he replied with warmth.

'So,' said Val, as we both sat down, 'we have some good news.'

I could feel him watching me.

'Now, I can't take credit for this –' she started.

I sensed what was coming and counter-attacked: 'It was a joint effort,' I offered, looking at her, not him, 'but I'm too close to it, too ensconced in the details – Val, why don't you explain it? You'll do it more concisely.'

'Nonsense,' she said, looking back at me expectantly. Her look said: *Please take the stage. I so want to be able to promote you. I so want you to have a valid answer when I am forced to ask you in your promotion interview that dreaded question: 'Can you give an example of a time you have shown initiative?'* Then she handed me the grey folder. I opened it and inside lay a few sheets of paper: an A3 blueprint of Eastbourne as it currently stood, the town's current house price information, a series of figures illustrating the impact of The Town Square – Stepanovich's scheme in Oxford – on both residential and commercial prices, and a short list of contacts at Citexel. That was Stepanovich's company. But as I laid them out on the table, all I could think about was the warmth of David's chest, his cigarette lips and the low rumble of his voice as he said: *I just want to stay in bed with you forever.*

I looked up and went to speak – he was scanning through a set of figures on the table – but my tongue was thick. 'You've probably heard of Nicolai Stepanovich,' I started, trying to control the pitch of my voice. 'And The Town Square in Oxfordshire.' I felt stupid. Childlike. I needed to pull it together.

David looked up at me, nodded, and his eyes met mine: a shot of adrenaline to the heart. *I'm married. We have an understanding.*

'Well, he has a new scheme ready to start construction down in Eastbourne,' I said, swallowing hard and trying to focus. 'It's another place-making scheme, but this one is aimed at the over sixty-fives.'

'Built-to-rent blocks,' Val interjected. 'A hospital. Shopping.'

'Yes.' I smiled at Val as I gained confidence. 'And one of the key investors is rumoured to have just pulled out.'

'Really?' he asked, glancing briefly back down at the papers then back up at me. 'That's great. Stepanovich is impossible to get in with. How did you find out?'

'A trustworthy source,' I said. Angus's face hung before me and I tried to focus on him instead. The man I loved.

'Right,' said David. His eyes returned to the steel-coloured sky, his expression turned pensive, and his stubble glimmered red and gold beneath the warmth of the light that hung above us.

'Well it would be phenomenal if we could pull this off,' he said. 'This is exactly the sort of opportunity I'm looking for.' Then he looked straight at me. 'Well done,' he said, taking a sip of what had to be lukewarm coffee.

My throat tightened and I tried to control the expression on my face. Because Val was watching the interaction between us, I needed to feign okay-ness; I needed to pretend I didn't know what he looked like naked. What his chest hair felt like as it pressed into my cheek. His warmth behind me. His eyes staring into me before I'd truly woken up – not into my eyes, into *me*. But how could I, when that's what they were doing at that very moment?

'Construction is scheduled to start in May, so they're already looking for a replacement – should we set up a meeting asap or do you want to run it past the board first?' Val asked, all business.

'I can meet with the board this afternoon, so I'll let you know for sure after that, but I'd say let's get something in with them as soon as possible.' Then he turned to me. 'Is there any way I could take you out for a business dinner to say thank you?' he offered. Smile.

Shit.

'Oh, that's kind, but totally unnecessary,' I said, a tight smile on my face.

'No, it would be my pleasure. Let me know when suits you,' he countered. I was thrown by the overt nature of his invitation. He wasn't even hiding it. My pulse sped up. *Can Val tell?*

'Sure, let me check my calendar,' I offered.

'Great,' he said.

'Great,' I repeated, trying not to look at him or at Val. 'Well, we best get back to it.'

'Okay,' said David as he watched me awkwardly gather the papers into a pile, smile and stand up. Val followed me to the door, then David did the same. She shook his hand as we walked him to the reception area. I didn't. I couldn't. Instead I smiled curtly and headed for the elevator.

'Did he just ask you out on a date?' Val whispered as she joined me by the lift.

'No. Of course not,' I replied, pressing and re-pressing the up button, my face aching from fake smiles. 'Isn't he married?'

'Probably,' she replied, 'but you know men. They turn on a dime. Just look at Angus.'

I smiled yet again and said nothing. Val had witnessed the fallout from Angus on a more moment-to-moment basis than anyone. She was not a big fan and I wasn't looking forward to telling her we were back together.

'Still, he *is* a client. If he insists on dinner, I'll come along as chaperone,' she laughed. 'That will shut him up.'

—

'So. What the fuck?'

That was Charlotte. 'I mean: what the actual *fuck*?' she repeated with animation, the gin and tonic in her hand splashing out of the glass. We were at a little wine bar in Leicester Square, a downstairs hole-in-the-wall place that smelled like a pet shop, had walls covered in Parisian posters and was easily missed by those blinded by the blinking lights of the theatre district and the pigeons of Trafalgar Square. All the regulars were British, and most of them academics of some sort. But despite the venue, Charlotte was a gin girl, through and through. I had a big glass of Malbec in front of me and was sipping on it, carefully choosing the right words for my reply.

'I know he's been awful,' I started, 'he even admits to that. But he's … he's in NA,' I said, lowering my voice. 'He's got a sponsor and everything. I really think it'll be different now.'

I wanted her to be happy for me but she looked worried. She'd never fallen for Angus's charms the way I had, and he'd never fallen for hers. Instead, he'd always accused her of poisoning the well, of turning me against him, but she didn't, she was just worried about me.

'People don't change,' she said, her forehead crinkling, 'not forever, at least. And he can't blame everything on drugs, babe. That's a total cop-out.' She slurped back the rest of her gin then sat sucking on an ice cube, I could see it pushing against her cheek as it melted. Charlotte was marijuana's greatest advocate and didn't take kindly to people speaking ill of drugs.

'I really hope you're wrong,' I said, looking down at the wooden table and taking a sip of my wine. It looked purple in the dim light and clung to the edge of the glass like mussels to a rock pool.

'I hope so too,' she said. 'But, babe. Seriously. I mean, take the tape and all the mind games out of it – he still took that other girl away skiing.'

This was why I'd never told Charlotte about the slap; about him grabbing me by the throat. She didn't know Angus the way I did: she'd only ever seen the dazzling façade he showed the world. She'd never seen the anguish in his eyes when he realised what he'd done. She couldn't possibly understand.

'I know, but I sort of did the same thing,' I said. I needed her to accept us getting back together.

'How? You mean the lawyer guy?'

Jamie, David, revenge …

'Him … and someone else,' I said, crinkling my nose.

She raised her eyebrows. 'When did this happen?'

'Friday night. This client from work was at the restaurant I had my shitty date at.'

And then Charlotte laughed. Loudly. 'Well, that's made my night. Well done, babe – serves fucking Angus right.'

She looked around and motioned to the waitress for another drink as my phone buzzed from the table. I looked down at the screen: *When will you be back? Miss you. A xx*

Charlotte turned back just as I picked it up; she didn't see the screen but she knew who it was from. She sighed, smiled, looked me dead in the eye and said, 'I know I can't talk you out of getting back together with him, but just be careful, okay?' Then she held up her hand, baby finger out.

'Okay,' I said, reaching my hand out to meet hers.

And we pinky swore.

tuesday

Master Sun said: *'Two armies may confront each other for several years for a single, decisive battle.'*

14 FEBRUARY

One hand was grabbing the back of my hair, the other was on my hipbone holding me in position as he moved. I was bent over, facing the mirror, and he was inside me. I'd just woken up and hadn't been ready, so I winced from the pain. But he'd woken me up like this many times before and I'd always liked it. There was no way he could know that all I wanted right now was for him to hold me, that I wanted something different for us this time.

'Look how pretty you are,' he said, gently pulling my hair back so I could see my face in the mirror.

I wasn't pretty. I looked tired, the night before tattooed on my face: puffy eyes and dry, wine-stained lips. But that didn't matter. Because the man inside me was not just any man. It was Angus. And not just any Angus. The Angus I'd fallen in love with, the one I'd always believed he still was deep down beneath the muck. The same man who, when I cut my finger with a handheld food processor while making him a cake one Sunday early in our relationship – vanilla sponge – bandaged me up, kissed it better, helped me ice the cake, and then ate it. Blood and all. Like it didn't matter one bit. The one who'd programmed, 'Love you!' as a daily reminder on my phone. And it was such a relief to finally have him back.

When I'd got home the night before – I was even referring to his apartment as 'home' again – he'd been waiting for me. We'd cuddled on the sofa sipping camomile tea. He'd wrapped his arms around me, I'd leaned back into the warmth of his chest and he'd asked me about my day: how Charlotte was, whether Val had been impressed by my Eastbourne idea, whether I was happy to be back together with him. And then we'd talked about other things too: about the breakup. About how sorry he was. About how much pain I'd been in – how much it had hurt me to see him with Kim in that photo. To know that he'd betrayed me in such an intimate way with that sex tape. I lowered the shield from my heart that night, and really let him in.

Though not *all* the way in.

Was I tempted by the relief of a full confession? Yes. But Charlotte's words rang sharp and bell-like in my ears: *Just be careful, okay?* So I was. I kept my secrets: the prostitutes, Felicia next door, my break-and-enter while he was away, Jamie and David. But they were all sitting there at the forefront of my mind, reminding me of my own misdemeanours. And maybe that's why I missed it – it was like a magic show, where you're so busy focusing on the magician's hands that you don't see his assistant place the bunny in the hat.

And so the return of rough sex didn't pose the warning to me that it could have.

He started moving faster. His grip tightened and he pulled my hair. Hard. My neck strained and I struggled to breathe.

'Ow, baby, you're hurting me,' I said.

'Sorry,' he grunted, and his hand released.

I let my head dangle, my neck grateful for the rest. Eyes closed, I searched for a hidden image, a feeling, anything, to turn me on. Anything to lessen the friction. I could hear him breathing heavily behind me and hoped that meant it was almost over. My mind sorted frantically through its many trash cans: *there must be something here somewhere*. But the things that turn me on have always been so abstract and elusive, and so hard to find on demand: whispered words, unbroken promises, shared secrets. So, I was searching frantically, but coming up empty.

But then, just as I was about to give up and ask him to stop, I found something: it was on our last holiday, just before Christmas. We'd escaped the London winter to Gran Canaria for five days. I was wearing my orange string bikini and one of his T-shirts, sitting on the white balcony drinking coffee with the warm morning light on my legs. He was standing looking out at the view – the water sparkling blue in the bay, sand turned yellow by the tide, guava walls, palm trees and tiny tourists laying towels out on the beach in the distance – and he'd looked over at me and said: 'I think we're really going to make it, darling. I've never loved anyone like I love you.' Things had been rocky over the months before that moment, and we'd made the tape with Holly shortly before leaving on holiday. But as soon as those syllables hit my eardrums it felt like agreeing to that threesome had been the best idea of my life – it seemed to have brought us back to that great place again. That warm place I'd missed so much.

'Me too,' I'd said, smiling and sipping my coffee.

And then he'd walked over to me, leaned down and kissed the top of my head and said, 'Though, come to think of it, I'm not sure it's you I really want, it's that orange string bikini. I might just have to take it.' He'd put his hands under my T-shirt and pulled the string on my back, and the knot came loose.

'Well, we come as a package deal, I'm afraid,' I'd said, looking up at him. And he'd smiled.

'Done.' Then he'd led me by my hand to the bed.

'You like that, don't you, baby,' he said, breaking my chain of thought. My eyes reopened, his pace quickened, his moans deepened and then it was over. He wove his arm around my waist, lifted my torso to vertical and kissed me on the back of the neck.

'Happy Valentine's Day, darling,' he said. And then he wandered through to the shower. I lay back down in bed. *Just two minutes. Then I'll get ready.* I was raw, but happy.

The shower faucet turned on. The hot water pipes creaked. His voice echoed against the bathroom tiles; he was trying to sing. My ears strained to identify the melody.

'Feeling good ...'

He was singing our song.

—

'Mum, stop it! Can't you just be happy for me?'

'How? Tell me how am I supposed to be happy for you?' she replied. 'He's an absolute shit.'

We were two minutes into the call I'd been dreading. I'd dropped the bomb after one, and her voice had been escalating in volume and pitch ever since.

'I know he hasn't always been great, but he …'

'He what?' she demanded.

'He's changed. He's really trying.' I was standing in the kitchen; it was one of the only places in the building with cell reception. And so my voice was low.

'People don't change, sweetheart,' she said, 'they just pretend.'

'Look, it's complicated with Angus, there are other things going on, things you don't know about,' I said, facing away from the office area.

'Sweetie, *life* is complicated. How people deal with difficulties is how you judge their character. Not how they deal with things when everything is hunky dory.'

She was right.

I took a deep breath. 'I know why you're worried, I get it,' I said, 'but I really feel like it will be different this time.'

She was quiet. I could hear her swallow. 'I'm just really scared for you, honey.'

The middle of my chest hurt. 'Mum, it will be okay,' I said. An image of her huddled on the sofa – shaking, crying, in a way I'd never seen her – flashed in front of me. It was just after she discovered the truth about my father. And it haunted me.

'I hope so,' she replied. 'I really hope so.' Her voice sounded so fragile and I wanted to reassure her. Because I knew what she was thinking. I could hear it without her even saying the words.

'Angus isn't Dad, Mum,' I said.

'I didn't say he was,' she replied, defensive.

'Okay,' I said. I didn't want to fight, I just wanted the call to be done and dusted.

Her deep disappointment robbed me of air. I knew she didn't like him. And I knew why. But I loved him. And I believed in him. And I thought things would be different. I really did.

'Well, that's great news then, darling,' she said, trying to sound happy. And that hurt far more than her concern.

'Thanks, Mum,' I said, smiling hard so she could hear it through the phone.

'You'll have to come out here for dinner, the two of you,' she said. 'I haven't seen Angus in months.'

'We will,' I said. 'Mum, please don't worry.'

'I can't help it, darling, I'm your mother. It's my job to worry.'

I gave a half-laugh in response.

'Just promise me one thing.'

'What's that?' I asked.

'If he gets violent again, you leave.'

'Okay, but he's not going to,' I said.

'I hope not.'

'But yes, I promise I'll leave.'

My mother was the only person I had told about Angus slapping me. I hadn't told her everything, though. Not about the rough sex that landed me at the GP. Or the time he banged my head against the wall, holding me there by the throat as I gasped like a goldfish. How could I possibly tell my mother something like that?

Loving Angus, and all the secrets it required, was the most exquisite sort of loneliness I'd ever felt. And somehow that made me feel even closer to him.

But I wasn't stupid.

I knew it wasn't *good* that Angus had a temper and a habit of shutting me out. It's just that when I'd read stories in magazines about women in abusive relationships, they'd had broken bones and black eyes. The signs were clear. Mine weren't – not to me, at least. Which left me questioning whether I was being melodramatic and unfair to him. Whether maybe it really *was* because I pushed him too far. I knew I talked back when I could have stayed quiet. And I reasoned with myself that it was true: the cocaine *did* make the whole thing worse. So it made sense that now that he was clean, now that he finally saw there was a problem, it really would be different. Because the way he'd acted wasn't *him*, it was just his behaviour. And, I reasoned, behaviour could be changed.

That explanation also accounted for the fact that the man I'd come to know and love was so different from the Angus he'd become. And it explained why the Angus who turned up on my doorstep, clean and sober – roses in his hands and tears in his eyes – was his better self again. His loving self. And it was the first time he'd ever made such a big stand for me. It felt like progress, so I intended to stand by him in return.

He'd go to Narcotics Anonymous. I'd be supportive and loving. We'd get back on track.

And in our case, everything really *would* be different this time.

I hung up and moved back to my desk.

Val smiled at me as I approached. I was dreading telling her too, so I decided to hold off for a day or so, let her focus on getting Citexel to talk to us. She'd taken over trying to arrange the meeting: her title had more clout than mine.

'Two pm today,' she said, grinning at me as I sat down. I looked at her, confused. 'David Turner, we got him in to speak to Citexel.'

'That's brilliant,' I said, glancing at the time: 10.52am.

'Yes,' she said, watching me. Then she added: 'And Angus called for you.'

Fuck.

'Thanks,' I said, staring at my screen.

'Back together?' she asked. She was frowning: she already knew the answer.

'Yes.'

'Okay, well, he'd better not mess it up again,' she said, rolling back to her side of the partition. A faulty bulb flickered above me. I picked up the phone and dialled.

'Good morning, Candice speaking.' Her voice was irritable, as though she'd been interrupted in the middle of performing complicated mental arithmetic.

'Hi Candice, can I speak to Angus, please?' I asked.

'May I ask who is calling?' she asked. Bitch. She knew exactly who it was – we'd spoken on the phone countless times.

'It's Taylor,' I replied, 'returning his call.'

'One moment,' she said.

And a moment later I was connected.

'Baby?' Angus said.

'Hey,' I replied.

'Hey darling, I really wanted us to do something special tonight, but I … well, there's a *meeting* I want to go to,' he whispered. 'I'm struggling a bit. A lot.'

'Oh,' I said, 'of course.' It was Valentine's Day and I'd thought we'd spend it together, but an NA meeting mattered more.

'Are you sure?' he said. 'I know it's Valentine's Day and all.'

'Of course,' I said. 'What time will you be back? Should I come over later or stay at mine?'

'I'll probably be quite late. Need to come back here and do a bit more work after the meeting – trying to keep in everyone's good graces what with the credit card debacle. Fucking nightmare. Maybe we should leave it till tomorrow?'

'Sure,' I said, 'of course.'

'Oh shit – sorry, darling, I hate to ask you this, but do you mind going past mine on your way home? I have Elena coming in the morning and what with everything going on I know I'll forget to go past a cash machine. There's a card to the other account in the top drawer of my study – can you go draw some money for her? Actually, can you draw out a thousand pounds? I have no cash on me at all at the moment.'

'Okay,' I said, 'but I don't have your –'

'Four-five-four-one,' he whispered into the phone. And with that one swift manoeuvre, that one show of ultimate trust, another piece of my armour fell to the floor. Give trust to get trust, I guess.

'Okay, love you,' I said. And then we hung up.

And as I looked up I saw Kevin weaving his way towards me, his mail trolley full of couriered flowers, red envelopes and packages amid the usual letterbox envelopes. A deep pang in my chest: had Angus really not got me anything?

A few minutes later Kevin arrived at my desk. He was tall and thin with dark curly hair, and always wore a tie. Today's was the colour of red wine, diagonal cream stripes running through it.

'Bonjour,' he said in an Englishman's French accent; he knew I'd been trying to learn a while back. 'I have something for you. Just arrived.'

'Oh?' I said, a wave of relief washing over me.

He reached into the bottom level of his trolley and pulled out a stark white box. There was a little envelope stuck to the outside and my name written on it.

'Thanks, Kevin,' I said as he laid it with both hands on my desk. I could feel Val watching as I opened the box and peered inside. Three little chocolate cakes – the patisserie type.

'Damn. Looks like I have some competition,' he said with a smile.

I could see Val in my peripheral vision and was so glad she could see that Angus was trying.

'Yes, but it's not the elevator trick, is it?' I said to Kevin with an awkward smile as I closed the box again.

He laughed at our only shared joke, about a trick I'd once seen him perform. We'd been down near the mailroom and it was lunchtime, so every floor was crowded with people too lazy to take the stairs. We were both lacking in patience that day, so as we got into the elevator he reached across and pressed two buttons: doors-closed and the number four, because that's where we were going. It was an emergency-services trick he'd found on the internet and it meant we skipped every level until we got to the fourth. I'd never actually tried it on my own and couldn't remember what order to press the buttons in, but it had been a source of conversation – a silence filler – ever since.

'Very true,' he said, winking and moving on to the next desk.

I leaned over the cake box, reopened the lid, and smiled: it was a thoughtful gift. Then I reached for the envelope and slid out the message card:

You never got to eat your cake. How about we do it properly this time – dinner? Happy Valentine's Day. Call me: 07700900154.

David x

~

I arrived home at about 6.30pm. I'd drawn Angus's cash as promised and then shared a tense elevator ride with Felicia on my way back to deliver it. But it was tense because of me, not her. She'd smiled at me when I'd stepped in, then ignored me in favour of her phone for the rest of the trip. I, on the other hand, had held my breath the whole way, trying not to blush with shame, wondering whether she was wearing the lingerie, whether it fit, and whether she'd figured out who '*Love, A xx*' was.

Chiara was waiting for me, meowing at the front door, when I arrived back at my place. She purred against my legs as I searched for my keys. Then as I pushed the door open she ran inside and I followed. I looked around me then closed the door – occasionally, very occasionally, I remembered that she wasn't *my* cat, that somebody might be looking for her, and that always made me feel a bit guilty. But nobody was calling for her, nobody was looking for her, so I dropped my handbag at the front door and closed it behind me. My fingers fumbled with the small plastic buttons on my shirt and I undid them as I walked towards the bed.

I slipped the shirt off my shoulders, unzipped my skirt, peeled off my pantyhose and then laid them all over the chair by the bathroom. I reached for my pyjama bottoms – shoved underneath my pillow – and dug out Angus's pink shirt from my second drawer. I put them on, picked up my laptop and left it starting up on my bed.

Chiara was meowing from the kitchen, staring at the fridge.

'Hello darling,' I said as I approached her. The meowing escalated. 'Do you want some milk?'

I opened the fridge. It was almost empty. But there was milk for Chiara and a bottle of sauvignon blanc lying at the bottom behind a row of nail polish and half a jar of jam. I poured the milk into a saucer and placed it on the floor by my feet, then a big glass of wine for myself. Cold. Tangy. I pulled the stark white box out of my handbag and moved over to the bed. I left the card in my bag.

The Art of War sat in the pile of books on the bedside table; it was still only half-read. The day Jamie gave it to me felt like months before, but it had only been a week. I put the cake down beside it, crawled beneath the covers and propped myself up with three brightly coloured throw pillows. Then I reached for the box and opened it.

David's voice rang in my head: *Did you plan on using that cake for something specific later?* And I could feel his warmth. See his naked chest as he danced in his bathrobe. And I almost emailed him, just to say thank you. But then his voice echoed in my mind again: *We have an understanding.* And that's the sort of thing I could have imagined my father saying. And so even if I hadn't been back together with Angus, I would have been cautious: I didn't want to be the scalpel that sliced open another woman's heart.

I reached for my computer, pulled up Netflix and took a sugary bite of cake.

And that was the last time I recall feeling entirely safe.

wednesday

Master Sun said: *'If trees move, he is coming.'*

15 FEBRUARY

Like most things, in hindsight I think I knew.

The air felt different: thicker, quieter, heavier. The newspaper headlines on the Tube looked bolder, as though trying to attract my eye. Trying to show me. The escalators at Green Park station were more packed than usual. The smell of urine on the stairs that led outside was stronger. And the London bus that passed as I emerged onto Piccadilly seemed redder, brighter, more dazzling. Something just felt off: I'd burned my tongue on my coffee, I'd almost choked trying to swallow my magnesium tablet, my airways felt blocked and my lungs felt tight. All the signs were there. Yes. Even the carpet leading the way towards my desk seemed to resemble bars in a way I'd never noticed before. And Val; well, Val was certifiably grey. Even greyer than usual.

She was sitting at my desk when I arrived, her eyes pinned to a newspaper in front of her.

'Oh honey, what have you done?' she asked quietly as I approached, not looking up.

I placed my bag on the floor and tried to catch my breath: 'Huh?'

She pushed the paper towards me: gracing the cover was a large photograph of a man with jowls, walking out of a building. The caption underneath it read: *Nicolai Stepanovich.* The headline read 'Russian tycoon's money laundering exposed' and it went on:

> *Nicolai Stepanovich (pictured above), the primary of Citexel International, has been linked to an elaborate property-based money laundering scheme, an investigation by the* Guardian *reveals. Leaked data shows that Stepanovich used a sophisticated web of shell companies to funnel over £500 million of illegal money into British circulation over the last eight years. The majority of these funds were moved through The Town Square regeneration in Oxfordshire; however, a duplicate scheme in Eastbourne is currently in the pipeline, with large swathes of land already purchased using illegal funds.*

I gulped and the air got stuck in my throat.

> *Planning permissions to transform the seaside town into a high-value retirement mecca over the next fifteen years have already been passed, with finance and multiple investors secured.*

My eyes skipped a couple of paragraphs – quotes from experts, some journalistic speculation – then stopped. Dead.

Inside sources report that local parties currently in conversation with Citexel include: KR Property International, Jenson and The Turner Group. These revelations highlight yet again how easily the light regulations of the British corporate landscape can be manipulated by those looking to launder money through the UK's property market.

'Fuck,' I said, looking up. 'How is this possible?'

Val just looked at me. Then she said: 'Where did you hear about Eastbourne needing an investor?'

I swallowed hard and my mind swirled. I couldn't tell her about Angus – not then, not as a reflex action without thinking through all of my options and talking to him first. What he'd told me was confidential – I couldn't risk it somehow getting back to his work and biting his friend on the arse. Not after all the trouble I'd caused him by ordering the prostitutes. Not when he'd been trying to help me.

So instead I lied. 'Someone mentioned it at the pub. I think he was from the trade press,' I said, vaguely. 'It was time sensitive so I brought it straight to you.' The trade press were renowned for knowing, but not printing, secrets so as not to spoil a deal. Yet as I listened to the lie spill out of my mouth, even I didn't believe me. And from the look in her eyes, neither did she.

'David Turner has been on the phone with Nigel this morning,' she said. 'He's *really* angry.'

I swallowed hard. 'But we only told him about it two days ago,' I said, louder than I'd planned.

'Yes. And then *I* put in a meeting for him at Citexel, Taylor. And then they *named* him in the newspaper.'

'But I didn't know Stepanovich was a criminal,' I said softly. My head was hot.

'It doesn't matter,' Val replied evenly. 'David is fuming.' She let out a heavy sigh. 'Shit.'

'I'm going to get sacked, aren't I?' I said, my eyes burning and my pulse quick.

She sighed heavily. She was trying to calm herself down. 'You should probably go home for the rest of the day,' she said, her voice icy and her jaw tight. 'I'm going to have to somehow explain all this to Nigel.'

'I'm so sorry, Val,' I said. The walls were moving towards me and my head was light. 'I just don't get how this happened.'

'I'll give you a call later on,' said Val quietly.

My thoughts quickly moved to David. I would call David. Sort this all out. My hands were clammy as I picked up my handbag and headed back towards the front door, searching through my bag for David's Valentine's Day card.

I found it. And as soon as I got out of the building I dialled his number, ducking into the small dark doorway of the building next door to muffle the sounds from the street.

It went to voicemail.

'David, look, I'm so sorry about everything. I have no idea what happened with Eastbourne. I didn't know. Of course I didn't know. I would never have suggested it if I did. Anyway, please call me back.'

Two long minutes later he still hadn't called back. So I dialled again.

This time he answered.

'David?' I asked. 'It's Taylor.'

'Hi,' he said. His voice was flat and hard.

'I'm so sorry, I have no idea how this happened.'

'I wish I could believe that,' he said.

It felt like I'd been punched. 'David,' my voice was high and shrill. I needed him to understand. 'Why would I do something like this on purpose? That would be career suicide.'

'I have no idea why women do what they do,' he said. 'Maybe some ridiculous attempt at revenge?' His voice raised in anger at the beginning of that sentence, but lowered again by the end. As though somebody in his office was listening.

'That's unfair!' I said quickly. 'I would nev–'

'Is it?' he interrupted. 'You could barely look me in the eye on Monday. Wouldn't even shake my hand. You don't think it seems a bit far-fetched to expect me to believe this is all a big coincidence? Jesus, Taylor. How could you do this to me? I championed it to my fucking board!'

I struggled to hold back tears and my voice shook as I spoke, 'David, I –'

'Do you have any idea how long it has taken me to build my reputation?' he asked. 'Or how difficult it was?'

'I'm so sorry, but I promise it wasn't inten–'

'Taylor, I have to go.'

And then he hung up.

Oh God.

By 9.07am I was weaving my way through the grey-suited stragglers and motorbike couriers. Thick, dark clouds hung heavy in the sky and the air was damp. My heart was still fast, but I felt calmer to be out in the open as I moved through Mayfair.

Green Park station had emptied by the time I made my way back down the grimy stairs that smelled of urine. Past the dry-cleaner. And as I hurried past the kiosk and glanced inside, I saw Nicolai's face staring back at me from the pile of newspapers stacked beside the Mars Bars and brightly coloured sweet wrappers all cheerfully reflecting the light.

I focused on the ground and moved towards the escalator and down to the platforms. There were only a handful of us waiting, watching as the lit-up board clicked down from three minutes to two to one. And when the train came, I took a seat near the doorway, exhaling as the doors beeped and closed. But then the man across from me opened up his newspaper and once again I was faced with the front page …

The French have a phrase for what my life had become – I'd noted it in my purple notebook when it was still my French phrase book: *à la débandade.*

A chaotic mess.

I called Angus when I got home. My face was puffy from tears and my nose blocked. I was lying in bed and my ears were thick with dread.

'Don't be silly, darling, of course you haven't been fired,' Angus said.

'I have. Well, basically I have,' I said. 'I will be, at least.'

He was silent on the other end of the phone, and I didn't have the energy to fill the void.

'Why, what for?' he asked.

And I paused before I told him: I didn't know how to say it without it coming out as an accusation.

'Eastbourne,' I said, my voice hoarse.

'What do you mean, Eastbourne?' he asked, his words clipped.

'Have you read the papers today?'

'I don't have time to read the paper every day and I'm late,' he said, sounding annoyed. 'What exactly happened?'

'Read the *Guardian*.' I sighed. 'You'll see.'

'Can't you just tell me?' he snapped.

'Stepanovich is a money launderer, Angus.' Then I took a deep breath and asked the question I had to ask. 'Did you know?'

'For fuck's sake, Taylor,' he said, 'are you really asking me that?' I heard him breathing on the other end of the line. 'How do you manage to make everything my fault?' he asked, defensive. 'I was trying to help you. Do you have any idea how many of these things cross my desk every week? And you want to know why I didn't know the inner workings of a man's business from eons ago who I didn't even end up working with? Have you listened to yourself?' I could hear traffic behind him and then a deep exhale. 'Fuck, you didn't tell them I gave you the idea, did you? I told you that in confidence.'

'No, of course not,' I replied, and I could feel my voice cracking. My life was falling apart; I needed him to be kind.

'Look, nobody reads the *Guardian* anyway, and no real damage has been done. It'll probably all blow over,' he said, his voice taking on a gentler timbre.

'No, this won't blow over,' I replied.

'Look, darling,' he said, his voice intense and low. 'I'm so sorry this has happened but I'm running into a meeting. I'll talk to you tonight, and don't worry, they're still pissed with me about those hookers here. Maybe we can go sign on together. It'll be romantic.'

My heart sank. *How have I fucked everything up to this level?* And I let out a loud sigh.

'Why don't you go over to my place, have a bath, make yourself comfy. I'll be back later on. Ask Charlotte to come round or something. Tell her to bring you a joint.'

'Okay, love you,' I said.

'Bye,' he said and the line clicked dead.

~

Charlotte arrived later that afternoon and we sat out on the balcony, looking out over the jagged and glittery London skyline. She was wearing jeans and a pink rope-knit jumper and I was in yoga pants, a black long-sleeved T-shirt and my navy coat. It had only been a few hours since I'd been sent home from work but I already looked unemployed.

'What the fuck are you going to do?' she said, coughing. We were getting high while Ed watched through the window from his cage, and we'd been out there for a while by then: me recounting my day and her listening. Our only interruption had been Val calling to suggest I take the next day off too.

'I really don't know,' I replied.

'God,' she said. 'You can't get into proper trouble though, right? Like, with the police?'

'No,' I said. 'At least I don't think so.' I inhaled and handed the joint back before I let a cloud of smoke and then a cough escape my lips. 'But I might lose my job.'

'How did you even come up with the idea?'

I took a deep breath.

'Angus,' I said. 'But he was trying to help me.' And then I waited for the avalanche.

'Oh for fuck's sake, of course he had something to do with it,' she said. 'What does he say about it all now?'

'No, it's not like that,' I said. 'I was really stuck for an idea, and he almost worked for Stepanovich a few months back. But he didn't know about the money laundering – how could he?' I said. 'Nobody knew, that's why it's news.'

'That's true. But seriously, he's always involved when shitty things happen to you – have you noticed that?' She tapped ash onto the floor. Angus would be pissed about that and I made a mental note to clean it up later.

'Do you want wine?' I asked as I stood up, my voice raspy from smoke and old tears. I moved towards the doorway.

Her eyebrows raised. 'Sure, why not,' she said, snuffing the joint out on the balcony wall.

'Red or white?' I called to her from the kitchen. It smelled of green apple cleaning fluid and furniture polish, the way it always did when Elena had been.

'White, definitely,' she called back. 'He's kind of pretty, you know.' She was looking at Ed.

I opened the fridge, grabbed a bottle of white and headed back outside to Charlotte with two glasses. London looked small from up there. Manageable.

'And there's something else. Another reason the client is cross.'

'What's that?' she asked, taking her wine.

'He's the one I slept with.'

Charlotte looked at me with wide eyes: 'What a fucking nightmare.' And then she started to laugh.

'It's not funny,' I said. 'He thinks I did it out of spite, because he didn't tell me he was married. He's out for blood now. I really can't afford to lose my job over this.'

'Oh please, like you'd bother.' She took a gulp. 'Why don't you call him?'

I cringed. *What would she think if she knew everything I had done?*

'I tried. He wouldn't listen.'

'Let him calm down, then try again,' she suggested.

'I will.' I sighed.

It was around then that Angus came home. I swivelled my head just in time to see him walk through the door and take off his shoes.

'Hi,' I said.

'How's the patient?' he called to us, dropping his briefcase by the door.

'She's okay,' called back Charlotte, 'all things considered.'

'Smells like she's well medicated,' he said.

'Yes,' she replied politely. But her tone said: *fuck you*.

'Shit, sorry honey,' I offered. 'We smoked outside …'

He appeared at the door with a smile. 'Do you have any you can leave here?' he asked Charlotte, 'just to get her through the next few days?'

Charlotte looked at me as if to say: *What? He hates you smoking.*

And I looked back as if to say: *See, I told you he'd changed.*

Then I stood up, wandered over to him, put my fingers through his hair and watched his eyes close.

'Of course,' said Charlotte, 'here you go. Keep it in the fridge if you aren't going to smoke it straightaway.' She tossed a little bag of weed at Angus. It hit him in the chest but he caught it.

'Thanks, Charlotte,' he said, his voice clipped.

'Anyway, I'd better get going,' she said, standing up and leaving her wine glass on the floor.

‘Thanks so much, honey,’ I said as I walked her to the front door.

‘Love you,’ she said as she hugged me. ‘Bye Angus,’ she said and waved at him.

And Angus put the weed in the fridge.

thursday

Master Sun said: '*When a general misjudges his enemy and sends a lesser force against a larger one the outcome is rout.*'

16 FEBRUARY

Please pick up dry-cleaning. A xx

That was the note Angus left me, scrawled on the back of a wrinkled petrol receipt. I smiled; petrol-station bathrooms had always been our thing. Next to it was a cold cup of tea and twenty pounds, presumably for the dry-cleaning. I was squinting at it through hazy eyes: I hadn't woken up naturally.

It was the phone that roused me. A tune I didn't recognise: high pitched and cheery. And muffled, possibly by walls. At first I thought it was part of a dream. But it wasn't. It was very real. And as I edged my way back into consciousness, out of the ashtray of my psyche, I could still hear it.

It must be a neighbour's phone.

But I didn't move. I just lay there, my heavy head nestled into the pillow and my eyes focusing on the darkening sky outside. It would rain later. I could feel it. And then I'd go outside and smell the rain. There's nothing like the smell of rain.

A constant stream of images flashed before my eyes: *Prostitutes. Felicia. Mrs Clifton. Lucky socks. His coke. David. Nicolai Stepanovich* …

I rolled over and squeezed my eyes shut.

At least he'd taken the sex tape down. Deleted every copy. It was almost like it had never happened. Almost.

But it was time to get up. My mouth was too dry, so I reached for the glass on the side table and took a sip. Cold. Wet. I glanced down at my phone: 10.40am. There was a missed call from my mother, two Facebook notifications and a text message from Never-call-he-just-wants-sex Anderson: *Therapy? xx*

Shit.

It had come in two hours before: had Angus seen it when he left his note? I flicked the phone off silent, put it back down beside me and lay staring at the ceiling, the knot in my stomach tightening as the cheery ring tone started up again.

I stood up and moved into the living room. The sound got louder. My eyes shifted from object to object, table to sofa, booze cabinet to kitchen, but I couldn't see it, so I moved towards the sound as if I was playing a game of Marco Polo.

I was standing in the middle of the living room looking around me, but I couldn't sense its direction …

The kitchen. I moved towards the kitchen. My legs were covered in a pair of Angus's old tracksuit pants and they were dragging along the floor, tripping me up as I moved. No. Not there. I moved back to the middle of the living room …

And then it stopped.

Fuck.

I felt like a failure. I was standing near the dining table: he'd left a copy of the *Telegraph* out for me. They'd picked up the story too, and Nicolai's face stared back at me from the front page. My eyes scanned it quickly but it told me nothing new.

Another ring tone started up, but this one I recognised. It was mine. I moved towards my phone, still charging beside the bed. And as I approached I watched its screen flash bright: No Caller ID.

My eyes landed on the note. Dry-cleaning. I could do that. Something I could succeed at. I waited for the call to go to voicemail.

A few moments later a notification popped up: No Caller ID had left a message. So I listened to it: Jenny, from HR.

Stomach. Wet cement.

She wanted me to come in. HR calling could only mean one thing. I swallowed hard as I looked around for a pen to write down her number but I couldn't find one, so I grabbed my eyeliner from the top of the dresser and flipped over Angus's note.

I jotted it down in thick, black kohl that smudged on my fingers and was difficult to read.

But as I began to dial her phone number, something caught my attention: the receipt was not just for petrol. It was for condoms too. Durex. *Angus never wears condoms with me.* He'd insisted I went on the pill because he hated them.

Kim.

The blood drained from my face and her smile on that mountaintop reappeared like a sinister hologram in front of me. *Bitch.*

The last time I'd discovered that Angus was cheating on me had been in a similar manner – via a note in his pocket. I'd just picked up his dry-cleaning: two coats and a pair of trousers. And as I'd stood by the closet door, peeling away the plastic from the wire coat hangers, I'd slipped my hand into each coat pocket, my fingers tracing the lining – I must have suspected something, why else would I have checked? And in the third pocket I found it: a torn-off scrap of paper. It had light blue lines on it.

And upon those light blue lines was a hand-drawn love heart with, '*A 4 K 4ever*' scrawled inside.

Frantically, my eyes searched for the date on the receipt. It was faint. I squinted. I could barely make it out; no, I couldn't make it out at all. The one part of a perfectly printed receipt that I needed had been worn away, probably by Angus's pocket or wallet.

I closed my eyes and willed the thought to leave as quickly as it had found me, told myself that vulnerability was making me irrational, and placed the call.

Angus had just bought his first vintage Porsche – it was black with chocolate brown seats. It'd taken three months and a small fortune to refurbish, and that was our first road trip. We were on our way to his parents' place in Wiltshire – Leigh Road – and I had just emerged from the petrol station mini-mart. I held two Cokes, a packet of salt-and-vinegar crisps and a novelty fluffy gearstick cover – a last-minute purchase I'd found by the cash register as I paid. It was a joke. He would hate it. But that was the first time he made love to me in a petrol-station bathroom.

There were no condoms. There was almost no noise. There was no light. It was just him, me, and a wobbly sink I used to keep my balance.

That was the first time.

—

It was 3.15pm when Jenny met me by the elevators. She smelled of hairspray and was wearing a herringbone dress. I followed her quietly down the corridor towards the small, windowless meeting room used for interviews and sackings. She opened the door and as I moved inside, my heart pounding, I saw Val – grey hair, grey suit – sitting on one of three chairs, her expression apologetic.

I took a seat. Jenny closed the door behind her and then sat down on the final empty seat.

'So, we have some news,' she said with misplaced cheeriness. I looked at her, waiting.

Her eyes moved to Val. 'We've managed to smooth things over with David Turner,' she said.

'What?' I asked, relieved. 'That's wonderful.'

'Yes,' Jenny continued, but her voice had taken on a sterner timbre and she was shifting her weight in her seat nervously. 'But, Taylor, as I'm sure you can understand, this is not the sort of thing we can have happen again. You should have taken more care, done more research before you brought an idea like this to a client.'

'I agree,' I said. There was no amount of research that could have protected me from what had happened. But if taking the blame meant keeping my job, I was willing to do that.

'Nigel insisted we chat to you,' Val interjected. There was a softness in her voice that warned me.

'Yes,' continued Jenny, 'it's important that we make this very clear to you.'

She paused and I waited for the axe to fall. 'So, Taylor, this meeting will go down on your record as a verbal warning. Do you understand what that means?'

My stomach filled with lead.

'Yes,' I said, 'I do.' I swallowed hard and a loud silence filled the room. A warning was better than losing my job, but I couldn't bring myself to look at Val.

'Why don't you take tomorrow off and come back to work on Monday?' Val said. Her voice was gentle.

I nodded. 'Okay.' Then I tried to smile.

She smiled back but I knew I'd let her down. I'd really let her down. And I wouldn't be getting a promotion any time soon.

Then Jenny stood up and opened the door. 'Thanks for coming in. We'll see you on Monday,' she said.

I moved through it and she closed it behind me with a click. I could hear the hum of them discussing my fall from grace as I turned and made my way towards the elevators. And as I pressed the button and waited for the doors to slide open, my phone buzzed from my coat pocket. I pulled it into view. My mother: *Hi darling, just checking all okay xx*

And I replied with a lie: *Yes, all okay. xx*

—

I have to fix this.

I was lying in the bathtub, my big toe inserting itself into the tap head. It fit perfectly. A candle flickered in the corner, its gradient light transforming rather ordinary tiles into quite the work of art. My catastrophe appeared to be drawing to a close and so my mind had reverted to Angus, yellow ribbons and seemingly impossible solutions. Because he had taken the sex tape down but I had no idea how to rectify my part.

All I knew was that I couldn't allow him to lose his job over something I'd done. It wasn't fair and yet I couldn't see a way out. The simplest solution, coming clean, wasn't an option: he'd never forgive me. I needed to find another way.

I turned on the hot tap once more and let it run, burning my feet just a little. They were becoming wrinkly. I drained the bath, wrapped myself in an oversized towel and wandered through to the bedroom just as the front door began to rattle.

I looked at the clock: it was 7.45pm already, Angus was home.

'Darling?' came his voice as the door opened.

'Hey,' I called back as I wandered through to greet him.

I watched him as he put his briefcase down by the door.

'So, how's my favourite reprobate?' he said, walking over to me and wrapping me in his arms.

'Okay,' I said, hugging him back and letting my towel fall to the floor. 'Hey, I think you left your phone here – it was ringing earlier.'

His eyes shifted, breaking his gaze. He looked to the left, then the right.

'Oh, no baby,' he said with a sheepish laugh, 'that's just my other phone. My sponsor made me get it. Supposed to keep me committed to my recovery. I'm not supposed to even put it on silent, so he's going to be super pissed with me that I forgot it.' He smiled. Then his hands found their way to my bottom and he squeezed it: 'I love this bum.'

'Do you just?' I said as I kissed him, me naked and him fully clothed.

'Yes,' he whispered as he carried me, my legs around his waist, through to the bedroom.

His mouth pressed down on mine, his hand frantically working upon his belt. Then I heard his zipper. He swivelled me to the side of the bed, my head hanging off the edge, his mouth between my legs. And just before I came he flipped me over so I was on my belly, facing the mirror.

'I want you to look yourself in the eyes and make yourself come,' he said.

And so I did.

–

Twenty minutes later I was lying with my head on his chest, his pink work shirt open.

'So, how was your day?' I asked, gently tugging at his chest hair with my teeth.

'Shit,' he said. 'I'm in the doghouse. Henry can barely meet my eye. Candice looks down on me. I'm sick of trying to convince them that I did nothing wrong. It's a nightmare.'

His eyes were to the ceiling. My throat was tight.

'Shall we run away to an island?' I whispered.

But I knew that was my chance. To tell the truth. To make it right. And I even opened my mouth to say the words. But the sounds just wouldn't form. And so I lay there, my mouth partially open, physically incapable of telling him what I'd done.

And instead I said: 'Jenny called this afternoon, the HR woman from work. I can go back to work on Monday.'

He rolled onto his side and stroked my cheek. 'Well, that's great,' he said.

'But they gave me a warning,' I added.

'You naughty girl,' he smiled. 'But you see? I told you it would all blow over.' He reached for my hand. 'So, what do you have planned for tomorrow, then?'

'Not sure. Charlotte's away in Scotland until Sunday, so I can't even play with her.'

'Jesus, doesn't she ever work?'

'Half-term,' I said.

And we lay there, our hands interwoven, for what felt like forever. My phone buzzed a couple of times, as did his, but we didn't care what the world wanted. So we didn't check. Nothing outside of that room mattered: it was a warm low-lit bubble, and there was nowhere else we wanted to be. It had been fifteen days since the break-up, thirteen since I saw the sex tape, ten since I'd first opened *The Art of War* and thirty-six hours since the Stepanovich story broke, and that was the first moment in that time when everything felt sane again. Calm.

Like every eye of the storm, I guess.

But then he reached for his phone.

'Fuck, Dad called,' he said. And just like that our cocoon had been pierced. So I reached for mine too: a Facebook message had come in. I was lying on my side, facing away from him, goose bumps forming on my arm as I read it:

Hi Taylor, I know you don't want to talk to me, but you need to. There's something you need to know. Please can we meet. And don't tell Angus.

It was from Kim.

My pulse quickened as I thought of the petrol receipt and the picture of them together on that ski slope. *What does she want? What could we possibly have to talk about? Should I tell him?*

But then the warmth of his hand was on my hip and the choice evaporated. He was looking over my shoulder and I didn't know how long he'd been there. What he'd seen.

'I just got a message from Kim!' I said, turning to look at him.

'What does she want?' he asked, his eyes wide and his jaw clenched.

'I don't know. She wants to meet, to talk.'

'Shit, baby, she's crazy,' he said, shaking his head. His fingers were in his hair. 'Darling, you need to block her. Immediately.' He moved towards me.

'Why?' I asked. I searched the thoughts behind his eyes for clues, but they were moving too fast.

'Look, I didn't want to worry you, but she's a bit obsessed with me. I've tried to be kind, tried to wean her off me … but she can't accept the fact that I chose you over her. She's angry. And I'm not sure what she's capable of. You need to block her.'

'I don't even know *how* to block someone,' I said, watching his face.

'Here, give it to me,' he said as he reached out and took my phone. A few seconds later she was blocked and he handed it back, then leaned forward and kissed me softly.

I reached my hand up and stroked his face: 'You chose me, did you?' I teased.

'Of course I chose you,' he said. Then he sighed, kissed my forehead and rolled out of bed. 'I better call Dad back,' he said as he stood up and walked out of the room with his phone. A moment later I heard his voice.

'Dad, you called?' His voice had taken on that plummy quality it always did when he spoke to his father. As if tone alone could make him feel good enough. His father had a presence that made everyone else in the room shrink into the cracks of the furniture. And I could tell the moment he first shook my hand – firm grip, empty eyes set deep in a shiny, balding head – that his was a world in which men didn't explain, women didn't question, children played quietly, a cleaner was a 'daily' and waiters had better never pour the wine without one hand behind their back. Defy those rules at your peril.

And every time we'd met since it had felt like yet another test I couldn't study for. I would come away with cheeks that ached from smiling and a mind tense from searching for clever anecdotes while trying not to insert them at the wrong time. I couldn't imagine growing up with a man like that. He made me feel lucky that my father had left.

The problem was: I knew I needed him to like me. If he didn't, Angus would never marry me. He wouldn't risk upsetting his biggest cash stream. Not even with his mother – white hair, blue eyes and skin that smelled of gardenia – on my side.

'They want us to come for lunch next Sunday,' Angus said as he came back through to the bedroom. 'Eleanor's back for the weekend.'

I'd just got up and put on my dressing gown. Eleanor was Angus's older sister and I'd only met her once, the Easter before. She lived in Guernsey with her husband, and she and Angus didn't get on. And she rarely found her way into conversation unless she was visiting.

'Great,' I said with a tight smile as I put on my slippers. *Fuck.*

And so the rest of my evening was spent short-listing books I could read over the next week to ensure I sounded smart enough – neuroplasticity? – and cataloguing dresses I could wear in order to look feminine enough to make his father's grade. All the while, watching the water turn cloudy as I stirred pasta and listened to Leonard Cohen croon about cracks letting in the proverbial light.

But what if the cracks let in the darkness instead?

By the time I was sprinkling parmesan into a little bowl on the table I had come to a non-negotiable conclusion: no matter what happened, I needed to deny that I had anything to do with ordering those prostitutes. I couldn't confess now, not after staying silent for so long. I would simply have to swallow the guilt and wait for the sour taste to fade.

But it didn't fade.

Instead it was simply replaced by something far worse.

friday

Master Sun said: *'At first, be like a maiden;*
when the enemy opens the door, be swift as a hare.'

17 FEBRUARY

The sky had been unseasonably blue that day; the kind of pastel blue that belongs in a kindergarten paint box. But by late afternoon it had been slashed up by the white trails left by a series of aircraft; white scars across a perfect sky. The window was open just a little and there was a breeze coming in through it, making the hinges creak every so often. That was the only sound in the flat that afternoon, aside from Ed's occasional shuffling around his cage – audible only if I really strained my ears – along with a distant hum from the streets outside and me opening and shutting drawers.

I was in Angus's study. I'd been rash to delete all our photographs together and now wanted them back. He had duplicates on his computer – it was me who put them there, neatly organised in an iPhoto folder named: 'Us' – so the plan was simply to copy them across and pretend the purge had never happened. But photos are big, too big for email. So my arm was elbow deep in his second drawer scouring for a thumb drive.

Bingo.

I pulled it into the light – it was green – and plugged it into his computer.

I clicked on the icon and got ready to copy across my photos. But it was already full of pictures, PDFs and a few Excel files with obscure names.

I couldn't just delete them all – I'd need to copy them onto the desktop in case they were important.

I clicked on the first one to see what it was: a spreadsheet. Tab after tab of figures. I looked at the file name: TTS_JN. What was I looking at?

So I clicked another file.

A photograph.

I recognise that man.

It was a face I'd become well acquainted with over the past couple of days. The lines that ran from beak-like nose to mouth, the thinning hair, the jowls.

It was Nicolai Stepanovich. He was walking out of a building with a big glass revolving door. He was carrying some sort of sports bag. His eyes were down.

The room spun and my blood raced as I quickly scanned the rest of the documents. There was only one text file and so I clicked on it. Watched as it slowly opened. A series of red comment bubbles ran down the left-hand margin.

Nicolai Stepanovich (Citexel International) was responsible for The Town Square development in Oxfordshire, a scheme that has been

> *instrumental in a large-scale operation to funnel illegal money out of his native Russia and into British circulation via a sophisticated web of shell companies.*

To the left of this sat a red bubble with the text: *please see spreadsheet TTS_JN for transactions.*

> *This is set to be duplicated with a new scheme in Eastbourne aimed at the over sixty-fives. This will involve an extensive regeneration, transforming the town into a high-value retirement village. Included in the plans are a number of built-to-rent blocks and a hospital. Planning perms have already been granted and finance/investors secured. All land acquisitions (already completed) have been via illegal streams. Construction of Phase One is set to start in May.*

And attached to that was a comment that read: *KR Property International and Jenson are currently in conversation regarding potential investment. Confirmation attached in PDF entitled Emails.*

I stared at the screen, confused: The Turner Group wasn't mentioned in this. And so I scrolled through the files, searching for that PDF. I found one entitled: *emails_UPDATED*. Clicked on it. And there, at the very top, was an email from Val confirming David Turner's interest in the Eastbourne scheme and his appointment at 2pm the previous Tuesday.

My skin prickled. My breath was quick and shallow. I stared at the screen, and the information swirled around my brain.

The spreadsheets. The photograph. The emails. The information contained in the dozen or so files I'd yet to open.

But most of all, that text file.

There was nothing in the *Guardian* article that wasn't in that file.

Sweat formed on my palms as I grabbed for the mouse and closed each document as quickly as I could.

I could never let Angus know I'd found them.

That I knew.

Because in that moment, I *did* know: Angus had set me up.

I unplugged the thumb drive and slipped it back into the drawer in which I'd found it, then slammed it shut.

I was dizzy and I held on to the edge of the desk for stability.

There was so much information on that thumb drive – he must have been collecting it for months. And newspapers fact check, which takes time too. He would have had to leak those files to the *Guardian* long before he suggested Eastbourne to me as a viable investment idea.

But why gather information on Stepanovich in the first place? It was dangerous at best – but to leak it to the papers? That was insane. And Angus was not the whistle-blowing type. Surely it had to be about something bigger than simply being pissed that he didn't get Stepanovich's business. And where did he even get all that information? Did he have a source working for Citexel? *He must do.* I thought of the spreadsheets. The emails. My mind moved back to the investor who fell away: was he a part of this? Did he know what was going on? Was *this* why he wanted out?

But I was tying myself up in knots about things that really didn't matter. Angus knew full well what he was planning. What the impact would be. And he'd intentionally tried to drown me in the storm. That was all I needed to know.

My throat tightened, and my vision liquefied.

I tried to get my thoughts in check.

This is ridiculous. It can't be true. Taylor, calm down.

The whole thing felt impossible. There *had* to be another explanation. Something more reasonable. But what other explanation was there?

I need to leave. Now.

I stood up and ran through to the bedroom. Slid open the closet door and started pulling out my clothes, throwing them into a pile on the bed. But then I just stood there, staring at the tangled mess, my fingers on my lips, not moving.

Because it wasn't that simple. I couldn't just leave.

Not without a good excuse.

If I did, he'd know I'd found out about Eastbourne, about what he'd done – why else would I have such a sudden change of heart? He'd know that I could potentially reveal him as the source of the leak and there was no telling what he'd do to protect himself.

An image of Val opening a link to my re-uploaded sex tape flashed before my eyes; I now knew that it was unlikely he'd destroyed all copies as promised. Then another, of that green thumb drive arriving in a yellow envelope on a tabloid magazine editor's desk, with a confession note speaking of how, while I couldn't disclose my sources, it was me who leaked the story and I was happy to go public; then it would be me in the firing line. The awful possibilities were endless.

So, no. I *had* to stay. At least for a little while.

Leaning over the bed I picked up a crocheted navy dress, slid it back onto its thick wooden hanger and returned it to the closet. Then I did the same with the rest of my clothes. Soon it looked like they'd never left the rail.

I slid the closet door shut and sat on the bed.

I had two choices. I could leave right then and there. He would register me as a potential threat, and I would remain an unwilling pawn in his game, never knowing which part of my life might implode next. Never feeling secure.

Or I could take back control. Orchestrate a safe exit.

In order to be safe from him I needed two things: a strong excuse to leave – something to allay any suspicion that I knew what he'd done – and something I could use against him once I was at a distance. Something that would make him as scared of me as I was of him. The information on the green thumb drive was a good start, but I needed more to tie him to it – what was to stop him from saying he'd never seen it before?

My eyes darted around the room. It still looked the same, smelled the same – fabric softener, furniture polish and a faint hint of his cologne – but everything had shifted. However, as it stood, I was in a strong position. I had easy access to his mail, his home, his phone, his wallet, his work diary, his neighbours, his credit card statements and his computer. Every morsel of his life was up for examination and tampering with, if I was brave enough to try.

All I needed to do was play the role he'd primed me for – the Sunday Girl. I would smile, defer to him, be charming and sweet, while covertly collecting what I needed to buy my freedom.

It was a good plan; I just wasn't sure I had the strength for it. Because how could two people who'd loved each other the way we had come to this? I thought of the tears in his eyes as he stood in my doorway, begging me for forgiveness just a week before. Of our in-jokes about orange string bikinis and our plans for the future. We'd had sex just the night before. Was everything a lie?

My phone was charging on the bedside table and I reached for it: it was 5:22pm.

I wanted to call Charlotte but I couldn't: even if she wasn't in the highlands of Scotland with shitty reception, she would tell me to leave. She would insist on it. But it was different for her. She didn't understand what it was like to live in the world with no money behind you. Nobody to pay your legal fees or fight your battles or make a call to get you a new job if you were fired under a dark cloud of sex-tape disgrace. I had nobody to make things go away.

And it wasn't her life that would blow up in the aftermath. She wasn't the one who would end up on the internet, unemployed or possibly far worse. I took a deep breath and stared out the window. The sky had turned a thick navy: Angus would be back soon and I couldn't risk him finding me mid-search.

I looked back at my phone, and came to a decision: I would call David. Tell him what I'd found; explain what had happened. I scrolled through my recent calls, found his number and listened as the line began to ring once, twice, three times. And then as quickly as I had dialled, I hung up. I wasn't thinking straight. What was I going to say? *'Hi David, it's me, sorry about the whole Citexel thing, but I just found this green thumb drive in my boyfriend's study. It turns out it was him who leaked the information, I think he's trying to destroy me and …'* It sounded ludicrous. Besides, the comments in that text file were all anonymous. So it was just my word against Angus's and who knew what version he'd spin if questioned before I had more evidence: *'Oh no, poor Taylor, she's a bit unbalanced. That's her thumb drive. Why? What's on there? Is she okay?'*

It could all blow up in my face. I'd have to wait until I had more against him before I could tell anybody about anything.

And so, I was back where I started.

We'd met at a party, on a boat, the August bank-holiday weekend. One of those glittery affairs that always made me feel out of my depth. I hadn't wanted to go, but Charlotte had begged me. She'd just met Ben, and Ben was an avid sailor. She'd offered to lend me a dress and promised me that the wine would counteract my natural propensity for motion sickness.

And so I went.

Of course, she'd been wrong. And at around 10pm I was on the lower deck, away from the noise, leaning over the edge of the boat with one hand grasping the railing and the other attempting to hold my hair back.

And so, busy as I was, I didn't hear him approach. I didn't sense it.

But out of the darkness came his voice. It was hypnotic: 'I've always had a soft spot for a vomiting woman.'

I turned, and I saw him. And in that moment everything finally made sense.

I can't recall what I said in response to his witty opening line. I probably just laughed. But whatever I did, it worked. Because my next recollection of that evening is dancing with him to a jazz band; a trumpet-led version of 'Feeling Good'. That would become our song, in time. And every time I heard it I would recall the golden intensity of that trumpet and the warmth of his breath as he whispered into my ear: 'You're in so much trouble, and you don't even know it yet.'

That was possibly the only truthful thing to ever pass his lips.

I was lying in the bathtub when he got home that night, running through our early history frame by frame – our meeting, our first date, Paris – searching for the clues I'd missed. But there was nothing there. Nothing to warn me it would come to *this*: that one day I'd be lying in the bathtub, I'd hear the front door open and my throat would tighten as I braced myself to lie to the man who was trying to destroy me.

'Darling,' came Angus's voice. The front door slammed and I sat up straight, hugging my knees with my arms.

'We have to be out at eight, remember?' he said, annoyance in his voice. He was tapping on the bathroom door and jiggling the handle. 'Why is this locked?' I needed more time before I could face him.

'Shit, sorry honey,' I called from the water. I could hear my heart beating in my ears. 'I'm really not well,' I said, working to control the timbre of my voice. 'Maybe you should go alone tonight?'

There was silence on the other side of the door. I could imagine his face, the irritation marked by creases on his forehead.

'What?' he asked, his voice high and clipped. 'What sort of sick?'

'I don't know,' I said. 'Maybe it's just nerves from the past couple of days, funny tummy. Just don't feel up to going out.'

'Oh,' he said.

I held my breath and waited.

'But you go,' I said. My voice was measured: one part kindness, two parts servitude.

'Are you sure?' he asked. It was Friday, and the only time we'd spent weekends apart was when we were broken up.

'Of course,' I said. We were supposed to be meeting Harry and whichever amateur stripper he was courting that week for dinner. But I had other plans: I was going to use the time to search the flat properly.

'No,' he said through the door, 'I'll stay here and we can watch a film. It'll be fun.'

Fuck.

'I really don't mind,' I said back. My stomach swirled. *Just go.*

'No, of course I'll stay with you,' he said. 'We can get them around for dinner tomorrow night instead. I'll ask Jeremy and Alison too.'

That sounded like hell on a stick: Harry was crass, whomever he was dating was bound to be awful, Alison was vacuous and medicated, and Jeremy – Alison's husband – was actually very nice but never said enough for it to matter. Aside from which, they would have all seen the photograph of Kim with Angus on that ski slope – hell, Harry had probably watched the sex tape – and I didn't want to have to squirm beneath their knowing glances.

But I couldn't say any of that. So instead I said: 'Okay, great.'

saturday

Master Sun said: *'"Deadlock" means that neither side finds it advantageous to make a move.'*

18 FEBRUARY

It was just after dinner when the subject of strip poker came up. I was in the middle of clearing away plates and Harry had just handed Angus a small bag of cocaine, a pink rubber band tying it shut. Angus was on his way to the bathroom to snort it, and I had just said, 'Darling, what are you doing?' It was the sort of thing I'd say if I still believed everything was fine between us.

But he'd shot me a red-flag warning of a look – the same one I had witnessed earlier in the day as I'd stood in the kitchen, wooden spoon in hand as I cooked for his friends; how dare I question his decision to pour himself his first Scotch in almost a week – and I'd cast my eyes down. I needed to stick to the plan and so couldn't afford to cause any more trouble. We'd already had an unspoken fight that evening. His eyes flaming. Mine apologising.

Because David had called me back. Mid-meal. And Angus had answered.

My phone had been lying on the dinner table along with everybody else's and, seeing the unmarked number flashing on the screen, Angus had picked it up like he owned it. 'Hello,' he'd said, and then, 'No, she can't. Who the fuck are you anyway?' Pause. 'David Turner?' His eyes glared at me, wide and angry. 'Well, *David Turner*, I'm her fiancé,' he'd said, 'and if you don't mind, I'd prefer it if you never fucking called her again.'

And then he'd terminated the call. Sighed loudly. Put my phone gently back on the table where he could see it. Continued eating his coq au vin like nothing had happened. And I'd been left reeling (fiancé?) and fending off questions from Alison about when I'd be getting a ring.

'Strip poker?' That was how it was said. By Alison: all chestnut hair, fake boobs and pout. A noun posed as a question. Flirty voice. Not even a sentence encasing it.

Angus stopped in his tracks and turned back to face me. There was a light fixture directly above his head and the shadows it cast rendered him ghoulish. The expression held in his eyes revealed that he expected me to say no.

Because I always said no.

'I'm in,' said Harry. 'How about you, darling?' He was addressing Emma. She was a pretty young Anglo-Indian girl: perfect dark skin, tiny waist, unpainted nails and wearing a crimson lace dress. She was very unlike his usual type and I wanted to warn her about Harry. He had blond hair and a cherub-like face, but a big black hole where his heart should be. Birds of a feather, I guess.

'Sure,' she said, scanning the table for reassurance.

'Yay,' said Alison, clapping her hands and looking to her husband.

'Of course,' Jeremy said, pulling a leather cigar case from his inner coat pocket like he'd been expecting it all along.

Angus raised his eyebrows at me and smiled. 'Sweetheart?'

This was my chance. So I lifted my eyes to his, and with a shy smile I said, 'Okay.'

Act coy. Smile. Play the part. Make him feel like he had total control. Make him believe I was guileless. Make him lower his guard far enough that I could navigate my way out of this mess.

Angus grinned, turned on his heel and continued on his way to the bathroom to snort his coke. I could hear him roughly opening the bathroom cabinet, the chinking of jars and toiletries as he looked for a small mirror, then the sound of glass smashing.

'Shit,' came Angus's voice. Then: 'Darling!'

A moment later he returned from the bathroom and sat at the table, his hands drumming a rhythm on the wood that jarred against the classical record he had playing softly in the background.

'Baby, I broke something in the bathroom,' he said, addressing me. 'Also, go get a pen and paper to keep score.' Even in the first flushes of love I'd hated him when he was on coke.

'And you, pussy.' He pointed an outstretched finger at Harry. 'Matchsticks or money?'

'Fuck off,' Harry replied. 'Money.'

Emma watched on silently while Jeremy bit off the end of his cigar.

'This is going to be so super fun!' Alison said, leaning forward to smile at Ed, whose cage had been moved to beside the table. His little feet were dancing back and forth in celebration. 'He's such a beautiful bird.'

'Of course he is,' Angus said.

'And clever. Watch this,' said Harry. ''Ello Ed!' he said.

''Ello Ed!' Ed replied.

I left them to it and went to find a pen. 'Honey, where are the pens?' I yelled back to Angus from his office.

'Fuck, I don't know, somewhere!' he called back.

I eyed the two highlighters in the mug by his computer. I decided on the pink one and took some paper from one of the printer trays.

'Cards?' I yelled again.

'Bottom drawer,' he yelled back, annoyance in his voice.

I opened the drawer and found them. But I didn't return to the table straightaway, I went through to the bedroom and put on a string of pearls and three bangles. I'd been wearing just five things: my navy blue dress, a pair of knickers, tights and two black kitten-heeled shoes. And, unlike Alison, I didn't plan on getting naked.

'Did you clean up the mess in the bathroom?' Angus asked as I placed the highlighter, paper and cards on the table.

'I'll do that now,' I replied. I went through to the kitchen to grab a rag.

He'd smashed a bottle of my eye serum. La Prairie. Expensive. And small glittery pieces of glass covered the bath mat and floor.

But I cleaned it up without complaint: The Sunday Girl never complains.

I returned to the table just in time to hear Angus announce that we would play Texas Hold'em.

'Okay,' I replied with a shrug, 'but I don't know how to play.'

That wasn't true: I'd gone to boarding school and had no pocket money. Poker was how I'd kept myself in diet pills, cough syrup and mascara.

Beside me sat the highlighter, a piece of paper and an untouched glass of winc.

'Oh darling, I'll walk you through it,' said Angus. 'Hang on, did you just put on jewellery?' he asked with a smile.

'Yes, I did; you guys need a handicap,' I said. 'Emma, do you want something?'

'I'm okay, thanks,' she replied, smiling. Her hands were under the table, presumably holding Harry's.

We were arranged boy – girl – boy – girl – boy – girl.

'Okay, whatever makes you happy, darling,' Angus said with a smile as he leaned over and gently squeezed my nose with two fingers.

I winced at the ease with which he could pretend he loved me.

'Seriously, I haven't played in years, and all I remember from back then is that I was totally crap,' I lied.

'Well, practice makes perfect, and the only reason you're crap at games like poker is that you are such a good person,' he said with a wink.

I smiled.

'But that's why I love you,' he added.

~

'Why do you love me?' I'd asked one night. We were in his bedroom, the light low, and we'd just made love.

'Because you're such a good person,' he'd said. 'You are the sort of person I need to marry.'

'Do you want to get married?' I'd asked, turning my head to gaze at him.

He rolled over to face me, our eyes met and the world went fuzzy. I would have given anything to be his wife back then. To call him mine.

'Of course. I need to get married,' he'd said.

'What do you mean?' I said. 'Why do you *need* to get married?' It had seemed like a strange choice of words.

'For work. You get over a certain age and you need to be married. People respond to you better. It makes it easier for them to relate to you.'

'But don't you want to get married for love?'

'You don't choose a wife because of love unless you are an idiot.'

'What?' I asked, and my insides ached.

'You choose somebody suitable. People judge you on your wife.'

'So, you don't love me?' An earthquake brewed in my chest.

'I love you as much as I can,' he'd said.

I should have left right then and there.

—

I handed the cards to Angus. He'd elected himself dealer and was sitting beside me, his thigh tight against mine.

'Let's ditch the small blind. Too few of us,' Angus said to the table as he took the cards and began to shuffle.

Alison, who had arrived in only a woollen dress, boots and a single bangle – and, with any luck, underwear – smiled eagerly. She arched her back, fiddled on her phone and then handed it to me.

'Here you go, this is a list of hands. The ones at the top are the best,' she said with a smile. I took her phone and pretended to study the screen.

'So, darling, essentially everyone gets two cards. Then we go around the table and bet on those cards. Then we put some more cards in the middle – that's called the flop – then bet again, put another in, bet again and then another. You're trying to form the best hand you can from a combination of the cards in your hand and those on the table … a bit like life. You'll get the hang of it.' He winked at me.

I smiled.

Jeremy lit his cigar and Alison shuffled around on her seat, probably wishing she still possessed some sort of pubic-hair cushioning. Harry whispered into Emma's ear, making her giggle. Angus dealt and I watched.

I had the Queen of Hearts and the Two of Spades. Alison was the first to bet: three fifty-pence pieces. Then Jeremy: he matched her. Emma and Harry followed suit. As did I. Then Angus.

Down came the flop: King of Hearts, Two of Diamonds, Ace of Hearts and Jack of Spades.

I looked at my hand and feigned confusion. Angus peered at me over his cards. 'That good, darling?' he asked, his foot touching mine.

I needed to flirt back.

'Maybe,' I smiled. Intimacy is disturbingly easy to fake.

'Really?' he laughed.

'Yes, amazing!' I fake laughed back, rolling my eyes.

'Oh my God, yes, yes, yes!' Alison said to her cards, never one to be outshone. She let out some sort of squeal and started bopping up and down.

Emma looked on, confused. Harry laughed. Jeremy sucked on his cigar. Angus frowned.

And then: 'Happy birthday, sir,' screeched Ed.

My ears rang.

My breath caught in my throat.

My demeanour was calm but my senses were straddling an electric fence.

I looked at Angus.

He was already looking at me.

'Is it your birthday?' asked Alison, her forehead crinkled and her voice high.

Jeremy exhaled a cloud of smoke, his eyes on Angus, and I wondered if he knew about the prostitutes. Then my eyes moved to Harry: did *he* know? My cheeks grew hot and my hands damp.

Angus laughed. 'No, it's not,' he said, then: 'It's a funny story, really … Darling, why don't you tell it?'

I swallowed hard and tried to read his face. But it was useless.

And my memory was failing me: I couldn't remember the exact details of Angus's prostitute disclosure. *Did he tell me about the prostitutes saying: 'Happy birthday, sir'?* I only remembered him talking about the yellow ribbons. *But then, why would he suggest that I tell the story?* Everyone was looking at me. And I was struggling to breathe, grasping for an excuse, a reason, something. But nothing came. So eventually I just said: 'Huh?' Then I pretended to focus on my cards and added: 'I don't know, Ed hates me.'

Angus's eyes were still on me, I could feel their heat, and a thin film of sweat was forming at my hairline.

'Oh, never mind,' Angus said, his leg still pressed hot against mine.

The betting continued around me and the game went on. But my mind was elsewhere. I tried to steady my shaking hands. I took a sip of water and willed my vision to unblur …

'Darling, it's your turn,' he said.

'Shit. Do I have to put in money?' I asked and he laughed.

'Yes, sweetheart.' His eyes darted to Harry and back again. 'You do. You have to match what everyone else bet, unless you fold.'

I looked at my cards: my hand was too strong.

'Okay, I fold,' I said.

'Are you sure? You can't unfold,' he warned.

'But I don't want to lose any money, so, I fold.'

He sat watching me, considering. 'Are your cards really that shit?'

'I don't know, sort of.'

'Why don't you go one more round.' It was posed as a question but sounded like an order. But if I went one more round I might win. And that was contrary to strategy.

'No, I fold.'

'Okay, do it your way,' he replied, 'but can I see your cards so I can help you?'

'Sure,' I said, turning them to face him.

He looked at me, annoyed. 'Those were great cards.'

'They were?' I said.

'Sweetheart, you can't just fold every time there's some risk, you know. The risk is where the fun is … it's like that song says: you gotta know when to bluff and when to run away.'

Even with the lyrics all scrambled and ruined, I couldn't help being struck by how succinctly a country song had essentially summed up *The Art of War*.

'Anyway, the cards you are dealt are just dumb luck. The key to this game is being able to read people,' he added.

'Any other tips?' I asked in my best rookie voice as I glanced around the table.

Emma shrugged.

'Never overplay your hand,' offered Jeremy.

'Never bet more than you can afford to lose,' said Harry.

'If in doubt, bluff,' said Alison.

'But most importantly,' said Angus, pausing for dramatic effect: 'Always choose a worthy opponent.'

Wink.

'It's more fun that way.'

—

Two hours later Angus was shirtless, Alison was happily naked (nothing most of us hadn't seen before), I'd spent a lot of time folding so had only relinquished my necklace, Emma and Harry had gone home after much whispering and giggling, and Jeremy, still smoking his cigars, was fully clothed, with little piles of money either side of him.

The room was thick with smoke and Angus had just returned from the kitchen with another bottle of wine.

'None for me,' I said, placing my hand over the top as he moved around to refill glasses.

'What? Nonsense,' he said. 'You love your wine.'

'I just don't feel great,' I said.

'You're not pregnant, are you?' asked Alison, all wide-eyed: first the fiancé comment, now this.

'No,' I laughed, aware that Angus was watching me. I needed to keep a clear head, couldn't let booze soften the edges.

'Darling, I'm going to fill it up anyway,' Angus said, 'just in case.'

I smiled.

'Unless … does darling want to do an itty-bitty line?'

'No sweetie, I'm fine,' I said, trying to soften the expression in my eyes.

'Nice hand,' he winked, having seen my cards. And there was nothing in that wink to warn me.

If I hadn't found that green thumb drive in his drawer the day before, there would be *nothing* in his eyes to betray who he really was. What he was capable of. Was there anything in mine to warn him?

'Sorry,' Alison yawned, covering her open mouth with her hands while happily exposing her naked chest. Her eyes were getting heavy and Jeremy's were red, it was just past 2am and we were almost at the end of another hand. I knew they'd leave soon and then I'd be left alone with Angus. And every time I imagined him touching me the little hairs on the back of my neck stood up. I didn't want them to go.

And that's when I had an idea.

'I'm so sorry, I'll be right back,' I said. 'Carry on without me if you want.' Then I got up and went quickly through to the bathroom. I reached into the cabinet below the sink and pulled out a tampon. I left the wrapper in full view in the bin and the box on the edge of the sink. And then I flushed the unused tampon down the loo.

Angus wouldn't touch me if he thought I had my period. He was squeamish about that. It wasn't due for a week, but unless Angus had been counting my little white pills, he wouldn't know that.

I got back just in time to find them standing up from the table, Angus fetching their coats.

'Thanks so much for coming,' I said; manners are manners. Then we air-kissed our goodbyes and they left.

We brushed our teeth in silence, my pulse thumping in my neck as I let him go into the bathroom first. Gave him time to notice the wrapper. The box. Then, just to drive it home, I called to him for two paracetamol.

I remained safe from Angus's touch that night. But even so, I couldn't sleep. And as he lay there, a heavy stranger snoring on the mattress beside me, I was still but violently awake, staring at him as I struggled to make sense of it all, and stuck on the same unanswerable question:

Why?

Then finally, at around 4am I drifted into sleep, my last thoughts on David and his phone call and the possibility that the following day I would finally have some time alone to search the flat for something I could use.

And then, back to David.

sunday

Master Sun said: *'On the day they are ordered into battle, they sit up and weep, wetting their clothes with their tears; they lie down and weep, wetting their cheeks.'*

19 FEBRUARY

Angus was already up. His weight was no longer behind me and the bed felt empty. Big. Cold. Colder than the air beyond it. My eyelids were heavy and the room was dark. But my mind, frantic the night before, was logical. The way it always is in the mornings. And it was working overtime. All I wanted was to find another explanation: another reason for why Angus might have had those files. But every time I tried to join the dots another way I'd remember that text document and the comments in the margin.

Everything in the *Guardian* article was right there on that thumb drive, just a little less eloquently phrased.

And that was where all alternate readings came unstuck.

I let out a small moan and my eyes flicked open: a glare was edging its way in from the sitting room, piercing the black. My phone was charging on the table by the bed and I reached for it: another missed call from my mother. I put it back down, exhaled loudly and stood up. The air was like ice and it prickled my skin, so I wrapped myself in a thick bathrobe then wandered through to the kitchen.

Flicking on the kettle, I spooned coffee into the cafetière and looked over at Ed. He was watching me from his new favourite spot near the balcony window and let out a wolf whistle.

Angus's running shoes were missing from the front door but I didn't know when he'd be back. I couldn't risk being caught rifling through drawers with no alibi, so I needed to wait.

My mind spiralled back to the night before – *Happy birthday, sir* – and my heart picked up speed.

How much danger was I really in?

The kettle boiled, I poured the steaming water and the smell of coffee overtook the kitchen. As I pushed down the plunger, my mind traced back over the events of the night before, of the week before: a finger trying to learn Braille, but failing.

The information was all there but nothing made sense.

Because there was such darkness, such smugness, in his eyes last night when he'd said: *'Darling, why don't you tell it?'* How could he possibly know it was me?

I opened the fridge and pulled out the milk. Charlotte's little packet of weed was still sitting there on the top shelf. I poured the coffee, added milk and took a sip. It was bitter.

Maybe it was a test. He suspects me and wanted to see how I'd react.

My mind flew back to that little bag of coke, a pink elastic band tying it shut, and all the booze he'd downed the night before.

What happened to NA? The meetings?

I hadn't witnessed him going to many meetings in the time we'd been back together, but I knew he'd gone to at least one on Valentine's Day. And he had a sponsor. People don't get a sponsor lightly. But then again, he'd taken that little bag of coke from Harry like it was nothing – it was as if he'd never given up in the first place. *But that makes no sense. I know he has a sponsor. I've heard him calling; I've heard the phone ring.*

Maybe it was a relapse. They call it 'addiction' for a reason.

And that was when I heard the door handle turn.

'Hey,' I said, trying to be normal, as he walked in and past me. He was wearing a pair of black running pants and a grey T-shirt. There were dark patches of sweat under the arms and around the neck. Angus didn't do come-downs, he sprinted it off.

'Hey,' he said, and wandered through to the bedroom, stripping off his T-shirt and throwing it on the chair in the corner.

I picked up my coffee and followed him through.

'What do you want to do today?' I asked, sitting on the edge of the bed, pretending to be perky. He'd been glued to my hip the whole weekend so far, and I needed time alone in his flat. I was on my side of the bed sipping coffee, and he was on his, standing by his bedside table and fiddling around on his phone. His earphones dangled by his knees.

He didn't answer.

'What do you want to do today?' I repeated.

'I have to work,' he said, not looking at me. Staring at his phone.

'On a Sunday?' I said, trying to sound disappointed.

'Yes,' he said, his voice tense. He still hadn't looked at me.

Something was wrong, I could feel it. He was acting strange. I needed to defuse any suspicion. Make him feel powerful. Do something to make him sure that I was still on his side. And there was only one way I could do that.

'Are you okay?' I asked as I put the coffee cup down and crawled across the bed. I dropped the dressing gown behind me and stripped off the T-shirt I'd slept in, then knelt there topless and freezing before him.

'Baby?' I said.

'What?' he asked, looking up from his phone.

I forced myself to reach for him, two arms outstretched before my nakedness, but his remained still. One holding his phone, the other by his side. His eyes stared straight through me, as though trying to make out the painting on the wall behind my head. Then he put down his phone, walked into the bathroom and slammed the door loudly behind him.

There are forty-five seconds between the moment when an iPhone is last touched, and the moment the screen locks: I'd Googled that months before, when I first suspected the affair with Kim and needed to check his messages. I got to his at about second twenty-five. I touched it and it sprung to life. Screen. Light. Action.

Maybe there's someone else. He's acting the same way he did when he was fucking Kim. Distant. Cold. There in body, but not in soul.

I had to know: if I could prove that there was someone else I could leave unhindered.

I scrolled through his call log. Nothing unusual there. Then I flipped to his messages. Only three – me, Harry and his mother. That in itself was suspicious. *Who has three messages in their inbox?* Clearly he had deleted some. *Why delete them if they're innocent?*

The hot-water pipes were humming and I could hear that he was standing in the shower, the drumming of droplets on the tiled floor disrupted every time he moved under the faucet. I imagined his soap-sudded hair, his eyes closed as he rinsed the foam down the drain.

I navigated to his photo roll.

A few screenshots of a computer screen with numbers on it. A photograph of his mother. I scrolled up. Then up further: a dick pic.

A new one.

One I'd never seen.

And if he hadn't taken it for me, who was it for? My mind reeled back to that petrol-station receipt for condoms, and the Facebook message from Kim. Was that what she wanted to tell me – that they were still seeing each other? And as I sat there on his bed, listening to him in the shower, our entire history – Eastbourne, the prostitutes, the ski trip, the sex tape, the violence, the lies, everything he'd put me through – came crashing over me like a tidal wave that had formed while I blinked. And it was all too much.

I needed an out.

And so I went into his messages, and I typed in a phone number: 0770 090 0007. Felicia, from next door. And then I sent her the new dick pic.

If I couldn't leave as a result of a genuine affair, I'd leave as a result of a fabricated one.

Then I put his phone back beside the bed and covered myself with the duvet.

The door opened and he walked back into the bedroom. His hair was plastered to his head and his amber eyes gleamed from behind those waterlogged lashes. He picked up his phone and looked at it. But he could look as much as he fancied. The evidence had been deleted, his phone screen was locked again and I was back in bed. Silently watching him dress.

The room was silent, that noisy kind of silent that makes your ears swell. I could hear my pulse. My blood. The crinkling of his light blue shirt as he quickly did up the buttons. And then the sound of him walking out of the room, towards the door and slamming it behind him without a goodbye.

But the moment he was gone I sprang into action.

First I searched the bedside tables. There was nothing interesting in there – just some lubricant and a few loose sheets of pills. Paracetamol. Aspirin. And one of my old hair ties.

I picked it up and my heart flinched. There were three long dark hairs caught in the little metal fixture that connected one end to the other. I was dark blonde. Kim was bleached blonde. How many of us were there? I threw it back into the drawer and slammed it shut.

The wardrobe. One of the sliding doors was open just a crack and I could see the navy blue sleeve of one of his suit jackets poking out through it. I moved towards it and swiftly searched each of his pockets. Jackets. Hanging trousers. Shirts.

Nothing.

Just some crumpled, old, illegible receipts and a few rogue coins.

Ed watched me from his cage as I moved past him, past the balcony window and into Angus's study. I worked my way through the drawers: methodically, strategically. I did not feel methodical.

A couple of bills with the date of payment written on the corner, two stamps, some envelopes, a spare pad of post-it notes, and the little green thumb drive. But I already knew what was on that. I placed each item back, exactly where I had found them.

On his desk lay a thin pile of papers.

A couple of work emails with some handwritten notes at the bottom. And a bank statement. My eyes scanned it quickly, searching for something, anything I could use: restaurant charges, Waitrose shopping trips, a couple from Peter Jones and a few other miscellaneous charges I didn't understand. But it didn't matter how thoroughly I searched, there was nothing there. Either he was too good at hiding things, or I was too bad at finding them.

I put down the statement and moved to the next piece of paper. It was a letter from the tenants' board. They were following up a complaint from Angus's downstairs neighbour, Mrs Clifton. It was regarding the leak. Damages. And suspected drug use. Something that had fallen onto her balcony. I felt my throat swell: *why didn't he mention the letter?*

I read further. It was a letter of warning. Further complaints may lead to eviction.

My mind flew back to the dick pic I had just sent his neighbour, Felicia.

Perfect.

My eyes stared at his computer screen. What was hidden in that computer of his? What would I discover if I opened Pandora's box? I turned it on.

Emails. There was nothing on his phone, but maybe he hadn't been as meticulous about cleaning out his emails. Maybe I could find an e-trail to prove he leaked that information to the *Guardian*.

I opened a private-browser window and logged into his email address: MrHollingsworthtoYou@hotmail.com.

My eyes scanned the list: Amazon. Viagra. Harry. And then something from a man named Cameron. No last name. Email address: Caz007@gmail.com. The subject read: *Sophie Reed.*

It had arrived early that morning and had already been read. I clicked on it.

Two words: Sophie Reed. Pick up your fucking phone or I will call the other number.

I'd never heard Angus mention a man named Cameron, or Caz. Nor had I heard the name Sophie Reed. I scrolled down. The email trail had begun just four days before:

15 February, 10.16am

Caz: *Angus, I've just read the papers. How could you leak that information? Do you have any idea what kind of danger you've put me in? Put my sources in? They'll trace it back to me. You said it was due diligence!?! And the rest of the money hasn't come in yet. Call me.*

15 February, 9.22pm

Angus: *It wasn't me. Who else did you give that information to? You will get your money. But it takes time.*

16 February, 11.05am

Caz: *You are the only person I gave those files to. I know it was you. We need to talk. I'm trying to call you, pick up your phone.*

17 February, 9.42am

Caz: *Angus, I mean it. Call me.*

18 February, 10.04pm

Angus: *I need you to find out whatever you can about a man named David Turner.*

18 February, 10.09pm

Caz: *I want my cash. I'm not going to be as patient as last time. Just remember, Stepanovich is not the only person I have dirt on. So pick up your fucking phone.*

19 February, 1.01am

Angus: *Don't threaten me.*

Hence Caz's most recent email that came in at five past six that morning.

Thoughts crashed into one another as my mind tried to process what was going on. *Who the fuck is Sophie Reed? What is 'the other number'? And why would Angus be looking for information on David?*

I scrolled back through the emails and looked at the timestamp: he'd asked for information on David just two hours after picking up his call to me. *Fuck.* If he did anything to harm David it would be my fault.

Then I opened another tab and typed 'Sophie Reed' into the search field. There were four pages of results, but nothing of interest: Sophie Reed was living happily in Surrey with her husband and golden retriever, working as a yoga instructor.

I clicked on the second page. Still nothing. A couple of comments on a blog about Spain by a girl who went by that name, but nothing suspicious. And then I clicked on the third page. Nothing. Nothing. Nothing.

It was only at the very bottom of that third page that I found a news article. It was dated December 2006.

And there was a third Sophie Reed.

She was dead.

I stared at the article, trying to make sense of it, trying to join the dots: she died in an attempted robbery in her hotel room, blunt trauma to the head, while on holiday in Cape Town.

With her boyfriend – an unnamed London banker.

Ice filled my lungs and my blood stuck to my veins.

No.

My breath was loud.

I swallowed hard as I remembered Angus's hands tight around my throat, his thumbs pushing into my windpipe, my head slamming against the wall by the bed, his pupils small, the blurry vision, sharp pain being replaced by a dull throb, and then the tide of heartfelt apologies.

I'll never do that again.

It's just because I love you so much.

Nobody else can affect me like you can.

My throat burned with the memory.

I sat staring at the screen, my eyes hot and a dark certainty pulsing through me. My ears roared as I stared at her picture. She looked a lot like me: same dark blonde hair, same physique, and from what I could make out from the picture, the same hopeful eyes. She was laughing, small creases around her eyes and her mouth just a little open.

Then I remembered the box. The shoebox with the photographs of Kim. The place Angus kept his secrets. There'd be something in there to tell me if I was right – something to confirm I wasn't making it all up in my head. I stood up from the computer and ran through to the bedroom. Opened the closet. And, kneeling on the carpet, burning my knees, I reached for the box.

I lifted the lid and pulled out a handful of photographs.

There were a lot of girls in there. All of them pretty. Brunettes. Blondes. Smiles. Angus looking cheerful. Sexy. Tanned.

And then there, towards the bottom, lay the proof.

She was smiling too. Just like the rest of them. Wearing a long dress that brushed the lawn on which she stood. And she was holding Angus's hand. He was in a tuxedo. They were going somewhere special. The sun was setting behind them, and so the picture had the telltale yellow glow of 35mm film.

I dropped the photograph back into the box. I was shaking and my breath was fast.

The danger bore down on me. And then I felt it: a movement of the air. Before I heard the door. But then the front door was opening. And someone was entering.

And Angus was calling out: 'Darling?'

I dropped the rest of the photographs back inside, put the cardboard top back on, replaced it behind his shoes and ran to the doorway. He was just coming inside. I needed to get back to the computer.

'Hi honey,' I said as I moved quickly by him.

I sat at his computer and scrambled for the mouse. I was trembling. I didn't have time to close the browser but I quickly pulled up another tab.

'What are you doing?' came Angus's voice.

I could hear him closing the door and his footsteps moving towards me. I typed into the search bar: 'destination weddings Fiji'.

'There you are,' he said as he moved into the room towards me. 'Are you okay?'

'Hey,' I said as he kissed the top of my head. Pictures of white sand and blue water sat before me. I turned around to smile at him. 'Just looking at options.'

He looked at the screen: 'Nice.'

'I thought you had to work, honey?' I asked, looking up at him so he'd have to hold my gaze.

'No, made some phone calls, all done.'

'Oh,' I said. 'Great, then we can spend the day together.' I was holding his hands.

He smiled at me then said, 'What about Bali?' and walked out of the room.

'I'll look,' I called after him and turned back to the screen.

My stomach had turned to oil and my head was full of fog. But I reached for the mouse, closed the windows and cleared the browser history. Then I sat for a long while staring at the empty screen.

I could hear him in the other room. In the distance. Talking to Ed. And, finally, I realised: he was the same man he'd always been. It was me who'd changed.

—

I was chopping carrots. Shaping them with a knife into pretty little orange stars in the same way I always did – anything to make him think things were the same – and he was out on the balcony, drinking his Scotch and looking out over London's twinkling skyline like he owned it.

I looked at the time: 5.57pm. Charlotte would be landing soon. But what could I tell her anyway? And how was I going to go back into work the next day and pretend everything was fine? How could

I call my mother back now, knowing what I knew? She'd hear it in my voice and she'd worry. A thousand thoughts tangled themselves throughout my mind like kites on a winter tree.

Angus killed Sophie Reed.

Cameron, whoever he is, has evidence of that.

He keeps calling Angus's other phone.

Angus's other phone.

The one I heard ringing.

And then one of those kites unravelled and revealed itself to me: *What if that phone isn't for NA at all? What if he's not even in NA and that was just the one story he knew I'd buy? The one excuse he'd never used. The dagger up his sleeve.*

So, yes, he had a second phone and it was somewhere in the flat, but it wasn't for his sponsor. It was for people like Caz. And Kim. And the owner of the dark hair in my hair tie. The calls he couldn't have coming in and puncturing the sheen of his daily life.

I needed to find that phone and whatever was on it. Use it to blackmail him into leaving me alone – or maybe use it to send him to prison – and I needed to do it before I got hurt.

monday

Master Sun said: *'But throw them where there is no escape, and they will fight with the courage of the heroes Shu and Gui.'*

20 FEBRUARY

It was lying at the bottom of my handbag: a little plastic zip-lock baggie. Full of pot. The one Charlotte had left in our fridge. But it had been left unsealed and so the leaves were everywhere: in the crevices of my mobile phone, stuck to my lipstick and gathering in the folds of the lining.

I knew what had happened the moment the smell – all sweetness and pastures – hit me: Angus had planted drugs in my bag, kissed me on the forehead and sent me off to work.

I'd been at my desk at the time, and had just opened my handbag in search of a Band-Aid for a paper cut incurred while trying to print an email. But now I was in the bathroom. It had been empty when I got there and I'd locked myself in the stall farthest from the door. The one with a small window.

I looked around me: loo roll, a tampon disposal unit and the toilet bowl. Reaching into my bag, I pulled out the baggie and what was left inside.

Then I looked up at the window: somebody might find it if I threw it outside. Worse yet, somebody might see it fall. The risk seemed too great, so I emptied it instead into the loo. A thick layer of brown-green leaves floated on the water, a few stuck to the white porcelain. Flush.

I crammed the little plastic bag in the tampon disposal unit and my eyes landed back on the bowl.

Fuck.

Leaves were still floating there. Not all of them. But some.

The muscles in my back ached.

I piled in more paper and waited for the water tank to refill. It took forever.

Angus is responsible.

Footsteps.

Someone was entering the bathroom. I heard them open a cubicle door and lock it, then a zip being unfastened and urine trickling into the water.

My head was light and I steadied myself against the side of the cubicle. I needed to be quiet. I needed to muffle my breath.

The girl in the other stall was reaching for the loo roll. I could hear it squeak as it unravelled. Then came a flush. The zipper. The cubicle door unlocking and opening. The water as she washed her hands. The hand dryer. And finally, the heavy door to the bathroom shutting again.

I frantically removed the contents of my bag and placed each item on the shiny, blue-tiled floor – wrinkled receipts, maxed-out credit cards, coffee loyalty cards, a couple of long-lost tampons with the plastic broken, and three lipsticks I hadn't worn in months. Then I upended my handbag over the loo in an attempt to empty it of the remaining leaves.

And out flew the little bag of coke.

Fuuuck.

I reached into the loo, fished it out with my fingers, and then put that into the tampon disposal unit too.

Then once again I flushed.

My cheeks were hot and my underarms damp. I reached for more loo roll and wiped out the inside of my bag, attempting to clear the odour, all the while listening for the sounds of anyone else entering. I piled paper into the loo, and as I pressed the button again, I had what I can only describe as a flash of utter clarity amid the fog:

I need to leave. Before this goes any further. Before something irreversible happens.

And that was it: the moment I could have changed everything. The moment I could have changed my destiny. The weak spot in Fate's carefully set up game of dominos. The only moment in which, had I chosen well, I could have stopped those pieces falling altogether. Stopped them in their tracks.

Because, in that moment, I could have chosen to leave; to never go back to Angus's building, to stay instead with my mother and forfeit the belongings I had left in his apartment. And if my computer hadn't been there – work documents and access to my email – I may well have chosen that path. I should have chosen that path. And maybe if I had, everything would have turned out differently.

But I didn't.

Instead, as I stood in that toilet cubicle waiting for the tank to refill, I concocted a plan: I would feign illness, leave work a little early, grab my stuff from his place and then leave. Forever. Before he got home.

And so the click-click-clicking of falling dominos resumed at full pace. Almost like they'd never paused at all.

The water settled and I stared into the bowl. The leaves were all gone, so I repacked my handbag, zipped it up and unlocked the cubicle door. Then I walked out and closed it gently behind me. The bathroom was empty again. It was just me and my harrowed reflection in the mirror.

I steadied my thoughts, slung my bag over my shoulder and went back to my desk.

'Are you ready?' asked Val as I sat down.

'Huh, do we have a meeting?' It was almost 4pm on my first day back. And as a rule she never scheduled anything after 2pm.

'No, that pee-test thing,' she replied, putting on her jacket.

'What?' I asked.

'Random drug testing, they emailed about it this morning. You need to read your emails.' Her voice was firm.

The room swirled. 'But I just peed,' was all I could manage.

I knew that there would be traces of weed in my urine – I'd smoked with Charlotte just five days before – and in my bag if they checked. I'd already received a verbal warning that week.

'Is it mandatory?' I asked. Heart fast.

Angus did this.

She looked at me with a shrug. 'Not sure. But it's a bit hard to say no without looking suspicious … come on, it'll be over soon.'

'It's just that I'm really not well,' I said as I held my abdomen. I could see Jenny from HR chatting to someone, hovering in the doorway. A young girl with dyed red hair was following her, a cardboard tray full of plastic cups with bright yellow lids in her arms.

'Oh,' she said, her voice softening as her eyes shifted to Jenny. 'Okay, look it's your first day back, just go home. But go that way,' she said, nodding towards the back stairs, 'so she doesn't see you. I'll tell her you did a half-day.'

'Thanks,' I said, picking up my bag.

'See you tomorrow,' she said.

And twenty minutes later I was sitting in traffic, making my way to Angus's place in a cab and texting Charlotte: *Can I come and stay with you for a couple of days? xx*

The flat was quiet. Eerily so. Even Ed was still. My heart beat quickly and the zippers on my boots echoed loudly as I removed them by the door. My palms were damp and my breath was shallow as I ran softly through to the bedroom. It was just before 5pm, so only just starting to get dark, the shadows from neighbouring buildings reflecting on the walls. The bed was bathed in a gentle light coming in through the window.

And I could smell his cologne.

It made me feel sick. Spice. Leather. Wood.

I reached under the bed for my suitcase. It still had the pink ribbon tied around the handle in wait of our ill-fated ski holiday. I laid it on the bed and did a quick sweep of the room. My make-up was lying on the top of the dresser, and I picked it up in rough handfuls, dropping the bottles and brushes into the case. Then my underwear. My dresses. And my turtlenecks.

My computer.

I rushed through to his study to grab it – I'd left it charging, plugged into the wall just behind Angus's chair.

The light in his study was on when I got there, a deep orange glow – *he must have forgotten to turn it off* – and the door was just ajar.

So I pushed it open, and the floorboards creaked as I stepped over the threshold.

Then as I lifted my eyes and they acclimatised to the light, I saw him, sitting in his aged leather chair, ankle over knee, the way men do. My purple notebook lying open on his lap.

I wanted to run. To scream. But I couldn't. And all I kept thinking as I looked into his smiling face was: *Sophie Reed probably felt like this. She probably sensed danger too.*

'*La magie dans la lumiere*,' came his voice. Thick. Dark. Low. He was reading from the notebook. 'I love that phrase,' he said. 'Do you remember when we wrote it down, darling?'

Paris. Lace curtains. Dusk. Wrinkled sheets.

I swallowed hard. 'What are you doing with my notebook?' My voice came out shaky and high. I could see my computer charging behind him but I couldn't reach it.

'I'm reading it,' he said as his index finger tapped hard on the page. Tap, tap, tap. 'I think it's time for us to have a little chat.'

'Okay, sure,' I said, 'but I'm supposed to be going to see Charlotte, she's expecting me, but later?' Then I smiled, nodded and turned to leave.

'No, Taylor. We're going to talk now,' he said. The calmness in his voice was menacing.

I turned back around. He was staring at me.

'What would you like to talk about?' I asked.

'This,' he said, his voice calm, lifting up my notebook.

'Where did you get that?' I asked.

'I found it,' he said. 'On Sunday while you were showering.'

'Well, nothing in that book means anything,' I said. I was trying to laugh it off but my smile was fake and tight. 'And you shouldn't be reading through my private things anyway. It's too easy to misinterpret them.'

'Is it?' he asked. His fingers flipped through a couple of pages, his eyes skimming them as he went. Then he started to read: '*I keep thinking about last year,*' he was imitating my voice, '*wondering where we went so wrong, and about the prostitutes turning up, wondering if I did the right thing.'* His voice was loud now, booming against the wall and his eyes cut through me like a sheet of ice.

I couldn't breathe: I knew that look. I stepped backwards and turned to run.

'Don't you fucking dare!' he yelled and my bones shook.

My mouth was open. Dry. But I turned back around to face him. 'I'd just seen the tape, Angus,' I said. 'I was so hurt.' My hands were shaking. My vision was splotchy.

'I was so hurt.' He was mimicking me again. 'Listen to yourself. Like you're the victim. You ordered prostitutes on my work credit card, you crazy bitch!' He took a deep breath, calming himself. 'Taylor, when did you become this person?'

'You went on our ski holiday with another woman, Angus,' I said. 'You uploaded a sex tape of me to the internet.' The less he thought I knew, the better.

He smiled. 'Yes,' he said, 'I suppose I did.' His eyes narrowed. 'But are you really going to stand there and pretend that you didn't sleep with anybody else while we were apart? Hmm?'

My mind moved to Jamie. To David. But he was guessing: sure, David had called me during dinner, but we worked together. And how could Angus possibly know anything more?

And then the horrible answer came hurtling into focus: *Therapy? xx*

His hand patted the arm of his chair and he let out a sharp exhale. 'Come here, darling. Come sit with me.'

But I was paralysed. I couldn't move towards him and I couldn't move away. My throat was closed and the soles of my feet ached.

'I can't, honey,' I said. 'I'm already late.' Then I turned and walked through to the bedroom. 'I'm going to see Charlotte,' I called over my shoulder.

'Like fuck you are,' he said in a low rumble. I heard his heavy footsteps on the floorboards behind me, but I didn't look back.

I slowed my breath and forced myself to speak in a calm and rational voice as my feet tripped towards the bedroom. 'Honey, I'll fix it,' I said, 'but if I don't go and see Charlotte now she'll know something's up –'

'You're not going anywhere,' he said as he walked into the bedroom after me. The air was stifling, thick, and as he sat on the bed it creaked with his weight. He held my purple notebook in his left hand, but it was closed now. I could feel the electricity pulsing through him, his breath coming in a deep, controlled rasp. I was standing near my half-packed suitcase and we were only ten inches apart.

'You know, darling,' he said, 'your biggest failing is simply that you don't know your place in the world.'

I was blinking fast as I watched his eyes, his thoughts. But they were barely moving. It was as though the words that fell from his mouth had been scripted, memorised, rehearsed. 'I mean, you really believe that you could win against somebody like me. But you can't. I'll always be one step ahead of you because I'm smarter than you. And I'll always win, because I'm stronger than you.' He took a deep breath. 'I mean, I could fucking pay to have you killed if I fancied. It's not even that expensive.' And there was an edge to his voice – I knew he meant it.

Sophie Reed's face flashed before me. And in that moment I knew: running out that door would do nothing to keep me safe. It would just make me more of a liability.

And so I stood dead still, watching as he tried to control himself. 'I just don't understand why you keep making it so fucking hard,' he said; his voice was high pitched and he was spitting out his words and shaking his head.

How am I going to get out of this?

'I mean, did you really think I wouldn't know that it was you?' he asked, his eyes wide with seething irritation. 'I knew the moment Candice called me. Long before I found this,' he said, waving my purple notebook around. 'I mean, who the fuck else would be dumb enough to do something like that? Maybe Candice, but let's be fair, she doesn't have it in her.'

My thoughts scrambled.

'Honestly, I didn't think you did either,' he continued. 'You surprised me. And you … well, you didn't have the faintest clue that I knew.' He smiled. 'You should have seen your face when I pulled out that yellow ribbon …' He laughed, like an evil child who'd caught a rabbit in a trap and was taunting it. 'But that ribbon was just as sexy the second time as the first.' Wink.

I could feel my face slacken.

'Although, I am intrigued, how did you know which girls I used the most? And who on earth did you tell them you were? My secretary?'

He was looking at me now: expectant. His monologue was over and he wanted an answer. And all I kept thinking was: *The Way of War is a Way of Deception.*

'I told them I was your girlfriend,' I said in a small voice, looking down at my suitcase. 'That it was a surprise and I'd be there too.' I looked back up at him and swallowed. Lying was dangerous, but I couldn't let him know I had access to his emails.

'Oh,' he said, 'you clever little minx.' Then he stood up and the mattress creaked. He moved towards me: I could smell the spice of his cologne as he reached one hand behind my head and ran his fingers through my hair.

His eyes were mere inches from mine: deep black pools where the whiskey hue usually lay.

Then he grabbed my hair and held me very still and seethed: 'But enough now.' His grip tightened and I let out a yelp. My breath was uneven and I could hear him swallow as he watched me with narrowed eyes.

I tried to nod but he was holding too tight and my eyes filled with tears. 'Okay,' I cried. 'I promise.'

Then he let go and my breath grew deep and raspy.

'Good. Because I wouldn't want you to do anything silly, darling. You might get hurt.' He was standing so close to me: I could feel the heat from his body and the hairs from his heritage green jumper – the one I'd bought him – on my bare arms. I looked down to avoid his gaze and shook my head fiercely. The tears that had been welling in my eyes rolled down my cheeks.

Then he cocked his head to the side and looked at me. 'How was your first day back at work today, darling?' he asked, and he gave a little smile.

'It was fine,' I said. Still looking down.

'Are you sure it was fine?' he asked. 'Or are you fibbing again?' His index finger found its way to underneath my chin and guided my head up to face him. 'You had a little test today? Didn't you?' he said, nodding.

I stared at him, mute.

'Oh hurry up, darling, just say yes, it's not that hard,' he said, impatient.

'Yes,' I said quickly. 'Why did you –' I started.

'Why did I do that?' he finished for me. 'Because, darling, I'm not sure I can trust you anymore. I mean, you *just* tried to lie to me. And you're far less dangerous to me if your drug use is on record.' He smiled sadly. 'Nobody believes the word of a pothead, do they?'

I looked at him, my face blank.

'You see? You're your own worst enemy, darling. You bring it on yourself.'

My mind whizzed. 'How did you even –'

'A phone call. A simple phone call saying I'd seen people smoking pot in the car park that morning. Easy-peasy.'

My lower lip quivered as he released me from his grip and sat back down on the bed. 'Darling,' he said, 'I'm not a bad person. And I don't want to hurt you. Really. I want to *marry* you.' His fingers interlaced with mine, and I forced myself to not jerk my hand away. 'That would be better. But that doesn't mean I *won't* hurt you. If I have to. So, it's your choice how this ends.'

I watched him. I think he actually believed what he was saying. That he was justified. Good, even.

That was when my phone started to ring: it was lying on the bed and we could both see Charlotte's name flashing back at us.

I looked at him and he looked at me. My pulse went wild.

'Let it go to voicemail,' he said. It was an order, and so we both stood there, watching it ring.

'Now send her a message and tell her that you'll see her some other night.'

I picked up my phone and typed in the message: *Hi honey, let's do another night, I'll call you tomorrow. xx*

'Show it to me,' he said. So I did. And then I pressed send.

'Well done, darling,' he said, taking the phone from my hands and throwing it back onto the bed.

'Now,' he said, gripping me by the wrist and leading me through to the sitting room. 'There are some things that need to happen for us to get back on track. First you need to call Candice and tell her that it was you, not me, who ordered those fucking prostitutes on that card.'

'Okay,' I said, my voice gentle. I needed to appease him.

He stood by the booze cabinet and poured himself a Scotch.

'Sit,' he said.

And I did as I was told.

I looked around the room: a lamp could be a weapon.

He picked up his glass and moved slowly towards the chair on the other side of the coffee table. I remained alone on his black leather sofa, my hands clasped in my lap.

'You see, darling,' he said as he sipped, 'we are actually sort of perfect for each other. All of this proves it. I mean, if you're really honest with yourself you'll see that we're the same.' He was nodding. 'I need a wife, and you need a … a me.'

I was listening. I was trying to compute. And all the while I just kept looking around the room, wondering where he kept that fucking phone.

'What about Kim? You don't want to marry *her*?' I asked. But my voice was small and desperate. And it made him smile.

'Absolutely not. Kim is too … I need someone more … someone like you. Someone who knows how to dress and can make conversation at business dinners. Besides, darling, you know too much about me now; I can't afford to have you wandering around out there.' He said this with a flick of his hand. 'You're mine.'

'Oh,' was all I could manage. My eyes burned, and I clenched my teeth.

'Jesus, woman,' he laughed. 'Are you ever happy? I mean, all you've wanted since we met was to get married. And I'm so far out of your league it's ridiculous. You should be thrilled,' he continued, his tone darkening. 'But, darling, my patience is running fucking thin, so you think hard before you do anything else stupid. This is the last chat like this we are going to have. Do you understand?'

His eyes bore into me and I nodded. 'Yes.'

'Good,' he said, a calm gaze landing on my face. 'So, yes, we'll get married. A nice spring wedding. If you want Fiji, we can do Fiji. And then, I suppose, babies,' he continued.

'Speaking of which, let's start practising.' He downed the rest of his drink and put his glass down heavily on the table beside him. Then he grabbed my hand and led me back through to the bedroom.

He threw me down roughly on the bed and lay on top of me. He was heavy on my ribcage and I struggled to breathe; I let out a small whimper and his hand reached into my underwear.

'I can't,' I lied as I pushed him away, 'I have my period.'

'Oh, don't piss me off,' he hissed into my ear, ripping at my knickers, 'I know you don't. I'm not a fucking idiot. But you know what, have it your way – just know that one way or the other I'm fucking you tonight. Darling.'

tuesday

Master Sun said: *'Seize something that he cherishes and he will do your will.'*

21 FEBRUARY

The nausea hit me in waves. I was frightened to blink. *If I keep my eyes open I won't see it. And if I don't see it, I won't remember.* My eyes stung, a wire coat hanger scraped the back of my throat, I sniffed back tears and a lack of sleep blurred my vision. Every sound, smell and movement felt menacing: the hum of the photocopier behind me, the flickering light overhead and the bitter smell of coffee drifting from my cup. Everything made me flinch.

Kevin was doing his mail round. I watched him start at the other end of the room and weave his way through the cubicles; to him, it was just like any other day. But if it were just like any other day I wouldn't have to concentrate to remember what came after 'breathe in'.

Breathe out.

My exhale was shaky. I hoped Val couldn't hear me. If she could, she pretended she couldn't. And for that I was grateful.

The last thing Angus had said as he walked out the door that morning was: 'See you tonight.' And the words rang in my ears.

I'd replied: 'See you then.'

But I wouldn't be going back there again.

I'd tried to fight him and I had failed. I'd tried to pry myself free and had ended up even more entangled. And so, in the early hours of the morning as I lay there dead still, trying not to wake him, I'd constructed a new plan. A plan for total escape.

Soon I would build upon the 'cramps' I'd experienced the day before. I'd clutch my abdomen. Then I'd go home – my home, not his – pack some things and leave for my mother's house. And I would never see that man again. Yes. I'd be on the train to East Sussex before he even realised I was gone.

Until then, I was safe at work. My laptop computer beside me.

I'd been reading more about Sophie that morning: she died during what was reported as a failed robbery attempt. Battered to death in her hotel room. Her boyfriend had sustained only one injury, a mild blow to the head that knocked him out. He awoke to find her body. She hadn't been raped. Nothing had been reported stolen. Nobody was ever arrested. And her parents, Justin and Lorraine Reed – a kind-looking couple based in Hampshire – fought for justice, reached out to the public for information and tried to get the British authorities involved, but failed.

My jaw was tight as I noted down their contact details in my phone: one day maybe I could tell them what I knew.

I tried to compose myself as Kevin wove his way towards me.

There had been an email from David in my inbox when I arrived that morning but I hadn't responded. It read: *Sorry about calling on Saturday. I hope I didn't cause problems for you and your fiancé … I think we should talk. I'll be in your office a little later, otherwise call me? David.*

And just like that I could see him there in front of me, grinning, feel the warmth of his hand on my lower back and his soft lower lip as we kissed.

I should have stayed. I should have stayed with him. None of this would have happened.

Kevin was getting closer. He was talking to Val, fiddling with his fuchsia tie and glancing in my direction.

I shut down my browser.

'And how are you today, mademoiselle?' He winked as he arrived at my desk and riffled through his cart.

'Really well.' I grinned. My eyes started tearing up, so I smiled harder. The harsh fluorescent office lights made it difficult not to squint.

'Here we go,' he said, handing me two items: a stationery brochure with a bright red hole punch on the cover, and a thin white package. 'For you.'

'Thanks,' I said. The stationery brochure went straight into the plastic rubbish bin under my desk, the thin white package remained in my hands. My name and work address were handwritten on the front. But there was no stamp: it had been couriered.

I recognised the writing immediately.

'Well, have a dandy day!' he said as he moved on.

'You too, Kevin.' My eyes were burning. My fingers ripped at the white envelope, as though trying to destroy its contents before I even knew what they were.

Inside was a DVD. And on the front was a smiley face, drawn in pink highlighter.

Breathe out.

But the arrival of that package didn't change my plan at all, it merely brought it forward an hour or so.

'I'm so sorry, Val, I'm still feeling really unwell,' I said in a monotone voice over the partition. 'Would it be okay if I work at home this afternoon?'

'Oh,' she replied, rolling her chair back to look at me with an irritated frown. 'Maybe you should go to the doctor?'

'Yes, I think I might,' I said, grabbing my handbag. And then I stood up and headed for the elevator.

I pressed the down button, then focused on the carpet. I still hadn't called my mother back and Charlotte had left two messages on my phone the night before, checking I was okay, so now I needed to call her back too. But all I could think about at that moment was what was on that white disk.

Ping.

The elevator opened and I looked up.

And there, in front of me, he stood.

David Turner: perfectly put together in his immaculate navy suit, white shirt and light pink tie. A man in control. And beside him stood Nigel, the head of research, his pinched face concentrating on what David had just said.

Fuck.

I stared at them, my breath quick. I was wearing a dirty pair of black trousers, an old grey jumper and my unwashed hair was up in a bun. I looked like I was coming apart at the seams. Nigel eyed me as they moved towards me and for a brief moment I thought they might walk straight past.

'Taylor,' David said, stopping in front of me. 'So nice to see you.' He smiled a professional smile for Nigel's benefit but he was standing so close to me I could smell the spiced lime of his shampoo and the familiar musk of his skin.

'Hello David,' I said. 'Hi Nigel.'

Nigel gave me a cold look. 'Hello,' he said. 'Nice to see you, Taylor.' His tone said otherwise.

'I'm glad we bumped into you,' David said. 'I was hoping to put in a meeting with you, get your initial thoughts on an idea I'm considering.'

The elevator doors closed over his shoulder, and that little white disk was burning hot in my bag.

'Of course, I'd be happy to,' I said, my voice steady but high. My heart was banging against my chest walls and Nigel was watching us, clearly confused by David's warmth.

'Great,' said David. 'I'll get my secretary to send through a request.' Our eyes met as I nodded. I could see him dancing in his bathrobe. Taste the cigarette we smoked out that hotel window. Feel his weight against me. And my cheeks grew hot.

'I look forward to it,' I said, glancing at Nigel. He was looking at his watch now.

'Wonderful,' David replied, eyes on mine, and then they continued to wherever they were going and I ran to the stairs.

~

Chiara was crying from inside the door, and that warned me that something was off. And so my hands shook a little as I slid the key into the lock: *How did she get in?* The DVD was in my handbag. And something deep inside me already knew what it contained. I turned the key, opened the door slowly and looked around me. Nothing. She ran out through my legs and I shut the door tightly behind me.

I dropped my computer and handbag by the door, pulled out that white envelope and rushed towards the DVD player. Power on. TV on. Open. Insert. Close. Wait.

Grabbing for the remote control I navigated to the DVD. A little round disk swirled as it connected. It took forever.

A sharp pain hit me right between the ribs as two boxes appeared. Even from a distance, even as thumbnails, I knew what they were.

I clicked on the first one.

And I think I recognised him long before I recognised myself.

His chest, broad and covered in soft dark hair, and his hands on my hips: his face was obscured and out of frame. And there was no sound. But there was something about the way he was moving. Or breathing. Something that was unmistakably him.

Me, I didn't get immediately.

Did I really look like that? All blotchy and contorted?

But as a hand came into frame and pulled my hair back, lifting my face to the camera – 'Look how pretty you are' – a wave of hot shame washed over me. And in an instant I knew exactly what I was watching. I knew exactly when it was taped.

What I didn't know was how.

Battery acid rose in my throat and I leaned forward over my knees. I couldn't help it. My stomach convulsed and I vomited. There, on the tassels of my red-and-beige hand-me-down rug.

I stared at the screen: there was still another film.

Wiping my mouth with the back of my hand, I sat back on the sofa, pointed the remote control at the screen and clicked on the second box.

It started to play and I cried out. I paused the tape. My breath was fast: I knew when it was taken. On the Thursday evening. I'd just stepped out of the bath, and he'd said he wanted to watch me make myself come. The towel was right there in frame, thrown by the side of the bed. And he was nowhere in sight. According to the tape, he was innocent and I was …

Another wave of nausea hit and I went to vomit again.

But how had he taped them? The video with Holly was taken using his phone. I knew he was taking it – I shouldn't have let him do it, but I knew it was happening.

But this?

I stared at the image on the screen. My face frozen in a horrible expression. I was looking right at the camera, nobody would believe that I didn't know it was there …

The mirror.

But how? It felt unreal, like nobody would be that malicious. And yet there it was, the proof, staring back at me in humiliating detail from the screen.

I didn't know what to do or who to tell. My whole body burned with shame as I moved through to the bathroom, where I grabbed a tissue from the box on the windowsill and roughly blew my nose. Vomit in the tissue. Bitterness in my mouth. And my reflection staring back at me from the mirror: I was spiritually splintered, red, white and pink.

I held on to the ceramic basin below it and sobbed. My shoulders heaved and my nose ran.

And then I heard a rap on the door.

Shit.

I thought it might be the neighbours: maybe they heard me crying and were worried. The walls were thin. I looked in the mirror and tried to straighten myself up, then I went to the front door.

'Hello,' I said, trying to sound okay.

'Open the door, darling.'

My heart shook and I stood still.

'Darling,' Angus said, 'open the door.'

But I couldn't let him in. My hands trembled.

How did he know I would come here?

'Taylor, I know you're in there, let me in,' he said in a calm voice. 'I'm not going to do anything with those tapes unless you force me to.'

My hand was covering my mouth, my breath was shallow.

I could feel him leaning up against the door.

'Taylor …' he said. 'I mean it. Let me in. Now.'

And so I reached up to the cold metal deadlock, turned it, and let him in.

'Good girl,' he said as he stepped inside and placed his briefcase by the door. 'That wasn't so hard, was it?'

I flinched at his touch as he took me in his arms. 'I have a key, darling, I cut it from yours ages ago. I would have just let myself in anyway, so that was a good choice. You should be proud.'

My sobs deepened and my shoulders shook.

'Stop crying, darling,' he said as we swayed, my head against his chest.

Then he took me by the hand and led me to the sofa.

'Sit down,' he said. Then he walked through to the kitchen, and I heard the cupboard open and the faucet turn on. 'Are you thirsty?' he called.

'Yes,' I said, my voice shaky, 'thank you.'

A moment later he was moving towards me and handing me a glass of water. I sipped it slowly, watching him.

'Darling, those tapes are not a problem unless you make them into a problem,' he said. His eyes were dark. I tried to steady my breath and wiped my running nose with my hand.

He put his empty glass down on the coffee table, right beside the vase of aging roses he'd brought me just a week before, then he took mine and did the same.

'That's not to say we don't have any problems, though,' he said, reaching for my hand. I hesitated but I gave it to him. What choice did I have? And he helped me to my feet, held my hand tenderly for a moment, and then with so much strength, so much brutality, he crushed it. The force was unbearable. My bones twisted and ached. He was so strong.

And I yelled out in pain.

'Ow, please, honey, don't,' I cried.

'Oh, shut up,' he seethed as he let go of my hand. I fell to the floor and lay there, buckled over, looking at him. He grabbed me by the hair and forced me to stand.

'You see, darling,' he hissed, 'I came here earlier today, it was going to be a surprise, but I found something that really fucking pissed me off.' His grip tightened and he walked me over to the bed. 'I was so cross I had to go for a walk to calm down so I didn't do anything harsh.' My legs struggled to keep up with him and the world was a blur through my tears. Everything hurt, even my nails. They ached.

He pushed me hard and I landed on the bed. Creak. I gasped for air. And just lay there, face down, watching him open the top drawer of my chest by the bed. That was where I kept my underwear.

'Darling,' he said through gritted teeth, as his hand fished around inside, 'what the fuck are these doing here?' His eyes flashed at me as he held up his lucky socks. That brown-and-black pin-striped ball.

Fuck.

I opened my mouth but no sound came out.

He just stood looking at me. Smiling. And then his hand reached into his back pocket, and he pulled something small and black into view.

'Of course, I found this at the same time,' he said, dangling a little black rectangle in front of him.

It was suspended by a thin thread in the corner, held between his index finger and thumb. And it was swaying.

I squinted at it, trying to make it out. But then I knew.

It was my bank keypad: access to my online banking. It lived in my underwear drawer, right by his lucky socks. It was part of a two-tier security system my bank had introduced to up security measures. That was how I got into my account: a code generated by the keypad plus the answers to two security questions.

He threw it at me but it missed and hit the floor with a small, sharp clack. Then he walked over to me slowly, reached into his pocket, pulled out his wallet, and threw four £20 notes at me;

they landed by my head. 'There you go, Fluffy, that should get you through till payday,' he said.

Fluffy.

Fluffy Kramer.

My prostitute name.

Favourite pet.

First street.

The answers to my banking security questions.

I didn't even need to log on to know what he'd done. I already knew that the £984 I'd squirrelled away over the past four months would no longer be there. He was doing everything he could to stop me leaving. And it was working. I wouldn't get paid until that Friday and had maxed my credit card months before on my flat deposit. So, as it stood, I had £80 to my name, three sex tapes in existence, a boyfriend who hated me and no visible path to escape.

He was right: he *was* smarter than I was.

And that would have to change.

He moved towards me, and before I could flinch he lifted his hand into a flat palm and rushed it towards my face. One swift, fluid movement. As though to slap. Hard. But he stopped just before impact. A small yelp escaped my lips and he laughed.

'I'll see you later on, darling,' he said, as he stood up straight. 'Have a shower or something.'

And then he walked towards the door and picked up his briefcase. Before he slammed the door behind him, he said: 'Don't do anything stupid, darling.'

Bang.

And I lay there, vomit in my hair, mascara clogging my eyes. I'd been so naïve: a leak in his kitchen sink, Felicia, Mrs Clifton, prostitutes. It was all so petty. So amateur. If I was going to escape I'd need to think like him.

That's when I picked up the phone and called Charlotte.

I was sitting on a grey plastic chair opposite a kind-looking man with glasses – I say 'man' but he must have been around twenty-two. That had been Charlotte's sensible advice: 'Go to the police!' she'd yelled down the phone. 'Then come stay here.'

I hadn't told her everything – to do that would mean relinquishing all control over how things turned out. But I *had* told her Angus was cheating on me again and that when I'd confronted him about it, he'd got angry and held me by the throat against the wall. A corroborative witness would be a useful thing to have, should he try to frame himself as the victim. And it occurred to me that she might be right: maybe it *was* smart to get something on record. And so, on my way back to Angus's apartment I'd done just that.

From the outside, the Belgravia police station looked like a badly designed university building, constructed sometime in the late seventies when brown brick and blue paint were considered the height of chic. It was marginally better inside. I was taking a sip of warm water from the filter and going over in my mind what

I wanted to say – what I needed to remember *not* to say – when a young detective with a trendy haircut, shaved at the sides, appeared. He greeted me with a handshake and asked me to follow him.

We walked through a well-lit corridor. Brown carpet. Strange, diamond-patterned wallpaper. And him, throwing smiles at me over his shoulder every seven steps or so. Step, step, step, step, step, step, step, smile, step … I followed him into a small office at the end. On his desk sat a picture of a woman with auburn hair. And a white stapler, much like Val's, lay on its side by his mouse pad.

He picked up a biro with a chewed end, opened a notebook and said, 'You'd like to report an incident?'

'Yes, sort of,' I replied. My fingernails bit into the palms of my hands.

'Why don't you tell me what happened.'

'It's my boyfriend. I … he's, well, he's got a cocaine problem and he's violent and he's threatening me. And I don't know what to do.'

'Oh,' he said, trying to write. The pen wouldn't work. So he picked up another.

'He's vicious,' I continued. 'He tried to get me fired. Twice.'

'Are you living with him?' he asked.

'No.'

'So, you've left him, and he won't stop bothering you?' he asked.

'No, not yet. I'm frightened to leave him,' I said.

He sighed. 'Would you like to press charges about the violence? Was it recent, do you have any bruises?'

I looked at him. 'Yes, it was recent but no bruises. He just grabbed me by the hair and threw me around the room.'

'Christ,' he said, and then added: 'Okay, look, I'll take a statement, and then we'll talk to him.'

I imagined an inept policeman turning up at Angus's apartment, or worse yet his office, and telling him not to be mean to me anymore. Angus would smile his hypnotic smile, throw around his Eton accent as though that rendered him above suspicion, assure the policeman that I was just being a silly and melodramatic woman, and then the policeman would go away. And I would be left to deal with the fallout.

'Do you have to talk to him?' I asked, and he shifted his weight in his seat.

'Yes,' he said, 'usually getting a warning is enough.' Another smile.

I was happy for them to take a statement – that could help me – but I couldn't risk them talking to him; him finding out I'd gone to the police would enrage him further. And if they couldn't even protect me from him physically, they sure as hell couldn't protect me from the insidious variety of life-ruining blows he seemed capable of dishing out.

'We just need you to make a formal statement,' he continued. 'Can you give me your full name?'

'Oh,' I said, standing up. 'Let me think about it.' Then I moved towards the door.

I rushed down that brown hallway, past the man at the front desk and out through those big glass doors onto Buckingham Palace

Road. And as I stood beneath a thick grey blanket of cloud, inhaling the fumes from red London buses and backfiring motorbikes as they whizzed by, a finely ground calmness settled on my soul: because I knew exactly what to do. And I knew how to do it.

It was 7.10pm and I was standing in the middle of the sitting room. I'd spent the last hour meticulously searching the cabinets in the bathroom then the cupboard and drawers in the bedroom. I was looking for his other phone. I'd been lying in bed when I first heard it ringing, so I knew he must keep it nearby. Hidden beneath a pile of jumpers in the closet. Maybe inside a shoe he never wore. I'd gone through it all carefully, strategically skirting the eyeline of the mirror – I didn't know whether his camera was recording continuously – but all I'd found was his silver cigarette tin, heavy with a new stash of cocaine.

So I'd moved through to the sitting room and that's when I'd heard the storage cupboard vibrating. My forehead crinkled as I registered both the source of the sound and its point of origin.

I moved quickly towards it, grabbed the handle and turned: it was locked. I don't know whether it had always been locked – I'd never needed to open it. I'd always just imagined it full of skis, golf clubs, smelly old shoes and boxes.

I pressed my ear to the door. It was definitely a phone. And just as quickly as it had started, it stopped. I moved my face away from the white-painted wood and stared at the door.

And then the vibrating started up again.

I moved to the fridge and lifted my hand to the terracotta bowl above it that held the spare keys. Tangled in elastic bands, buried beneath the pens and bottle opener, lay three small keys, all on the same flimsy metal loop. I rushed with them to the door, then one by one I tried them in the lock. First: no. Second: no. Third: no.

Fuck.

I walked the keys back to their home above the fridge, and glanced at my watch. Angus would be back soon.

I picked up my handbag, went to the bathroom and locked myself inside.

Now that I knew where his other phone was, I could put my plan into action.

I turned on the taps, and as the bathroom filled with steam I texted my mother and told her I was fine and would call her soon. Then I texted Charlotte to say: *Going home for the night and turning off my phone so he can't call me. Can I come stay from tomorrow? xx*

Then I turned off my phone so neither could check. I needed to do this alone.

I got into the bathtub, and lay there long past the point I heard him arrive home, long past the point my toes began to wrinkle. And all the while the same image of Sophie Reed flashed before me: the picture used in most of the articles showed her wearing a blue satin dress that hit the floor, and her smile was big and bright. Then, still frames of her lying on the floor, blood coming from her pretty head, filled mine. He would hurt me too one day, I could feel it.

But that DVD had shown me that I was right all along: I couldn't just leave. I couldn't just disappear like they do in the movies. That train to East Sussex was a nice idea in theory, but in real life I'd have to deal with the fallout. With his rage. I knew what he was capable of now and it was far worse than sex tapes – Stepanovich and Sophie Reed had shown me that. The best-case scenario was that it would end in humiliation. The worst was unthinkable. Un-riskable. A fabricated crime that could cost me my freedom. An 'accident' that may cost me my life. And as my trip to the station had shown me, the police couldn't protect me.

I would have to protect myself.

I just had to survive one more night with him.

wednesday

Master Sun said: *'Discard rules.*
Follow the enemy to fight the decisive battle.'

22 FEBRUARY

That was the day I bought a gun.

And I almost wish it was harder. But it wasn't. All it took was a phone call, nineteen minutes on the Tube to Brixton and half a Valium.

I was sitting in a greasy spoon across from Hayley Cravick: Charlotte's ex-weed-dealer from when we used to live together. I'd only met her once before and I'd had to sift through my old messages from 2015 to find her number – but now there I was. Except I wasn't there for weed. I was there for the 'other' thing she dealt in. The reason Charlotte got scared and stopped using her. Guns. Small ones. The kind that fit into your pocket. The kind I needed.

The kind she was about to sell to me.

Because nobody runs at a girl who's holding a gun. Not even Angus. A knife, maybe, but not a gun.

And so there I sat, my blood racing, trying to pass the little money I had left in the world to her under that plastic table, the underside of which was full of old chewing gum. All I wanted was for her to take the money, give me the gun and for everything to be over.

But even then I knew it wouldn't be *that* easy.

My eyelids were heavy. I hadn't slept. There was wet cotton wool in my head and an electric knot in my stomach. And as hard as I tried, my mind wouldn't let go of the morning's events. It was trying to find a hole in my plan, anything I might need to plug up.

'Come here,' he'd ordered, standing by the open door. It was 7.56am and I was dressed in a pencil skirt, pantyhose and a crisp white shirt. I had a mascara wand in my hand and was about to apply a second coat. To an onlooker I was getting ready for work. But I wasn't.

I walked over to him.

'Don't look so scared,' he'd laughed, an awful smug laugh. 'I just want to kiss you goodbye.'

His lips found my forehead in a gesture of false tenderness, then: 'Maybe we'll make another video later.' Wink.

Then he'd picked up his briefcase, turned and walked out the door. It had echoed as it closed behind him and I remember squeezing my eyes shut and thinking: *I have fifteen minutes to pack.*

Then I'd stood there by the door, still as stone, listening as his footsteps faded to silence. Waiting until I knew I was safe. I'd run through to the bedroom, pulled out my suitcase and laid it on the bed. Reaching for my phone I'd sent three communiqués.

One: an email to Val, telling her I had just discovered that Angus was cheating on me again and I needed two days to move my things out of his flat and get my head straight. She replied with a short, sharp message saying I'd need to take them as 'leave' days.

Two: a text message to Charlotte, letting her know I'd be there late morning. She wrote straight back to remind me that the key was underneath the money frog to the left of the front door.

Three: a text message to David, asking to see him on Friday evening to talk. I suggested the Coach and Horses. 8pm. And he immediately wrote back to say yes. I was going to warn him that Angus was investigating him, of what he was capable. That I knew that even if Angus couldn't find genuine dirt on David, he'd fabricate something, so he needed to be stopped. Now. Then to prove my point I would hand David the green thumb drive and Angus's second phone. Because if there was one call Caz would definitely pick up, it was one he thought was coming from Angus. And maybe, when he answered, David could offer to pay Caz for information on Angus instead …

Then I'd packed. Quickly. Efficiently. Quite unlike my previous attempt two days before. First, everything hanging in the closet went into my suitcase, laid flat, folded over. Then the contents of my drawers went in. My toiletries and make-up. And I moved through to the sitting room: I was looking for the five paper reasons I'd had to get through one more night.

It was Wednesday. And that meant Elena, the cleaning lady, would be there by 8.30am at the latest. Angus had left five £20 notes on the coffee table for her. Apparently her market rate was higher than mine.

I picked them up and slipped them into my pocket, adding to the £80 he had given me and the £38 I had in my bag. My sum value as I walked out that door was £218.

Can £218 buy a gun?

Probably. According to Google, £250 could buy me a grenade. My eyes glanced at my watch: 8.13am.

I needed to be gone before she arrived – and not only because I'd taken her money. She might have told Angus if I was still there and then he'd want to know why I wasn't at work. It would alert him, and I couldn't risk that.

Five minutes later, I rolled my suitcase past Jake and stood on the kerb waiting for an orange taxi sign to save me – I had no money left in my account and no space left on my credit card, so the fare would need to come out of my £218 cash.

I watched the door at Starbucks across the road open and close as people came and went and the traffic lights cycle through green, orange, red. And then a cab stopped.

I hadn't seen it approaching. I gave him Charlotte's address, he put my bags in his boot and we drove away.

Forty-five minutes later I was inside Charlotte's flat, dropping off my suitcase, then just as quickly as I'd arrived, I was leaving again, the spare key in my pocket.

I was heading to Brixton, to the little restaurant with the yellow plastic tables and old chewing gum. Hayley's suggestion.

And now she sat across from me: Louis Vuitton handbag beside her, thick black liner on her lids, and her expression stating clearly that she didn't want to take money from me in a public place. I slipped my remaining £190 into my handbag.

My mouth was dry, so I took a sip of water. The glass smelled like it had been dried with a dirty rag.

She was trying to give me a crash course in shooting, but it was proving troublesome because I'd never held a gun before. She was using a teaspoon as a prop and a ketchup bottle as her target. And I was looking at her confused.

What the fuck am I doing?

'You try,' she said, handing me the spoon.

But it made no sense. There was no handle, no trigger, no safety catch (everybody knows that there's supposed to be a safety catch). My breath was shallow and my pulse thumped.

She watched me awkwardly clutch the spoon, her eyes scanned my businesslike outfit, and I saw pity flicker behind those kohl-framed blue eyes.

'Let's go to my place and try with the real thing,' she said, leaning in towards me. Her voice was older than her face.

'Great,' I said. Relieved.

'I live just around the corner.'

I nodded. Then I dropped the teaspoon and motioned for the bill. It came quickly, I paid – I was now down to £184 – and we left.

She lived in a bedsit, with an unmade double bed and a mezzanine up a rickety wooden ladder, the rungs threaded with fairy lights.

The room smelled of weed but there was an innocence about it. Around the mirror that hung in the middle of the wall were photographs of her, laughing and smiling, with one boy in particular.

'Right,' she said, pulling the gun from her bag.

I flinched.

She giggled. 'Calm down, there aren't any bullets in it yet. Besides, you see this?' she asked, pointing to a small part of the trigger. 'If this isn't held down with a finger it won't shoot. Not even if you drop it.'

'But where's the safety catch?' I asked.

'That *is* the safety catch,' she said. 'Now, you hold it like this.' She demonstrated, one hand grasping the handle, finger on the trigger and the other steadying it.

She handed me the gun. 'You try.'

A shiver ran up my neck and goose bumps appeared on my arms as I tried to mimic what she had just done. 'Good,' she said gently. 'The hardest part is aiming. If you can do it at super-close range it will be way easier. The further away you get the harder it is. But you know, with self-defence it's usually at close range, so you'll be fine.'

I'd told her I had a stalker ex-boyfriend and the gun was just to make me feel less frightened. And she'd nodded in a knowing sort of way, as though most of her clientele had similar issues.

'Try pulling the trigger,' she urged. I hesitated. Then I aimed at the window and pulled the trigger. It was stickier than I expected and required more pressure.

I glanced down at my watch: I wanted to get lost in the crowds of rush hour, so I needed to hurry.

'Bullets are extra,' she said. 'So is the silencer.'

'Shit, how much is it all together?' I asked, worried.

'One eighty?' she asked.

My stomach dropped: I couldn't give her everything I had.

'I only have one-seventy,' I lied, eyes to the floor.

Her eyes were on me, I could feel their heat.

'Can I give you the rest in a few days? I promise I'm good for it,' I said, looking up.

She smiled kindly. 'That's okay, don't worry about it, one seventy is fine,' she said. 'You bought tea.' Then her eyes moved back to the gun. 'Now, the silencer screws on like this.' Eyes back to me. 'But a silencer doesn't actually make it silent. It just means you won't blow your eardrums. So be careful. And the bullets like so.' I watched as she slid them into the inside part of the handle then click, it was back in place.

Two minutes later, with £14 to my name and a loaded gun in my bag, I left.

It began to drizzle, and I ran towards the station. There was a small stationery store I'd noticed a couple of hours earlier when I'd arrived. It had a blue fluorescent 'Open' sign on the door and a handwritten note on the window that read: 'Quick Cheep Printing'.

The typo made me smile.

I was met by a young man, paid him £5 to use one of the computers and typed out a single line of text: *Felicia:* 0770 090 0007, 0207 946 0139.

And then I pressed 'Print', 'Close' and 'Don't save'.

I would leave Brixton that day with £9, a gun and that printed piece of paper.

—

'Oh my God, are you okay?'

It was around 7pm and Charlotte had just arrived home. She was in the kitchen pouring heavy-handed gin-and-tonics into red-wine glasses. Ben was at a play rehearsal and so it was just us.

She came through and handed me a glass, sitting down next to me, her face tight with concern: 'Tell me exactly what happened.'

And so I told her my intricate lie. I'd been refining it since I got home from Brixton.

'It was horrible,' I said. 'It was yesterday morning, and he was in the kitchen. I was late for work and looking for my hairbrush and I couldn't find it anywhere. So I looked under the bed.' I paused and took a deep breath, looking down at my glass. 'And there were a pair of dirty knickers under there.' I looked up at her. 'They weren't mine.' My shoulders were slumped forward and I hoped I looked believable.

'Oh my God,' she said, disgusted. 'What did fucking Angus say?'

'Well, I took them through to him and showed him,' I said. 'I was pretty cross. I was yelling, and things got out of hand.' My mouth was freezing up the way it always does when I lie, and I willed it to relax. 'Maybe it was my fault.'

'It was *not* your fault,' she said. Firm. And I wondered what she'd think if she knew the whole story. If she knew there was a loaded gun hidden at the bottom of my suitcase.

'Anyway, he just started screaming about how I didn't trust him and then the next thing I knew he was holding me against the wall.'

'Fuck.' Her eyes were narrow and her forehead creased. 'Of course you don't trust him. Did you go to the police like I told you?'

'Yes, but they wanted to go and talk to him,' I said.

'So let them,' she said loudly, her hands gesturing wildly. 'It might do him some good to be scared.'

I took a sip of my drink and weighed my words. 'Honey, I don't want to make it any worse,' I said. 'I just want to never see him again.'

That was when my phone beeped. I reached across to pull it from my bag and my throat grew tight.

'I *knew* something like this would happen,' she said, her face scrunched up. 'I actually thought it already had.'

I was staring at my phone screen.

'Is that him?' asked Charlotte.

I showed her the screen: *Where the fuck are you?*

'Well, at least he doesn't know where you are,' she said.

And as I looked up at her I could feel my eyes filling with tears.

'Oh darling, it will be okay,' she said, her eyes maternal as she hugged me. 'Just don't reply to him.' Then she headed back into the kitchen with her drink in her hand.

My phone beeped again: *Get the fuck back here now.*

I could feel my heartbeat at the base of my throat.

I had been expecting those messages and knew I would have to manage him; I just didn't expect it to be so hard. I was sitting on the same mustard leather sofa Charlotte and I had bought back when we lived together, when London was new and anything was possible. The day we left that first flat she took the sofa and I took the fridge. But time had changed things. I could no longer feel the excitement of possibility propping me up. Possibility was now an abstract concept – a small pinprick of light in the distance. It was just a matter of time before it was snuffed out.

But ignoring him wasn't an option, not yet. I had to answer. Charlotte didn't understand the stakes.

Me: *I'll be back tomorrow, I just need some space.*

Beep: *No. Come back now.*

'Pizza or Thai?' Charlotte called to me from the kitchen.

'Pizza?' I said, my ears buzzing. My reply to Angus had to placate him. It had to buy time. My mind ran through response options … but then he texted first.

Beep: *Okay. Well, you have 24 hours to be back here or I'll be sending a little something to your mother. And your boss. And maybe even …*

Beep: *David Turner.*

David. Caz's comment about looking for dirt on David came spiralling back; I needed to warn him. If anything else happened it would all be my fault.

Me: *You realise I could just go to the police, right?* He didn't need to know I'd already been.

Beep: *Why would you go to the police? It should be me doing that, not you.*

Me: *???*

Beep: *Well, darling, you're the one who was stealing from me to pay for your weed and god knows what else. Not vice versa.*

Me: *What are you talking about? I never stole from you!*

Beep: *Really? You didn't go to my apartment when I wasn't there, take my bank card and PIN that I keep in my underwear drawer for emergencies and then go to an ATM and withdraw 1000 pounds? How high did you get that you don't even remember?*

The edges of my vision became white.

Beep: *The security camera at the ATM you went to will have footage of you doing it if you don't remember …*

Beep: *Or ask the doorman, he would have seen you come, go and then come back to return the card.*

My pulse sped up. And the texts kept coming.

Beep: *I mean, I do appreciate that you paid me back … but you shouldn't steal in the first place. You can always ask me. Always.*

My forehead crinkled: what was he talking about? And then I knew: the £984 he had taken from my account. He was covering his tracks. Creating backstory. Making me seem like the unreliable, crazy one. Anyone reading those messages would think it was me who had done the wrong thing – not him. I was the drug-addict girlfriend breaking into his apartment to take his bank card to draw money for drugs while he was at work. And he was the concerned and loving victim. The money that had been transferred out of my account to his, by him, was now just me paying him back …

I could finally see through him, but it would do me no good.

Beep: *Nor should you have broken into my home while I was away skiing …*

My breath caught in my throat. There was no way he could know that.

Beep: *Cat got your tongue?*

Beep: *Be silent then. 24 hours.*

Me: *Okay. I will be back soon. I promise. xx*

Beep: *Goodnight, darling.*

'Pizza will be here in twenty. I got half-mushroom, half-meat-lovers,' Charlotte announced. 'All about balance. Shit, are you okay?'

That's when I realised I was crying.

That mustard-yellow sofa was my bed that night. Ben set it up for me when he got home, stuffing extra cushions into the bits that sagged and jamming folded pieces of paper under the support to make sure it didn't wobble. And as I lay there, the old springs digging into my middle back, my mind swung from thought to thought. Chiara.

My flat. Val: what would she would think of me if Angus sent her those tapes? Cameron: Caz007. Sophie Reed. Angus's shoebox. RedTube. The videos. My mother. The green thumb drive. What Angus would do if he knew I'd found it. The gun in my suitcase. Hayley. Jake. The other phone. Alison's fake chest. Jamie. Cigars. Angus. The version I loved. The version I hated. Yellow ribbons. Prostitutes. Felicia. The lingerie. Kim: why had she messaged me? Should I have messaged her back? Ski slopes. David. Ed. 'Happy birthday, sir.' My purple notebook. Master Sun Tzu. A lemon-yellow pillowcase. Cigarettes and spiced lime.

Yes, I thought of a million things that night. And yet I really only thought of one: my alibi.

thursday

Master Sun said: *'Let your plans be dark and impenetrable as night, and when you move, fall like a thunderbolt.'*

23 FEBRUARY

Beep: *What the fuck did you do? Joe from next door just came over and said I sent a dick pic to his fiancée! Are you insane?*

That was the first text of the day. It arrived just before 9am. I was only halfway into my first cup of coffee, looking through Charlotte's kitchen drawers for loose coins to supplement the £9 I had until Friday. She would have lent me money if I'd asked, but I was running out of plausible explanations.

Me: *What?*

I stared at my phone and my stomach contracted. I'd hoped Felicia would only think to consult Jake's laminated list of contact numbers and tie the dick pic to Angus *after* I was gone. The printout from the day before was to help her piece it together.

Beep: *Don't you dare lie to me.*

Me: *I really don't know what you're talking about.*

Then the phone started to ring: his name and a smiling photograph I'd assigned to his contact information back when things were good flashed back at me from the screen.

Fuck.

'Hello,' I answered sweetly, focusing on my breath just like he'd taught me. I needed him to believe that I really was returning that evening as promised.

'What have you done?' he seethed into the phone.

'Nothing –' I started, but he cut me off.

'I could get evicted! This is fucking serious … and Candice said you haven't called her. I want the prostitute saga dealt with today,' he said, his voice cracking.

'Can we talk about it later?' I asked softly, closing the kitchen drawer. There was no money in there – £9 would have to do – but I *had* found duct tape under the sink and a pair of nail scissors in the bathroom. The two things I'd need, according to the YouTube video I'd watched that morning.

'I have a late meeting, I'll be home at eight. But I expect you to be there when I get back.'

'Okay,' I said, 'I will be.'

And then we hung up.

My throat felt thick, like a bathroom drain clogged with hair. I wouldn't be there at eight when he got back, and I was frightened of the aftermath. But I *would* have an alibi. I *would* be able to tell him to call the yoga studio. Then I would tell him I was too frightened of him to return. And he would harshly, then gently, try to coax me back. I knew the choreography. I could predict the steps. And that would buy me wiggle room: by the time he figured out that the videos had been deleted and his second phone was missing, I would know what was on it; I would already be using it against him.

~

It was a Thursday. And I had two remaining yoga classes on a pre-paid pack of ten. That meant there was a 6.45pm class I could register for and not actually attend, in the same way Charlotte and I used to do.

I arrived at the studio at 6.38pm, at the height of the post-work rush, so it was easy to go unnoticed. Then I stood in line, booked myself in, paid a £5 deposit and took my locker key: number 31. I was now electronically logged as having attended, and I had until 8pm to get back.

Then I followed the crowd into the change room and put on black yoga pants and an oversized grey pullover. I opened the locker door and left my belongings inside: handbag, jeans, phone, gloves, coat, baseball cap, crumpled piece of paper, duct tape, nail scissors, silencer and gun.

Then I zipped the key into the front pocket of my yoga pants and went into one of the loos. I stayed perched there on that porcelain seat until the room fell silent. When I was sure it was empty I crept out, unlocked the locker, put on my gloves and stuffed the hat into the waistband of my lycra pants. Then the gun went into one pocket of my fleece pullover and the silencer – together with the crumpled piece of paper I planned on dropping onto Mrs Clifton's balcony to help Felicia with her case – went into the other. I glanced at myself in the mirror: everything was concealed.

I grabbed for the duct tape, used the nail scissors to cut off a piece the length of my hand and then shut everything back inside the locker.

It was 6.47pm when I exited through the emergency door and closed it gently behind me, the duct tape secured over the latch to ensure it wouldn't deadlock.

And by 6.56pm I could see Angus's building on the corner. It had been raining earlier and streetlights were reflected on the mirrored streets as I jogged towards it. I couldn't afford a cab, after paying the locker deposit I only had £4 left.

I entered through the side entrance of the garage, using the key I'd taken from the terracotta bowl above Angus's fridge, back when I thought a leak constituted revenge. As the door closed behind me, the light that had been thrown in from the outside was eclipsed, and I was shrouded in a veil of pitch black. But I knew that garage well and could navigate my way through the dark.

My gloved hands guided me along the rough wall, through the CCTV's blind spot, past the assembly of rubbish bins awaiting collection, and towards the heavy door to the stairwell. The CCTV wouldn't have switched on yet, so I was less likely to be seen if I took the stairs rather than the lift. I pushed the door open and, holding on to the banister, I started my upward climb.

It was 7.06pm as I walked towards his door. I put my key into the lock. Turned it. And it opened. I was hit by the smell of furniture polish and green apple cleaning fluid: Elena. I closed it quietly behind me and took off my shoes, then ran through to his computer.

Sitting on the chair, I jiggled the mouse and brought his screen to life. Then I navigated to the home movies tab on his iTunes. And there they were, in plain sight. A snake of shame twisted in my stomach at the thought of my mother seeing those videos. I recognised the four of me immediately – they'd been branded on my psyche – but scattered amid mine were many others. Other women. One was entitled 'Kim3Valentine'. It was sitting near the top, so I clicked on it and checked when it had been added: the day after Valentine's Day. While I'd been imagining him in an NA meeting, sharing heartfelt stories with strangers, he'd been in bed with Kim. That was the night I went past and got that money for him – I must have just missed them in the elevator.

That's probably why Kim wrote to me two days later. And why Angus had me block her …

There were twelve in all. I dragged every last one of them into the trash, pressed empty, and then pulled up a browser window. Then I logged into Angus's emails and scrolled through them until I found the one from Caz.

Two words: Sophie Reed.

I forwarded it to a new email and typed 'I'm sorry' into the body of the message. I left 'FW: Sophie Reed' in the subject field. I copied the email address for Justin and Lorraine Reed I'd taken from that newspaper article the day before into the addressee field.

I took a deep breath, and pressed send. Then I deleted both the original and forwarded emails.

I stared back at his empty home movies pane. He would know it was me who deleted them, and he would be angry. And so he would call me in a rage and tell me that of course he had back-ups, and exactly how he was going to use them.

And when he did, I would calmly mention that I had his second phone.

That I was happy to use *that* in retaliation.

My heart thumped against my ribs as I reached across and opened his drawers, one by one, searching for the key to the storage cupboard. First the top one. Nothing. Then the second. Towards the back lay my favourite little green thumb drive, so I took it and slipped it into my pocket. Then the third. Nothing.

Swivelling around, I checked the bookcase. It was sparse and it didn't take long to search, and while I didn't find a key, I *did* find my purple notebook hidden behind an old encyclopaedia. I left the notebook where it was and moved through to the living room.

A shuffle. Jumper cable to the heart. Ed. I stared at his cage, a silhouette against the window.

Where the fuck would he hide that key?

I was running out of ideas: I'd searched the cupboards in the bedroom and bathroom just two days before. And it wasn't in his office or on top of the fridge.

Does he keep it with him?

That was when I heard the jangling. The sound of his key fitting into the front door lock.

I will never forget that sound.

I ran into the bedroom and hid.

My watch said 7.21pm. He had said 8pm.

I heard his footsteps as he entered. The flick of the light switch. Him putting down his briefcase by the front door. Then he took off his shoes, and his pace became lighter as he moved towards his booze cabinet. I couldn't hear the Scotch pour, but I knew him well enough to know that's what he would be doing: two Scotches out on the balcony.

My breath was shallow and my heart wild as I reached into my pocket and wrapped my fingers around the gun. I pulled the silencer from the other pocket and screwed it on. Then I waited. Soon I would hear the rusty key turn and the creak of the balcony door opening. And the moment he walked out, I would make a run for it.

Three-quarters of my plan had been accomplished: hard drive, email and videos. But I still didn't have the phone, and a thick danger swirled around me. What was going to happen when he saw I'd deleted the videos? If he noticed the thumb drive was gone? That I wasn't back there when I said I would be? What would he do? I clenched my eyes shut. There was no telling how long it might take for Sophie's parents to read the email I'd just sent – for the police to act on it – and anything could have happened by then. I needed that phone as collateral. Something that linked him to Caz and Sophie and Stepanovich and the information on that green drive; something I could hide away, in case. Because the only thing that would stop Angus coming after me – hurting me – was knowing I could hurt him more. I would have to come back for it.

I looked towards the front door and my ears strained against the silence, searching for his movements. His location.

I swallowed, hard. And it echoed through the room. But then came the sound I'd been waiting for: the familiar creak of the balcony door. I counted to five, calculating that he would be outside by then, standing by the railing looking out at the view. And then, with my hand clenched around the cold handle of the gun, my finger carefully avoiding the trigger, I took a deep breath and I ran.

But the moment I moved out from my hiding place, a strong arm reached around my waist. He had been waiting for me. The gun flew out of my hands. I heard it bounce across the floor. He was behind me. He was so strong.

The arm that wasn't around my waist pinned my arms to my sides.

'You fucking bitch,' he whispered in my ear as he swung me away from the front door. 'Did you really think you could outsmart me?'

We were moving towards the balcony. I reached back with my hand and grabbed hold of his crotch. I squeezed with everything I had: hand, gloved nails, everything. He crumpled. I went to punch him in the head but I fumbled and he grabbed for me. I could see him recovering almost immediately. My mouth was dry. My throat was tight.

I ran outside, through that balcony door.

I will scream. The neighbours will hear me.

But he was right behind me. I opened my mouth to scream. To bite. And his hand reached around in front of my face to stop me. He could read my every thought. He knew what I was going to do before I did.

I turned my head quickly and ducked out of his grasp. His forward motion propelled him towards the balcony wall. He hit it hard and I turned to run. But he grabbed for me before I was out of range. Before I was free. He caught my wrist with a cold, harsh hand and he pulled me towards him with a force I couldn't fight. Only the sleeve of my pullover stood between his hand and my skin. I pulled away with all my might, but he was stronger. He was drawing me towards him. I ripped frantically at his shirt with my free arm and let out a yelp when he pulled harder. When he pulled harder, so did I.

And then, somehow, I slipped free. He tumbled backwards, his feet wrestling with the rain-streaked slats. His feet won. He was leaning against the railing. Grinning. And I could have run, I could have left, I could have taken my chances.

But I didn't.

Instead I ran towards him. And with everything I had, every ounce of my weight, I pushed. I pushed that heavy torso of his and as it toppled over the balcony wall it dragged his legs with it like an iron weight. One swift movement. One single moment. One decision. And he was gone.

My lungs drew in a deep frozen breath. My eyes were pinned open, and I stared at the slice of moon that stood in his place.

What have I done?

My pulse was quick as I turned my head: left then right. *Did anyone see me?* A heavy layer of soot settled on my conscience and the weight cemented my feet in place.

I had just killed a man.

His body, the body of the man I'd loved, was lying on the street below – it would be seeping a thick, dark red substance, a burgundy set of wings. And the impact as he hit the pavement would have changed him; his limbs would be limp, and he would be gathering attention. *Angus is gone forever.* I had done it. I had seen it. And yet it didn't feel real.

But the faint sound of sirens in the distance punctured my paralysis: I needed to keep moving, to think clearly, rationally, strategically. If I didn't, I would be caught. The sirens were getting louder.

I forced myself to breathe. I needed to get out of that building and back to the yoga studio by 8pm. I turned away from the moon and walked back through that creaky door, leaving it open and unlocked. My head was clear and my heart was numb: the sting of sadness held at bay by shock.

Once inside, I dealt with the evidence: I put the key to the side entrance back in the terracotta bowl above the fridge. I ran through to his bedroom, took the packet of cocaine from the silver tin in his sock drawer, and quickly moved through to his study. I retrieved my purple notebook from his bookcase and then picked up the gun on my way to the front door. With my notebook under my arm, I unscrewed the silencer and placed the pieces back into their relative pockets. Then I slipped on my shoes. Put the cap on my head. And dropped exhibits A, B and C into the front pocket of his briefcase: the cocaine, the green thumb drive, and the crumpled piece of paper containing Felicia's details.

And just like that I wrote his headline: *Angus Hollingsworth, sexual predator, cocaine addict, banker with strong ties to money launderer Nicolai Stepanovich, committed suicide by jumping from his eighth-storey balcony. He left no suicide note, but shortly before he died he forwarded an email to the parents of murdered ex-girlfriend Sophie Reed suggesting that he was responsible for her death.*

An image of his mangled body lying on the pavement flashed before my eyes. The sirens were louder now. I wouldn't have time to retrieve the phone from the storage cupboard, but it no longer mattered: he couldn't hurt me anymore. And anything found on there could only further solidify any theory of suicide and possibly shine light on the fate of Sophie Reed.

I closed the door behind me and moved quickly towards the stairwell, my eyes briefly scanning my watch: 7.33pm. *Fuck.* I fought the urge to flick on the light as I entered. Instead I used the banister to guide me. It was safer that way; if anybody else entered the stairwell, the light would warn me.

But I would have to swap to the lift for a short portion of my journey, because the CCTV would now be on. I counted the flights of stairs: seventh, sixth, fifth, fourth, third, second. I moved to the stairwell door and looked through the window out into the hallway. It was deserted. I opened the door, walked briskly towards the lift and pressed the down button. And when it came I got in. I pressed the button for the basement and, just before the doors closed, I remembered Kevin's trick with the buttons. And so, holding the basement button down, I pressed the 'Doors closed' button too. Then, watching as the doors slid shut, I prayed.

'Please God, please help me, please help me, please help me, please help me.'

The elevator whirred, it began to move and I watched the lights glow red: seventh, sixth, fifth, fourth. I took a deep breath. Third, second, first.

Basement.

Ping.

The doors slid open and I moved to the wall for support, trying to focus on the location of the cameras. And after three seconds, the lift doors closed again and with them, all light disappeared. I followed the rough walls in the dark, past the stairwell, past the assembly of rubbish bins and towards the side entrance. When I got there, I felt for the big round button that would let me exit. Pressed it. Pushed the door. And walked into the road.

The sirens were almost there. I walked down that road with a gun in my pocket, away from his building and the crowd that would be gathering around or running from his body. My hair was damp with fear beneath my cap. But people sweat in yoga, right?

How did I feel? It would be easier to say how I *didn't* feel. I *didn't* feel like a girl who had just committed murder – I'm not that girl.

Nobody noticed me as I wove my way through those backstreets towards the yoga studio. My mind was frantic but I just kept moving my feet, one and then the other. And only one person passed me on the street that night – a woman deeply ensconced in an imaginary argument, her lips mouthing objections and her forehead crinkling. And she didn't notice me. Why would she? I was just a girl in yoga pants, walking down a London street with a purple notebook in her hands, and tattered old cap on her head.

~

My watch told me it was 7.53pm when I slipped in through the back door, pulling the duct tape off the latch and holding it tightly in my hand as I let it close quietly behind me. Nothing else was scheduled until 8.30pm – I'd checked the timetable – so I should have been safe. It should have been empty.

But when I entered, one of the bathroom stalls was occupied.

Did they hear me come in? What could I say? That I was smoking outside?

I ran across the room and locked myself in one of the loos and tried to steady my breath. Then I stuffed my gloves and hat into the pockets of my pullover, took it off and folded it into an unsuspicious I-just-got-hot ball. My blood was fast and my breath was still quick but soon that steady stream of om-ed out women began to fill the change room and it was time to go.

I opened the door and went straight to my locker, trying not to make eye contact. Hairdryers sounded behind me as I opened it. Then I put my pullover bundle safely inside, changed back into my jeans and put on my coat. I grabbed my things, returned my locker key to the front desk, retrieved my £5 key deposit, and made my way to the Tube. Just like I'd planned.

~

I was standing outside Charlotte's front door but I couldn't make myself go in. I felt like a liar. I *was* a liar. How can you keep something like that from your best friend? So I stood there staring at the old brown mat beneath my feet, self-soothing, telling myself to go inside: *It will be okay*. But that was another lie. It wouldn't be okay because it couldn't be okay. And so, despite the warmth of the yellow light that beckoned from her sitting room, I remained frozen. Breathing, in and out. In and out. As though frightened I might forget how.

But eventually I entered. I smiled my hellos. I moved towards my suitcase – it was in plain view, just beside the sofa. And with Charlotte scolding me from the kitchen as she boiled the kettle – 'You should have told me you were going to yoga, babe, I would have come. I wouldn't have *liked* it, but I would have come' – I unzipped my suitcase, wrapped the gun in my lilac bra and stuffed it, along with the silencer, towards the bottom. I zipped it up again just as she moved towards me with two cups of cocoa. Three melting marshmallows bobbed on the top – two pink, one white. We sipped our cocoa, Charlotte lamented what a dick Angus was, and I sat there numb, silent and nodding, certain that I would never be the same person ever again. I would have no obituary, but that didn't mean a large portion of *me* didn't die on the pavement that night too.

friday

Master Sun said: *'Victorious campaigns are unrepeatable. They take form in response to the infinite varieties of circumstance.'*

24 FEBRUARY – DAYTIME

I went to work the next day. Maybe that makes me heartless, maybe it makes me cold, and in the eyes of a jury it would probably be quite damning. But it also makes me smart. Because I knew that turning up to work was necessary.

That said, it wasn't easy. Charlotte certainly didn't advise it. She'd reasoned with me over a bowl of cornflakes and burnt toast, saying: 'That's what sick days are for.' Ben, nursing a cup of tea while standing in a Guns N' Roses T-shirt and a pair of blue pyjama bottoms, had agreed with her: 'Nobody will think badly of you, love,' he'd said.

But I'd insisted. I'd pulled my hair back into a ponytail, put on mascara, and marched past that yellow-eyed money frog, over the brown welcome mat and out into the world.

I'd held it together on the Tube. Instead of wallowing, I'd searched its sea of downcast, deadened eyes for understanding, shared experience, a glint of something that would tell me that somebody, anybody, in London had done something as terrible as I had. That I was not alone. That there was somebody out there who would understand.

I'd found nothing of the sort. Instead, I'd spent the journey scanning my horoscope for confirmation of my impending doom, looking over the shoulder of a middle-aged woman who, it became apparent during an unexpected jolt when I'd lost my balance and made my presence known, didn't enjoy the intrusion.

Val wasn't at her desk when I got in, so I didn't have to answer questions right off the bat. Instead I focused on behaving normally: checking my bank balance – it was payday – and forcing myself not to Google Angus's name. I didn't even Google the news that morning – nothing that might draw suspicion if examined at a later date.

Instead, I made my morning coffee, did the familiar 9am tearoom dance: a hive of worker bees trying to negotiate the limited counter space and badly placed mini fridge, each with an outward smile and an inward chorus of 'Get the fuck out of my way'. I had – and lost – a fight with the printer when I tried to print an email. And I calculated that every workday consisted of 8 hours, or 480 minutes, or 28,800 seconds. Then I set up an internal betting pool as to when that inevitable tap on my shoulder, telling me about what had happened to Angus, would come. My guess sat at 11am.

It was 10.03am when Val got to her desk.

'Are you okay?' she asked, wheeling her chair into my cubicle and placing her hand on my shoulder.

And that's when the anaesthesia of early shock finally began to wear off and the tears started to fall.

But they were deceptive: they spoke of betrayal but they embodied a funny mix of fear, relief and a flatness I didn't understand.

So, by 10.05am, my goal in forcing myself to go to work had been met: I was a mess. An obvious mess. And anyone walking past could attest to that. Not an 'I just committed homicide' sort of mess, more a 'That arsehole just screwed me over again' sort of mess. A loveable mess. A blameless mess. A mess that didn't know how to hold a gun and had never read *The Art of War*.

Because it is almost inconceivable that a girl could kill someone and then turn up to work the next day.

And that's why I *had* to do it.

Even my clothes said 'mess': my shirt had a drip of old coffee on the left breast and the crinkles and fold-marks of the skirt I had fished out from the very bottom of my suitcase looked even crinklier under the bright fluorescent globe that flickered above me.

'What exactly happened? You only just got back together,' Val said softly. Discreetly.

And so I retold it, my story of woe. The panties I had allegedly discovered under our bed had taken on a colour and fabric by that point: a sort of washing-machine-induced-greyed-out pink lace. It seemed nuanced enough to be true.

'I'm so sorry,' she said with a heavy sigh. 'Are you okay to be here?'

'Yes, it's *better* for me to be here, occupied,' I replied. She gave one last stroke to my shoulder then wheeled herself back to her side of the partition.

But 11am came and went, and the phone remained silent.

All the time spent practising my shocked face ('What? He's *dead*?') had been for naught.

So instead I went to the bathroom and called my mother.

'Oh,' she said. Gentle. 'That's horrible, darling.'

'Yes,' I sniffed.

'Sweetheart, I really think you should come home for a bit,' she said. 'If you want to, of course.'

'Maybe,' I said. 'I can't really take too much more time off work.'

We sat in silence, on either end of the phone line. She could hear my sobs and I could hear her breath. It was comforting.

'Well, darling, at least you know for sure now,' she said, piercing the silence.

We ended the phone call without her ever uttering the phrase I feared most: *I told you so*. And with me never breaking the news I wasn't meant to know yet: that he was dead. And I went back to my desk.

The computer screen stared back at me, I pretended to read emails, and every so often I thought: *You had no other choice.*

It was only at around 2pm that the call finally came.

I'd been reorganising my stationery drawer at the time. Paperclips. They tried my mobile phone first but I didn't recognise the number, so I didn't pick up. But a moment later Val was looking at me with a worried expression on her face. If I didn't already know who it was, that might have warned me.

'Um, it's the' – her voice lowered – 'police.' Her voice was soft but her lips mouthed it loudly.

She passed me her receiver. The cord was barely long enough to reach me. And an entire lifetime passed in the moments between when I pressed that cold receiver to my ear and when the voice on the other end of it finally spoke.

It belonged to a woman.

The first syllables floated by without comprehension, as though they were intended for somebody else. I found myself blinking hard, trying wake myself up. I could hear her in the distance saying: 'Is this Taylor Bishop?'

And then I could hear myself saying, 'Yes.'

'My name is Detective Rouhani, I'm calling from Belgravia police station. Would I be able to come and see you this evening?' she said.

'What?' I asked. 'Why? What is this about?' I could feel my pulse beating hard through my skin.

'It would be better if we could talk in person,' she said, her voice low and steady.

'Why, is something wrong?' I asked.

I heard her breathing – she was weighing up her options – and I saw a group of girls huddling around a pink box of cupcakes through the open door of the kitchen.

'I'm so sorry to tell you this,' she said, 'but there has been an accident.'

'Oh God, what's going on? Is it Mum? Is she okay?' I said. I'd practised that at home.

I swallowed hard.

'No,' she replied. 'Angus Hollingsworth. He fell from the balcony. It happened last night. I'm sorry.'

'What?' I asked. 'What do you mean? How?' My voice was cracking under the pressure. I was cracking.

'It looks like it was intentional at this stage. I am so sorry for your loss.' Her words were sympathetic, but her voice was hard-boiled. It had delivered this sort of news many times before.

'It's all my fault,' I said, my voice husky. 'I shouldn't have left him – we just broke up a few days ago.' I was covering my tracks.

'These things tend to be complicated. Could I pop in this evening and ask a few questions about Angus?' she asked.

'Of course,' I said. 'Or I could come in there,' I offered, wiping my wet nose with the back of my hand.

'That would be very helpful,' she said. 'When would you be able to get here?'

I looked across at Val, who was watching me with concern. The whir of the photocopier filled my free ear with the normality I was no longer a part of.

'I could be there in a couple of hours,' I said, looking through my now-tidy drawer for a pen. 'Sorry, what did you say your name was?'

'Detective Rouhani,' she said. 'Ask for me at the front desk.' Then she added: 'Do you have someone who can come with you? These sorts of things can be a big shock to the system.'

'I'll be okay,' I said in a small voice, looking around for a piece of paper. There wasn't one, just a red pen, so I wrote her name on my palm.

She hung up and I handed the receiver back to Val. Her eyes were searching mine for answers and her lips twitched with involuntary questions she was trying hard not to ask.

'Angus is dead,' I said. My voice was a broken whisper. No amount of rehearsal had prepared me for the confusion of real emotion splashing against the tide of what I thought I *should* be feeling. What I *would* be feeling, if the situation I was presenting were accurate.

My eyes were heavy; they just wanted to go to bed. My breath, shallow and quick while on the phone, had slowed to a deep, lagging rhythm.

I just have to answer some questions. Then this will all be over.

'They think it might have been suicide,' I added as I grabbed around beneath my desk for my handbag.

'Oh my God!' Val's gasp was real and her hand moved to cover her heart.

'I have to go into the police station to answer some questions about Angus,' I said, standing up. My eyes avoided hers.

'Of course,' she said, a voice in the distance. I threw her a half-smile, walked past the reception desk, down the four flights of stairs, and through that revolving door into the cold London air. I waited for it to shake me from my trance. But it didn't.

I headed to the bus stop, my eyes half-opened, my heart already closed. The C2 would deliver me almost directly to Detective Rouhani, and the trip would take just a little longer than the Tube. I needed the extra time to double-check my alibi, iron out any last-minute kinks. It was never meant to stand up to police scrutiny – it was just supposed to buy me time with Angus. Now it had to keep me out of prison.

And so I needed to keep my head when I spoke to her. Not tell her anything that might suggest I had a motive to hurt Angus.

But with every step the lead marbles of guilt and paranoia weighed heavier in my pockets and it was harder and harder to move. The only thing I could do to lighten the load as I made my way towards her was remind myself: *It was him or me.*

friday evening

Master Sun said: *'The warrior skilled in indirect warfare is infinite.'*

24 FEBRUARY – LATER

'Victoria Station.'

The voice jarred me into alertness and my eyes searched for the familiar pavement through the dirty bus window. I got up and made my way down the stairs to the door as the bus jerked and swayed to a stop. As my feet hit the pavement, the smell of French fries washed over me in a wave – salt, oil – but there was no McDonald's in my eyeline, just tourists and suitcases and traffic.

The police station – brown brick, blue plastic – was waiting for me in the distance to my left. And directly across from it stood a high cream tower with a clockface at the top: 2.55pm. I swallowed and walked towards it.

My hands were trembling by the time I got to the station. And I thought I might not be able to go in. But I forced myself to move up those stairs, one by one. To push through the big glass doors. I tried to unclench my jaw, tried to act the way an innocent person might. But guilt oozed out of every pore.

The young policeman with the glasses, the same one from a few days before, was sitting at the front desk. He looked at me, concerned. And I knew why: I'd caught a glimpse of myself in the bus window and my eyes were still red and puffy.

'Are you okay, Miss?' he asked.

I nodded in response, then said, 'I'm here to see Detective Rouhani.' My nails bit into my palms as I tried to relax my jaw.

He smiled kindly, motioned towards the row of grey plastic chairs that lined the large front window, and said: 'She won't be long, take a seat.'

I sat on the one in the corner near the water cooler, calmed my breath, and looked out the window at some evergreen shrubbery and a collection of mottled-yellow cigarette stubs.

My pulse sped up – I must have sensed her coming – and when I swivelled my head there she was, walking towards me. Holding a notepad. Long dark hair draped over one shoulder, dark unblemished skin and the bright and cunning eyes of a fox.

'Thank you for coming in, Taylor,' she said. 'I'm Detective Rouhani.'

She extended her hand towards me, and when I stood up and took it, she motioned for me to follow her towards the hallway. 'Do you mind if we take a couple of swabs?' She was talking to me over her shoulder. 'It's just protocol.'

'Okay,' I said. *If they think it's suicide, why are they checking DNA?*

It was the second time I'd had that brown carpet under my feet in a week. I'd preferred the first time. Detective Rouhani led me into a small room, where I was greeted by another woman. She was older: a splash of silver-grey hair and a set of deep lines etched into her forehead; she looked like she had been surprised often in her lifetime. She sat me down on some kind of massage table – it was covered in paper towel – then put a cotton swab into my mouth, rubbed it in a circular motion across the inside of my left cheek and then slid it into a small glass bottle.

I watched as she fastened a yellow lid onto it and wrote out a label with a fat black pen before repeating the process once more.

'Great, all done,' she said with a smile. I couldn't be bothered smiling back but I forced it, my lip quivering a little.

Rouhani led me back out of the room and we walked into her office.

'Are you okay?' she asked me from across her oak desk. My silent tears had started up again. I could feel them dripping down my cheek.

She passed a business card across the table. The shiny black type was embossed and it read: *Kate Stapleton, Family Liaison Officer*. There was a phone number underneath the name.

'We have services to help with the shock,' Detective Rouhani said. 'Sometimes the best thing to do is just talk.'

'Thanks,' I said, forcing a smile.

'Take your time,' she said, handing me a box of tissues.

'Thanks,' I said, taking a handful and forcing myself to look her straight in the eye. 'What happened?'

'Like I said on the phone, it looks like suicide. We've been putting out feelers, asking neighbours what they saw, but so far nobody has come forward. Aside from a couple of people walking past when he fell.'

My eyes cast down, my cheeks hot with tears. *How did I get here?*

'We'd just broken up,' I said, looking up at her. 'I feel like this is all my fault.'

The tears kept coming, but I wasn't acting. I was buckling.

'We found cocaine in his briefcase – heavy drug use does tend to lead to these sorts of things. There were also opiate painkillers in his bathroom. Did you know about the drugs?' she asked.

'I knew about the cocaine. Not the pills,' I said. 'But he was in the program, had a sponsor and everything.'

'There were other things we found in his briefcase which are confusing,' she continued. 'How well do you know his neighbour –' She read from her notepad: 'Felicia Jones?'

'I don't really know her at all,' I replied. 'I mean, I know who she is but I don't know-know her. Why?'

'Her name and contact details were in his briefcase,' she said. There was a flicker of movement outside her office window and she looked towards it.

'Oh.' I feigned confusion. 'Maybe you should ask her? Maybe she was going away and wanted Angus to watch her flat or water her plants or something?' I said, the way an innocent girl might.

She sighed. I watched her eyes move back from the window to her pad; they jumped a couple of lines, and I could feel her trying to choose between two options, one of which ran the risk of upsetting me further.

'We did ask her,' she started. She'd clearly chosen option B. 'Look, I don't want to upset you any further, but Felicia has been experiencing a level of harassment over the past couple of weeks. Unwanted gifts. Unwanted graphic text messages. Phone calls. We know now that it was Angus who was responsible.'

I looked at her with what I hoped was horror. 'What do you mean?' I said. 'Angus barely knows her.'

She exhaled loudly and uncrossed her legs.

'Yes, but the graphic messages came from his number,' she said softly. 'And there's something else.' She took a moment to inhale. 'In his briefcase was a thumb drive. It contained a lot of information about a man named Nicolai Stepanovich.'

I swallowed hard. 'Huh?' I said. My forehead crinkled. I let my eyes wander. And I tried to look confused. 'That's weird,' I said, eyes back to her.

'How so?' she asked.

'Well, I know who Nicolai Stepanovich is. He runs Citexel. I was doing this work project – God, it's so complicated – I was looking for an investment opportunity and suggested their new development down in Eastbourne. But then it all got leaked to the press and I almost got fired,' I said.

'Sorry, I don't follow,' she said. 'What do you mean it got leaked to the press?'

'Well, it turned out that Stepanovich had been laundering money. Through property schemes. It was all over the papers.' My voice was small and feeble. It sounded like it belonged to someone else. A child. And I only became aware that my tears had started up again when she handed me a tissue box.

'It's the shock,' she said.

'But why would Angus have information on him?' I asked, leading the witness. 'Oh,' I added, 'maybe it's because he was pitching for business from him a few months ago?' I was trying to walk the delicate line between being helpful and too in-the-know. And her poker face made it hard to judge how I was doing.

'Maybe. But the information on it was quite extensive,' she said. 'Anyway, we'll be calling his office later.'

'Talk to Candice Breen,' I said. 'She's his secretary. *Was* his secretary.' I hear my voice tremor.

She looked down at her pad again and scribbled Candice's name. The pages were angled so that I could see its contents: a list, some things crossed off, and something of a mind map on the opposite page. Circles and lines. It seemed like a lot of information for an open-and-shut case.

She changed tack: 'What can you tell me about Angus's frame of mind before his death?'

'God, I don't know, same as usual I guess,' I said. 'A bit agitated, but normal-ish. He was always a bit high strung.'

'So, you said you knew about the drugs …' The expression on her face said: *Please elaborate*.

I sighed. 'Yes, he had a bit of a coke habit. He was in NA but kept relapsing.'

'NA? Narcotics Anonymous?' she asked, noting it down.

'Yes,' I replied. 'Like I said, he had a sponsor. Had a special phone for him and everything.'

She looked at me, surprised. *Clearly they haven't found that phone yet. But they will.* It was waiting for them in the storage cupboard, if only they would look.

'I have one other question,' she said gently. 'Do you think he might have been cheating on you?'

I tried to maintain eye contact but failed. 'Yes. That's why we broke up. I found a pair of dirty underwear under his bed that weren't mine.'

'Do you have any idea who he might have been cheating with? We just need to talk to anyone who might be able to shed light on Angus's mindset.'

'I'm not sure,' I lied.

'Okay,' she said, glancing down at her pad then back up at me. 'There is one final thing you should probably know about. We found some videos on his computer.'

I stared at her. Clearly upsetting me was no longer a mitigating factor in her line of questioning. Her human kindness had been vetoed by her desire for the truth.

'Videos?' I said.

'Yes,' she said, watching me, waiting.

'Of me?' I asked in a small voice.

'Yes,' she replied.

I let my head dangle forward, my eyes dropped and I felt my face flush. I was embarrassed. For real. And for the first time in my life I was deeply grateful for my blush reflex.

'I know about that video. He uploaded that to the internet a couple of weeks ago, but he took it down.' I looked up and met her eyes.

She was frowning at me. 'You say it as though there was only one?'

'There *is* only one,' I said. *Lies. Lies. Lies.*

And her eyes changed.

'Taylor, there were a few on his computer,' she said. 'He tried to delete them but they were still there on the hard drive … and on his phone.' She was watching me, waiting for a reaction. 'And you weren't the only one he'd taped.'

I flinched. My eyes welled and I could feel my cheeks grow red. It was clearly the reaction she wanted.

'Look,' she said, 'this is all a big shock. Go home, rest, call the number on that card, and take care of yourself. We'll be in touch if anything else comes up.'

'Okay,' I said. But I made no move to leave.

'Do you have somewhere you can go, people you can be with?' she asked.

'Yes, I'm staying with friends,' I said. 'I've been staying with them since the break-up. It's better to be with people.'

She stood up and I followed her lead. And a few moments later I walked out the door.

—

Meat was frying in the kitchen and a Doors record filled the silence that I couldn't. Ben was making tacos, and Charlotte and I were sitting around the small table by the living-room window, a yellow-and-brown light shade hanging above us. It was dark outside, and the lights shining out from the apartment windows in the distance looked like little yellow stars. There was a bowl of ripening bananas in the middle of the table – I could smell their sweetness just above the meat – and beside them sat a bottle of wine. Charlotte had been peeling off its label for the past ten minutes, and the scraps of paper were gathering in a pile at the base of the bottle.

'God, I never pegged Angus for the suicidal type. Just goes to show, you never really know,' she said, taking a sip from her glass.

And I was silent. I had to be: I knew that if I spoke right then, I would tell her everything. Because it's hard to keep a secret. And lonely. It grows like a protected flame inside of you, burning your insides, killing you from the inside out. I knew that already and it was only day one.

Maybe Angus will win after all.

'I know,' I replied, licking what remained of the red-inked *Rouhani* on my palm and trying to wipe it off on my jeans.

'Are you sure you don't want some wine?' The kindness in her eyes made me wince. *I am an awful person.*

'No, I feel weird,' I said. Which was true. Adrenaline coursed through my veins, but that wasn't why I was sipping water instead of wine. I had to keep a clear head, and a strong hold over my tongue. Confessing felt like it would be a relief, but I sensed it wouldn't.

My phone had been buzzing in my pocket since I turned it back on, but every time I looked at the screen I was stabbed anew: Angus's mother had called three times already. I knew I had to call her back eventually, but how could I face her? I pulled it from my pocket and glanced through squinted eyes at the screen. But it wasn't his mother, it was a missed call from David. I'd forgotten to cancel him. *I'll call him tomorrow …*

'Five minutes,' came Ben's voice from the kitchen door. He was all wild-haired and holding a spatula.

'Lots of cheese!' called back Charlotte with a smile as 'Riders on the Storm' with its thunder and lightning and electric keys filled the air.

saturday

Master Sun said: *'Be ready for the unexpected.'*

25 FEBRUARY

Chiara was next to me, purring and clawing at my legs as I sat between the brightly coloured cushions of my sofa. I'd run out of clean underwear at Charlotte's place so had gone home to replenish. Well, that's what I'd told her. But the real reason I had to go home was the same thing that had kept me up all night, tossing and turning on her sofa bed, tangling myself in damp sheets: there was evidence I needed to destroy, and I couldn't do it at her place.

My handbag was resting on the floor beside the coffee table – and in it lay my purple notebook and the gun. The latter was still loaded and wrapped in my lilac bra.

I reached for the notebook, pulled it out and in one jagged movement ripped a handful of pages out; I did it roughly. I wanted them gone. Then I tore them into little pieces, letting them collect in a pile on the coffee table.

I stared at them. I needed to make them unreadable – unstick-togetherable – so I did the only thing I could think of: I put a handful of them into my mouth and chewed. I could smell the paper, feel the hard edges getting soft. And when it was a soft pulpy ball in my mouth, rolled together by my tongue, I spat it out into my hand then placed it on the table. Then I chewed another handful. Soon I had three little balls of mushed-up paper in front of me. Nobody was piecing that together.

I moved through to the kitchen and threw them into the orange plastic bag suspended by a knob on a cabinet beneath the sink that I'd been using as a rubbish bin since I moved in. The stalks from the old, dying roses Angus gave me were still poking out the top, the sickly sweet smell of aging petals filling the room.

My phone was ringing: it was sitting on the table next to my bed, plugged into the charger, so I ran towards it. *Mum* was flashing up on the screen. I couldn't talk to her. Not now.

The card for the Family Liaison Officer sat beside my phone. Kate Stapleton. I imagined Kate Stapleton all perfect and matching, pearls around her neck, nodding sympathetically at me while using my name five times in the first five minutes to establish trust. I definitely couldn't risk talking to her.

And I kept imagining what he might have done to me if I hadn't pushed him first. How he might have hurt me the way he hurt Sophie. And somehow the worse I made the scenario in my head, the better I felt about how things turned out – it was a sick, sick game, but I couldn't stop playing. The image running through my mind at that moment was one of him having slit my throat, laughing as he watched me bleed out.

But no matter how hard I tried to push the alternate possibility aside, it always swung back: maybe he wouldn't have done anything at all.

Maybe he would have just let me leave …

I squeezed my eyes shut to push out the thought, only to hear a low gentle tapping that sounded exactly like Angus knocking on my door, and for a moment I thought it might be him.

It took a full second before I realised that it couldn't be. It never would be again. Which only left one other person: Charlotte. She would be checking on me.

I moved towards the door, Chiara purring and circling my feet as I looked through the peephole.

Two police officers stood outside: Detective Rouhani and another one I'd never seen before.

My heart lurched up into my throat and I swallowed hard.

Fuck.

But I opened the door. Of course I opened the door.

'Hi,' I said. I was frowning. I could feel it. So I tried to relax my forehead. 'What are you doing here?'

I was wearing a pair of dirty jeans and a white T-shirt turned grey from the wash.

'Hi Taylor, this is Detective Stowe,' Rouhani said, eyes to the man beside her. 'Look, sorry to bother you on a Saturday, but we need to ask you a few more questions. Some new information has come to light.'

I swallowed again and felt my jaw tense up.

'Can we come in?' Detective Stowe asked.

'Of course,' I said, leading them inside. A dark leaden balloon began to inflate around me. *They must know.*

I gestured towards the sofa. 'Would you like a cup of tea?' I asked.

'Yes please,' said Stowe.

'Thanks,' said Detective Rouhani.

'How do you take it?' I asked with a tight smile.

'White and two,' said Detective Stowe, 'unless you have honey?'

'Sure,' I said and looked at Detective Rouhani.

'White,' she said, 'thanks.'

I walked through to the kitchen and flicked on the kettle. Red light. Low hum. I tried to calm my wild mind, tell myself it would all be okay, but my hands were shaking as I opened the cupboard and pulled out three cups. My palms sweaty as I reached for the milk.

I took the tea back to the sofa – first theirs, then mine – then sat myself down with care. I needed to look unbothered. Like I wasn't scared. But we were sitting in a triangular formation: them on the sofa, me on a chair. And I felt like I was already on trial.

'So, what do you need to know?' I asked.

Detective Stowe looked at Detective Rouhani as though asking permission, and then he spoke: 'New evidence has come to light. We are no longer sure it was a suicide.'

'What?' I said, my shock genuine. 'What evidence?'

'We think someone was there,' he continued.

'Oh my God,' I said, putting down my cup. 'That's awful.' My hand had found its way to my mouth.

Do not put your hand over your mouth or touch your nose. Those things make people think you are lying: body language 101.

Detective Rouhani was watching me. Her eyes were on my hand.

'We just have to rule things out,' offered Detective Stowe.

'So, what were you doing when he fell, on the night of Thursday, February twenty-third?' Detective Rouhani stepped in. No warning. Bam. Like fireworks at midday.

I felt saliva pooling in my mouth.

'Don't be alarmed,' she added with kindness. But the kindness was in her voice, not in her eyes. They had changed in the past twenty-four hours – now they suspected me. I could feel it. 'This is just standard protocol.'

Bullshit. That was what she said about the DNA swabs. What have they found?

'Of course,' I said. 'Angus and I had just broken up again, I was upset and staying with a friend – two friends, actually, Ben and Charlotte – and so I went to yoga. It's supposed to calm you down,' I said, taking a sip of my tea.

'Right,' she said, eyes to her pad. She wasn't holding a pen. Not yet. She was just reading from it.

'And that was at what time?'

'The class started at 6.45,' I said.

'And then you left the class at what time?' she asked, her eyes burning into me. Like they could see the truth I was hiding.

'Well,' I said, steadying my gaze on hers, 'they last around an hour and fifteen and then there's about ten minutes fiddling around in the change room afterwards, so around 8.10 I guess.' Then I attempted a smile. I took a sip of tea and Detective Stowe smiled back at me.

It was a struggle but I was controlling my breath.

'And then where did you go?'

'Home – to Charlotte and Ben,' I said. 'Like I said, I was staying with them. I still am. I don't really want to be alone – I just came back this morning to grab more clothes.'

'We're lucky to have caught you, then,' said Detective Stowe, trying to be merry.

'Yes.' I smiled back at him, shifting my weight. The chair wobbled.

'It's just that, like we said, we've found new evidence. A button. There was a button found on his balcony,' said Detective Rouhani, 'between the wooden slats.'

'I don't follow, what does a button have to do with anything?' I asked.

'It appears that the button came from the shirt he was wearing when he died.'

'Okay, so …?' I asked. I didn't have to fake confusion: I really didn't understand.

'We initially thought that his shirt tore loose with the impact. But if a button was on the balcony, then it implies a struggle of some sort before he fell, something that would have ripped the shirt open.'

'Oh, God,' I said. 'That's really terrible.'

'Yes,' Detective Stowe replied.

'Do you have any leads?' I asked.

'A few,' Detective Rouhani said.

'So, how can I help? Do you want me to look at the button?'

Detective Stowe smiled. He believed me.

'No,' he said, 'we're just covering all our bases.'

'Because the button isn't the only thing,' Detective Rouhani added.

'Oh?' I asked.

'No, there is also the CCTV footage.'

She's bluffing. I avoided that entirely. I know I did.

'Oh, well, that should provide a good clue as to who you are looking for then, shouldn't it?' I said.

She looked at me with narrowed eyes.

'Well, can't you ID them from the tapes?' I added.

'No,' she said, 'that isn't what was on the footage.'

Swallow.

'Oh?'

'No,' she said. 'One of the doormen pointed it out. We missed it when we watched the tapes the first time.'

Fucking Jake.

'What do you mean?' I asked. 'If not a person, then what?' My blood turned electric.

'Light,' she said. 'The doorman pointed out a shard of light, cast from a streetlight. Once at 6.59pm and again at 7.38pm –

it shines across an otherwise dark frame. It would have come in from the side door of the garage – it was the garage tape that picked it up. Which means someone exited the building that way. Most people would either drive out or leave via the front door. Why leave that way? And if it *was* murder, 7.38pm is precisely around the time the perpetrator would be leaving. He fell at 7.27pm. Almost hit someone on the way down.'

'Oh, God,' I said. 'I see what you mean.'

I was speechless. I hadn't counted on the light. I hadn't thought of that.

'And then there is the neighbour,' said Detective Stowe.

'Felicia?' I asked.

They looked at each other.

'No,' said Detective Stowe, 'the one across the way. He wasn't close enough to be able to provide a real description, but he saw somebody in the flat at around 7.30pm.'

'Maybe it was Angus and he got the time a bit wrong?' *Shit.*

'No, Angus was 6'2". The person he saw wasn't nearly that tall,' he said.

'Well, could they give you any description at all?' I asked.

I was getting dizzy but needed to stay calm.

'Not really, it was quite a distance,' said Stowe.

'But someone else was definitely there?' I asked.

'Yes,' said Detective Stowe. 'We're hoping someone else comes forward with more information.'

'God. Poor Angus,' I said.

'You had a key, right?' Rouhani asked.

My eyes moved to hers. 'Yes, I still had a key, why?'

'It's just that there was no sign of forced entry.'

'Oh,' I said, my eyes opened just a fraction too wide for genuine shock. 'God, you don't think I had anything to do with this, do you?'

'We aren't saying that,' Detective Stowe interjected, 'we're just trying to look at it from all angles. Cover our bases.' That seemed to be his catchphrase.

'Other people could have got a key too,' I said. 'He had a cleaning lady; she's sweet, though, I can't see her doing anything like this … The tenants' board has a key … And who knows who else does.'

Detective Rouhani had taken out a pen and was making notes. She looked up. 'It's just that in the text messages found on his phone, he said something about you breaking into his apartment? About you stealing from him?'

I forced my breath to stabilise. 'I didn't steal from him,' I said. 'He asked me to draw that money for the cleaning lady, that was him messing with my head. But I did go to his apartment when he wasn't there.' Tears began to form and their timing couldn't have been better. 'But I didn't *know* he wasn't there. We'd just broken up. I went there to apologise and surprise him. I never guessed for a moment that he would've gone on our holiday without me,' I said. The remembered pain of that incident struck my heart anew, and I hoped the blow registered on my face.

They were exchanging looks.

'Did you manage to speak to his work? To Candice?' I asked, shifting focus.

'Yes,' she said. 'I called her right after you left yesterday. Apparently he was in trouble for ordering prostitutes on a work credit card.' Rouhani looked like she wanted to say something else but stopped herself.

'Yeah,' I said, 'but he said he didn't do that … he wouldn't do that.' False allegiance. 'Did she tell you what the Nicolai Stepanovich stuff was?'

'They said he shouldn't have had all of that information. But we've sent it over to them to verify that Angus collected it on his own. That it wasn't part of his pitch,' Rouhani said.

'What do you mean not a part of his pitch?' I asked. 'Why else would he have – Oh. You think it was Angus who leaked it?' My voice cracked like it was the first time the thought had occurred to me.

'We're not sure,' she replied. 'But at this stage we just needed to clarify your whereabouts.'

'Oh, okay. Well, I told you. Yoga.' I took a sip of tea.

'You know,' she said, 'it would be understandable.'

My eyebrows raised involuntarily and I willed them still.

'If you hurt him,' she said. 'You were clearly having problems.'

'Everyone has problems. We'd broken up,' I said.

'Yes, but when you came in to chat to me the other day, both the policeman at the front desk and one of my colleagues recognised you. They asked me about you, were worried. They said you'd been in there a few days before, inquiring about how to report domestic violence?'

'Angus had quite a temper,' I said, looking down. I was trying to avoid bringing up the violence – yes, it would provide an excuse but it also gave me a reason to harm him.

'Yes, we know that. The escort agency told Candice that Angus had been violent with one of the girls for not saying the right thing. They were threatening to press charges – so, he was clearly quite a volatile character. It would be understandable if you defended yourself. What with the cheating, the prostitutes, and the videos we found on his computer, uploading one of you to the internet … It just feels like you might have had motive.'

'Motive for what?' I asked.

'You must have been angry,' said Detective Rouhani.

I looked at her, feigning shock.

'All we're saying is we understand what a bad situation you were in,' said Detective Stowe. 'We've read through his text messages to you. They sounded threatening. It was clearly a tumultuous relationship. We're just trying to get to the bottom of all this.'

'Motive for what?' I repeated.

'To harm him. To try to escape,' she jumped in. 'I mean, you must have been angry about those tapes. About the violence. About the cheating. *I'd* be angry.'

'Do we need to keep repeating it all? I know how horrible it all was,' I said. 'I was living it.' Strong. 'And yes, I was upset. And angry. That was why I left. I probably should never have gone back to him in the first place. But I sure as hell didn't kill him. I would have been too freaking scared to even try!' My voice was rising. Then I stopped talking and we sat in loaded silence.

'Do you have a phone?' Rouhani asked after a few moments.

'Of course,' I said.

'Great, would you mind if we take it – run some tests on it? You can have it back on Monday.'

'Oh,' I said. 'That's a long time.' My mind tried to run through everything on it but it was impossible. I had no idea what they might find, but I needed to look compliant.

'It would be so helpful,' Stowe said.

'Sure, I suppose so,' I said. Then I walked over to the bed, picked it up off the bedside table, returned to the sofa and handed it to him. 'Here you go.' At least I'd have a valid excuse for not calling his mother back for a few days.

'Thanks,' he said, handing it to Rouhani.

My eyes landed on my handbag, still on the floor by Detective Stowe's feet, and my pulse thumped. I imagined him catching sight of my gun, the shape of the handle, then the barrel, as he slowly unzipped it. The expression on his face as he registered what it was …

I was hot. My mouth dry. I needed them to leave. Immediately. So I remained standing, as a cue for them to go.

'Speaking of phones, have you spoken to his sponsor?' I asked as I led them to the door. 'Maybe he can shed some light on what was going on with Angus?' I suggested.

Please just find the other phone.

'It's on the list,' Detective Stowe said, smiling.

I opened the door for them and they left.

And so once again I was alone, in silence, with just Chiara, three half-drunk cups of tea, and a gun. I took it from my bag and rushed through to the bedroom, burying it beneath layers of mismatched socks and G-strings. But I needed to find a safer place to keep it. Or better yet, a way to dispose of it. And soon.

sunday

Master Sun said: *'If I do not wish to engage, I distract him in a different direction.'*

26 FEBRUARY

I'd cocooned myself in dirty sheets, my regrets gathering in their creases. Around me lay screwed-up tissues and a half-eaten sheet of paracetamol. The heavy blue curtains had remained drawn since the detectives left the day before, but morning was announcing itself through a bright crack in the centre. I hadn't gone back to Charlotte's house after my 'chat' with the law. I couldn't face it: the Tube ride, fluorescent lights and my shaky pretence of sanity.

So instead I had put myself to bed beneath the ashen cloud that hung just below my ceiling. I'd hoped it might dissipate in the night, but it hadn't. It had swollen further: it was Sunday and if Angus were still alive we'd be going to his parents' house for lunch that day. His mother's delicate face flashed before me. Her unanswered calls. My phone.

I let out a small moan and rolled over, the guilt pressing down on my chest.

My eyes were focused on my chest of drawers: I needed to dispose of my gun. It was still nestled beneath my bras and panties. I ran through the options in my head: river, dumpster, grave. *At least I never used it.* Never pulled that cold trigger. So it couldn't link me to anything solid – but given the cellophane nature of my façade of innocence, I couldn't risk anyone finding it.

I need to change the sheets. They'd watched him grab me by the hair and find his lucky socks. They spoke of tears. Vomit. And deafening grief.

But my head was heavy and the pillow soft. I needed to rest. To churn and process in silence. And so my plan was to stay there, amid the dirty sheets, until the bright crack of light between the curtains faded once more and the dark of the night sky finally matched my internal landscape.

So there I was, lying in bed with my eyes and my fists squeezed tight. That's when I heard it: a gentle tap.

I knew exactly what it was that time. I was no longer a stranger to people knocking on my door. But I was tired, so tired, so I just lay there for a little while, my eyes finally open, listening to it: tap, tap, tap.

What if it's the police again?

I forced myself to sit up. To get out of bed. And to walk the long walk to the front door, dragging my heavy limbs.

'I can hear you on the other side of the door,' came his voice, 'so at least I know you're not dead. That's a positive.'

I looked through the peephole.

It was David.

'Hi,' I said. 'I'm really not well, David.'

'Okay,' he said. 'Actually I'm quite grateful for that. Because it was so odd just not turning up like that and then disappearing. I was really worried.'

'I'm so sorry,' I said through the door. My voice was husky.

'Are you going to open the door?' he asked.

Shit.

I took the chain off and opened it.

'Sorry I'm such a mess,' I said, 'but I've been really ill.'

'That's totally fine,' he said. He was dressed in jeans and a navy blue V-necked jumper that brought out his eyes. 'I'm just glad you're okay.'

He stood there looking at me.

'Would you like to come in?' I asked.

'Sure,' he said as he moved inside, holding up a brown paper bag as he passed. 'I brought pastries.'

The air was stale, I hadn't noticed till opening the door and breathing in fresh air, so I moved to open a window.

I need to brush my teeth.

David placed the bag on the coffee table and sat on my sofa – the same sofa Angus had sat on not long before. He was staring at me with those navy eyes of his, their little green middles made all the more apparent by the light coming in through the window.

His eyes were scanning mine for answers; scanning me in the way Detective Rouhani had done the day before, but the answers he was looking for were gentler. Kinder. And not going to place me behind iron bars. David's unspoken questions pertained to the state of my heart. Not my whereabouts.

The air between us was thick, and that night in that restaurant when he'd said, 'Let's escape' felt like it had happened in another lifetime. To another girl. The anger in his voice when I'd called him after the Stepanovich story broke was gone, but the memory of it cast a dark shadow by his feet. Yet his body language – wrists facing up in the most open and vulnerable of stances, body and eyes to me – suggested that he came in peace.

'So …' I said. I remained standing, unsure what to do with my hands. The smell of croissants or something similar wafted up from the bag lying on the coffee table between us, oil slowly staining the paper.

'So,' he said, 'what's going on?' His face was serious. 'First you call me and hang up before I can answer, then you all but run away from me in the office and then you stand me up on Friday night.'

'I'm sorry,' I said, 'I should've called to cancel.' I let out a sigh. 'Would you like a cup of tea?'

His eyes were darting between my face, my grey-and-pink pyjamas and the dirty floor.

'Um, yes, that would be lovely, thanks,' he said.

I walked through to the kitchen and flicked on the kettle, resting my hand on its side to assess its trajectory towards warmth. My fingers grew hot, then my palm as the kettle began to purr. I pulled two mugs down from the cupboard, and I could feel him there, in the other room, sitting on the sofa. Waiting for me. This man who had no idea what I had done.

Tears were rolling down my cheeks but I swallowed hard, trying not to make a noise.

'Do you take milk?' I called through a forced smile. But it didn't fool him.

'Yes,' he said, appearing at the door. He moved towards me, took the mugs from my hands and wrapped me in his arms. 'Whatever it is, it isn't that bad,' he said, his seriousness softening. 'Why don't you go sit down? I'll make tea.'

But I didn't sit down. Instead, I went to the bathroom and brushed my teeth.

And as I squeezed toothpaste onto my brush, I heard him through the thin wall: opening and closing the fridge door; shuffling around the cutlery drawers in search of a teaspoon. As I ran the tap and brushed my teeth I imagined him pouring the hot water. The sound of metal on ceramic as he stirred.

I went back through to the sitting room.

'So?' he asked, eyebrows raised as he walked towards me. 'Tell me.'

'How did you even find me?' I asked.

'Driver's licence, remember?' he replied. 'Bolton Gardens is pretty memorable.'

I took a deep breath, put my mug on the table, crossed my hands in my lap and looked at him. 'You remember how that information about Nicolai Stepanovich and The Town Square and Eastbourne got leaked to the press?' I asked.

'No. Have totally forgotten.' He smiled, taking a sip of his tea.

'Be serious, David,' I said. 'I have something to tell you.' Eyes to him.

'Okay, well, of course I remember,' he said. 'And just so you know, I called that annoying woman in HR the moment I got off the phone with you … I'm really sorry about that. I feel terrible for how I spoke to you that day.' His eyebrows were raised and his glance cast down. 'It's no excuse, but I was very upset. I don't like being on the back foot.' He smiled and looked to me. 'But I know I was being illogical: of course you didn't know. Nobody did. That's why it made the papers. It was just fucking unfortunate.'

I sighed. 'No,' I said, 'it wasn't just unfortunate.'

'How do you mean?' he asked, taking another sip. I glanced at my own cup sitting on the table. It was making a wet ring at its base.

'I found out about the Eastbourne scheme from my ex-boyfriend.'

I could feel him harden again. 'You mean your fiancé?' he asked.

'He's not my fiancé,' I said. My sense of humour had evaporated the moment Angus fell. 'But he's the one who told me an investor had pulled out, suggested it as an idea for you. He didn't tell me about the rest of it, obviously. He saved that part for the papers.'

'What? Why would he do that to you?' David asked, squinting his eyes with a scepticism I understood. He was warming his hands with his tea but not drinking it.

'Who knows,' I said. 'We didn't have a great relationship.'

David looked at me, confused. 'But that's insane. I can understand leaking it – once you knew about something like that you'd have to do *something* – but why drag you into it?'

'I really don't know,' I said, reaching for my tea. 'But that's what happened.'

David was looking around the room, like the answers were hiding in the bookshelves or in the brightly coloured stitching of the cushions on the sofa.

'Well, did you ask him?' he asked.

'No,' I said.

'Maybe you should?' David said, eyebrows raised.

I took a sip of my tea, then set my cup down.

'I can't,' I said. 'He died, David. He killed himself.'

'What?' David asked, almost spilling his tea. He put his cup next to mine. 'When?'

'On Thursday night,' I said.

'Jesus, why didn't you tell me?' His face was contorted.

'I don't know.' Tears were now rolling down my cheeks.

'God, I'm so sorry. You poor thing,' he said, moving towards me. Hugging me.

'So am I,' I mumbled. And I was.

I still am.

'God,' he said after a few long moments of silence. 'Suicide.'

'I know. The police have been asking so many questions, it's been so stressful.'

'I bet.' His arms were warm. Tight.

'Is there anything I can do?' he asked, pulling away and looking at me.

'No,' I said, 'but thanks.'

I let him hold me. Sway me. And we sat there in the calm, in the quiet, for a while.

'Truth or dare,' he said eventually into the top of my head. There was a gentle mischief in his voice and it was such a relief.

'Dare,' I said. I needed the light.

He pulled away from me just a little and I looked up at him. 'I dare you to come away with me next weekend.'

And a smile cracked my face for the first time in a while as I nestled back against him. 'Where to?' I asked. Allowing myself to imagine, just for a moment. Because it didn't matter where – I would most likely be trying to scrape together bail.

'Paris,' he said. 'I have to go anyway, for work. You should come with me. It'll be fun.' I could see him trying to make things better for me. But he couldn't.

'You have a wife, David,' I said. My voice was small. 'In fact, it's the weekend, shouldn't you be in the country with her?'

I could feel his chest expand with each inhale as he held me.

'I told you, we have an understanding,' he said.

I pulled away and looked up at him through tired eyes. 'What sort of understanding, David?' The question I should have asked in that hotel room.

'Taylor, we haven't slept together in over three years and she basically lives in our house in Cornwall,' he said. 'It's just that divorce is extremely slow and expensive. But she knows I date. She does too. You can meet her if you want?'

'No thanks,' I said, taking a deep breath and looking down. 'Please don't lie to me, David.'

'I'm not. I'll be officially divorced in two, possibly three, months,' he said. 'Can't we just have a torrid affair in Paris until then?'

I didn't want to go to Paris. Ever again. Angus and I had left a snail trail of memories throughout that city of lights; the glittery hope I felt back then probably still glimmered from the cracks in the pavement after dark.

'Can we do that?' he asked, resting his chin on my head.

'Okay,' I said. 'But can it be somewhere else?' Images from Jim Morrison's grave bombarded me: Angus kissing me roughly behind a tomb, pushing me against it, my arms at my sides, moss under my fingernails; the smell of cut grass. The Eurostar: the sound of a small child's voice singing 'The wheels on the bus go round and round' flying at me from the seat behind us, and him whispering in my ear, 'Darling, touch me.' His coat flung over his lap, a makeshift blanket, and me unzipping his trousers, doing what he asked … then stillness as the coffee cart came past. And throughout it all, the lyrics continued, 'The wheels on the bus go round and round'. While the pink sky with its fraudulent cheer smiled back at me from behind foggy windows, never once warning me of what was to come. I blinked hard and tried to blot the memories out.

'Why? Paris is amazing.'

'Too many memories,' I said, my eyes cast down.

'We'll make new ones,' he offered.

I smiled and fell back into his embrace.

monday

Master Sun said: *'To be victorious in battle and to be acclaimed for one's skill, is no true skill.'*

27 FEBRUARY

I woke up violently that morning: adrenaline pulsing through my veins as heavy rain hit the windows and thick streams of water dripped down from the gutters above. David was asleep behind me, his face in my hair. It was still dark outside and the soft yellow glow of a streetlight was creeping around the edge of the curtains. It was beautiful. My heart was fluttering in my chest and in the warmth and safety of my bed, silent tears streaked my cheeks, their salt landing on my lips. My life was going to change that day, I could feel it.

My night had been spent drifting in and out of sleep, cataloguing the contents of my phone: messages to and from Angus, the call to David, photos, emails I'd sent from my account – none of that was incriminating. And I'd intentionally forwarded Caz's email from Angus's computer, his IP address, so they couldn't tie me to that in any way. But no matter how forensically

I ran through everything in my mind, I couldn't find peace. Because I just had no idea which way the dominos would fall that day.

She put my phone down on the wooden table. Heavily. The bang echoed through the small room.

'You can have that back,' she said. She threw me a quick look and walked to the window. It stretched the length of one of the walls and faced out onto the brown hallway.

I stared at my phone: they'd found something on there, I could feel it in my bones.

Detective Rouhani's footsteps as she paced back and forth along the window of her dingy office were the only sound in that small room. But I could faintly make out the hum of life continuing downstairs, on the other side of the wall.

My trousers, wet from the rain, were stuck to my legs. My socks were damp. The hard plastic chair was making my bottom numb and a blister was forming on the back of my left foot.

Having gathered her thoughts or grown tired of pacing, Detective Rouhani moved back towards me and the messy desk my phone lay on. I was too scared to reach for it, as if touching it would be an admission of guilt.

She sat on the edge of the table's ragged wood, her eyes on me. I looked up at her and then picked up my phone.

'Thanks,' I said. 'Did you find anything useful on it?' *No. Please say no.*

I braced myself for an unexpected question, something I hadn't thought of and couldn't prepare for.

'Yes,' she replied, 'we did.'

Here we go.

My teeth chewed on my inner cheek, I remembered the warmth of David's breath on my neck, and my heart froze mid-beat.

'Would you like a cup of tea?' she asked.

'No thanks,' I said. Why was she stalling?

She picked up a notepad that was lying on her desk, then asked as though it was of no consequence: 'You said you knew about Angus's drug habit?'

'Yes, he did coke. But he gave up. Or I thought he'd given up.' *Just tell me what you found on my phone!*

Her eyes squinted: 'We found a large amount of cocaine duct taped to the bottom of his sofa. You didn't know about that?'

Of course I knew about it. And I was glad they'd finally found it: maybe that meant they'd found his other phone too. I felt my own eyes widen, as though trying to telepathically unsquint hers: 'No, not at all. I mean, he kept small amounts around, but usually they were only about this big,' I said, holding up my two forefingers to indicate a small rectangle.

Her eyes returned to her notepad: 'And do you recognise this phone number?' she asked, swivelling the pad so I could see it. It was covered in stars and scribbled notes, and at the bottom of the page was a phone number. It had been circled to the point where the paper had started to tear.

I looked at the digits and could honestly say: 'No.'

'It belongs to a man called Cameron, or Caz. Have you ever heard that name before?'

They found the phone.

'I don't think so,' I said, 'not in relation to Angus. I mean, I've heard the name Cameron before but I don't know anybody by that name myself.'

'Okay,' she said, looking down again. Scanning.

'Who is he?' I asked.

'A private investigator,' she said, looking up. 'We found a number of missed calls from him on another phone in Angus's flat. It was under a pile of old clothing in a storage cupboard. Do you know anything about that?'

'No,' I said.

'We'll keep trying to get in touch with him,' she said. 'But just so you know, that was how he made the videos. We found the camera in that cupboard too. A two-way mirror. Quite the set-up.'

I swallowed hard and cast my eyes down, imagining a group of policemen all laughing as they watched my tapes.

'But my phone was helpful?' I asked. I wanted a solid answer. I needed one.

'Yes.' She smiled – but I couldn't read her smile. I didn't know if it was self-congratulatory or reassuring. 'Our analysts assessed it.'

She put down her notepad and picked up a couple of pieces of paper that were stapled together in the corner.

'Great,' I said. 'Can I turn it on?'

Master Sun said: 'When weak, act strong.'

'Of course,' she said. As I fumbled with the on button my mind jumped to Jamie and that fateful encounter. Naked, funny, charming Jamie with his lemon-yellow pillow cases, menthol smoke and *The Art of War*.

Maybe he'll represent me.

'The thing with iPhones is you can track them.'

Shit.

'And, as I am sure you are aware, yours …' She took a deep breath and looked down at the stapled report in her hands. 'Yours turned up at the yoga studio at 6.38pm. It stayed at yoga. And when it left, a bit after 8pm, it went to East London. Just like you said.'

'Of course,' I replied, 'but did you find anything on there to help you with your investigation?' I said it quickly. Like there was never any doubt in my mind as to the result.

I left it in my locker. Thank God I left it in my locker.

'So, that corroborates your story,' she said. But she was watching me. Like she was confused, or didn't quite believe the evidence – I couldn't tell which. It felt as though she was trying to put her finger on something but didn't know what, the way I'd done for so many months with Angus.

'What I don't understand is: if you were frightened of Angus, if he had a temper and you were considering pressing domestic-violence charges, why didn't you revoke his "Find My Friends" permissions? He could have found you whenever he wanted to.'

Find My Friends. I'd gone to a party in Dalston when Angus and I had just started dating. He wasn't a fan of East London – said he needed vaccinations to go there – and was worried about me going to the party alone. But because it was too new a relationship for him to simply tell me I wasn't allowed to go – that would come later – he'd added me on Find My Friends instead. And he'd watched my blue dot make its way home as he sat at a business dinner. He'd made sure I was safe.

I'd thought it was sweet and caring. But Charlotte, upon hearing of it, insisted it was 'creepy as all hell' and made me delete the app immediately. Which I'd done. Not that I'd ever mentioned that to Angus. And he'd never asked.

'Oh, I don't have that app anymore,' I said. 'I deleted it.'

'Deleting the app doesn't stop someone you've given permission to from watching where you go,' she said.

That's how he knew I'd broken into his flat while he was away – that was probably partially what pissed him off so much. And that was what he meant by: 'Did you really think you could outsmart me?' on the night he died; he thought I'd left my phone in the yoga locker on purpose to throw him off the scent. It was how he knew I was in my apartment, not his, watching the DVD; how he was waiting for me with my purple notebook in his lap when I rushed to his apartment to pack. He wasn't reading my mind at all. He was just watching my little blue dot.

'We also spoke to the studio receptionist who was on duty on the evening in question,' she said, breaking my daisy chain of thought.

I felt my heart pick up speed.

'Really?' I asked, suddenly filled with dread. 'And?'

Silence.

'He corroborated your story too. Said you'd "worked hard", those were his words, said you were sweaty.'

Hair damp with fear beneath that cap. She picked up the notepad again and I watched her eyes scan through it.

Then she looked up at me. 'Can you think of anyone, anyone at all, who might have wanted to harm Angus? Anyone else who might have had access to his flat?'

I let my eyes wander around the room, frowned a little and shook my head. 'No,' I said. 'Besides, I was thinking about it after Saturday, and for someone to get in, they would need more than a key to his apartment – and you could totally pick that lock – they would also need access to the building. But they change the downstairs code all the time and anyone who comes in through the front entrance would have to sign in with the doorman, so there would be a record of it. Maybe he really did just jump.'

She looked at me, mildly impressed. 'Maybe.' But I could tell from the tone in her voice and the look in her eyes that she wasn't convinced.

'It just doesn't add up,' she said. 'We know someone else was there, given what the neighbour saw and the light on the CCTV footage … but who?'

'Well, what about Stepanovich? If it really *was* Angus who told the papers, maybe Stepanovich found out and hired someone? Someone who could figure out how to get in through coded entrances without a code. I mean, he must have been kind of pissed, right?'

'We're not sure. But we need to rule out the simplest solutions first,' she said. Matter-of-fact.

Then her eyes returned once more to her notebook. And then she looked up, met my gaze and said: 'Anyway, thanks for coming in, and let me know if anything else occurs to you.'

Then she stood up and it was time to leave.

'Sure,' I said, as I followed her to the door.

My head was light and we moved in silence. She opened the door and let me out.

And then she closed it behind me.

And I walked down that brown hallway for the sixth time that week, past its diamond wallpaper, past the sign that said 'Incident Room', past the young policeman at the front desk who'd clearly told on me, and through the heavy front doors. I stepped out into the chilly London air. A red bus flashed by.

And I breathed in.

friday

Master Sun said: *'War is a grave affair of state; it is a place of life and death, a road to survival and extinction, a matter to be pondered carefully.'*

10 MARCH

I watched the houses blur by: washing lines, lives, deception. We were getting to the edge of London; it was early afternoon and the sky was electric blue. Spring was coming: the daffodils were already sprouting in Green Park. My face reflected faintly in the window, and beside it I could see David's. Soon there would be greenery. Then the darkness of the Chunnel. Then there would be light. French greenery. Grey rooftops. And finally, Paris. I knew what was coming, and I squeezed David's hand.

He was sitting beside me, reading the paper. I held an empty cup of coffee in my other hand, and the Eurostar was loud as it rolled along the tracks. I couldn't tear my eyes away from the window: I was looking for an answer out there, considering my options. I still needed to get rid of the gun, but how? *A river. A bridge. A dumpster. A neighbour's rubbish bin.* I just didn't know.

My head was still heavy. My heart was still shocked. And every time I closed my eyes I still saw Sophie Reed's face. Imagined Angus's dark eyes just before she died. And I wondered what her parents had done with the email I sent – whether they had read it yet, passed it on. Whether Detective Rouhani would find out about it from Caz when they finally spoke. Surely he would say something now that Angus was dead?

Those same thoughts would play in a continual loop through my mind, rarely changing order, for months on end. They would usually be followed by me wondering what Angus would have done to me if he'd lived, if he'd realised I'd sent that email and I didn't have what was on that phone to protect me. And sometimes I thought of Kim too. Wondered what would have happened if I'd messaged her back instead of letting Angus block her. Whether she would have told Angus. What he would have done then. And then I'd run through how things might have gone if I'd told Charlotte what was going on, if I'd taken what I knew her advice would be: 'Just leave.' And I'd question over and over again whether I made the right choices.

But eventually I'd always come to the same conclusion: yes, I could have made a different choice at any time, flicked a different domino, set off a different chain of events. But who's to say an alternate pattern would have turned out any better? If I couldn't predict how a Google search, a sick day and my first attempts at revenge would turn out, how could I possibly know the outcome of a choice I never made? And in a small way that brings me solace.

I'd called his mother back, with my excuse about the police having needed my phone. We'd both sobbed, and then again at the funeral a week later. I'd stood in their row during the service, the priest's voice booming off the walls, Eleanor sniffling and his father's eyes dry. It was held in the same Wiltshire church Angus was christened in – old stone walls, hip-height ceramic vases full of white flowers and greenery and the smell of lilies throughout the church.

I haven't spoken to Alison or Harry since the funeral. But Jeremy checked in on me every month or so for a while. He was kind at the funeral too, seeking me out and checking I was okay, shuffling me away from Kim when she arrived in her big black sunglasses. But eventually that faded away as well. As did my fear that I would be found out.

But it's a funny thing to get away with murder. You think there will be relief when you're home free, but there's not. There's just this darkness that settles on your soul. And a realisation that nobody will ever really know you again. That you will never again be able to choose 'truth' in a game of 'truth or dare'.

Because it doesn't matter how well David and I knit our lives together, how closely our souls intertwine; there will always be a part of mine that he will never see. A little ball of bramble that I will have to deal with all alone. And that's as close to a happy ending as I will ever get.

But I like the way he looks at me – like I'm still the girl I was – and the way he feels behind me when we sleep. And I know that one day I will stop thinking of Angus. I will no longer fear turning on the radio in case they're playing our song. I know that one day he will become just another thing that changed me, that made me who I am. Because that's how life works: Some love affairs change you forever. Someone comes into your orbit and swivels you on your axis, like the wind working on a rooftop weather vane. And when they leave, as the wind always does, you are different; you have a new direction. And it's not always north.

Acknowledgements

The only reason *The Sunday Girl* is out in the world is because a group of amazing people took a chance on me. So first of all: thank you to the brilliant team at Simon & Schuster Australia. Fiona Henderson for not only publishing me but always being 100% in my corner (you are gold), Dan Ruffino for your encouragement (like sunlight for writers) and willingness to help me get there, Sheila Vijeyarasa for passing my manuscript along in the first place (not to mention being a next-level-amazing human being). Thank you too to Michelle Swainson for your watchful eye, and Jamie Criswell and the marketing team for all your work. And to my editors: Vanessa Mickan and Claire de Medici. Without your eagle-eyed ability to point out the sticky bits and my blind spots, this wouldn't be half what it is.

Then there is Bella Zanesco: thank you for getting the whole ball rolling. Bells, without your friendship and pep-talks, who knows how long it might have taken to get this onto the shelves. Ben Evans for your guidance and encouragement on my earliest drafts. To my parents for always being there; for encouraging me to be curious, take risks and find my own path even when it didn't go to plan; *especially* when it didn't go to plan. To my sister for your friendship and love; for being my biggest fan and always telling me I could 'do it' no matter what 'it' was. My uncle, Michael Herbert: despite being an English Literature professor more accustomed to the likes of *Ulysses*, you supported my writing from the very first time you read it. I was still so fragile back then and that made all the difference.

Tabitha Wrathall for being such a great friend and willing accomplice on our 'research trips'. Reinet Keyter for your love and consistent emotional support before, during and after my heart-break season. Asher Crawford for calling me on my bullshit every damned time (Paris, anyone?) and loving me anyway. Kerrianne Blondel for all our hilarious chats about psychopaths, players and narcissists and the hours we've spent laughing about them until we cried. To Tana Adelmann for answering all my questions regarding the law and police procedures: without you I would have had to get arrested so I saw how things ran. To Daleya Marohn for being a magical photographer and serendipity connoisseur. Delia Hendrie for your kindness and chats in the kitchen. And to my friends in finance and property, who patiently answered a myriad of questions.

And finally, thank you to the men in my life: the ones who showed me how to trust again *and* the ones that burned me to a crisp. Without you, I wouldn't be the woman I am now. And for that I am eternally grateful.

About the author

Pip Drysdale is a writer, actor and musician who grew up in Africa and Australia. At 20 she moved to New York to study acting, worked in indie films and off-off Broadway theatre, started writing songs and made four records. After graduating with a BA in English, Pip moved to London where she dated some interesting men and played shows across Europe. *The Sunday Girl* is her first novel and she is working on a second.

To find out more about Pip head to:

pipdrysdale.com

Facebook.com/pipdrysdale

Instagram @pipdrysdale